Past
Perfect
Terror

Anthony French

Past Perfect Tense
expresses the idea that something occurred before
another action or before a specific time in the past.

Past Perfect Terror
Dee Johansen is running from her past when she,
literally by accident, meets Jeff Westman, who
appears to have no past at all.

They form a somewhat rocky partnership, and with
each new revelation their lives become increasingly
entangled--with terrifying results.

Second Edition published by
Create Space 2017

1

For Cerene and Riley

We've pasts of our own

Prologue

"Oh, I'm so glad you're home, Lila. I need to talk to you in the worst way."

One of the reasons Deeana had worked out so well as a roomie, apart from always coughing up her share of expenses, was that she tended to be pretty level-headed, taking most of life's little bumps in stride. She never complained about the apartment's messiness, or having to spend the night out when Lila was entertaining a new guy, nor did she seem to mind the occasional lapse in Lila's cash flow. That quality allowed Lila to put up with Deeana Jones' all-too-cheery disposition and cloying niceness. This sudden outburst, though, was totally out of character. Lila folded her magazine to mark her place and took a second, longer look at her roommate.

Deeana discarded her purse on the carpet as she started pacing. Lila took in the wringing hands, deep breathing, and wild-eyed look. Had she not known her blonde buddy avoided drugs and barely even drank much she'd have thought the girl was high, but whatever the cause it was clear something had seriously upset her.

"What's up kid? You look like you've seen a ghost."

"Maybe I have...my own. I don't know if it's real or if I'm just being paranoid."

"You know what they say--it's not paranoia if they really are out to get you."

4

"It's Mr. Malavesi..."

"Rico?" Lila set her magazine aside and flipped a wisp of auburn hair out of her eyes as she unfolded her long legs. Rico Malavesi could be a real teddy-bear at times but Lila also knew the man could be downright nasty when crossed. Deeana had that kind of farm girl, peaches-and-cream look that Rico went for. A lot of guys would go for those big, innocent blue eyes, curly blonde hair, and that perky body which hadn't yet succumbed to the forces of gravity--which was exactly why Lila wanted her out of sight any time she brought home a new mark. If Deeana had crossed Rico...

"Something strange is going on at that club of his. I don't mean the gambling, I knew about that when I took the job. It's more than that."

"Slow down. And sit down, will ya? That pacing gives me a headache."

Deeana obliged by perching on the edge of the fake leather armchair, but her wringing hands and darting eyes belied any suggestion she had relaxed. Lila forgot about the confession magazine, settled herself in for a long, juicy tale. She adopted a sincere and supportive attitude, tried to appear patient as Deeana recited details of her part-time clerical job with which Lila was all too familiar.

"I don't want you to think I'm not grateful for your recommendation, but right now I wish I'd stuck to that Welcome Wagon job. The hours interfered with my audition schedule but at least..."

"I hope this isn't about your missing another audition."

"No! This is serious!"

Lila idly wondered what could be more serious than money in the bank, but avoided voicing her thoughts. She wasn't in the mood for another of the blonde's inane little lectures about "art".

"This afternoon a man came into the office and started hollering at the bookkeeper about how he'd had to work overtime on this person who wasn't keeping up his end of the receipts, whatever that means. I tried to focus on my typing but it was hard to ignore his curses and shouting. I got the distinct impression he had beaten up the man he was talking about. The bookkeeper finally told the man to shut up and grabbed him by the arm and took him into Mr. Malavesi's office."

Lila was disappointed. "That's it?"

"No, that was just the beginning. A little later the bookkeeper and the other man came out of the office. The man left and the bookkeeper told me Mr. Malavesi wanted to see me." Deeana got to her feet and resumed her pacing.

"Remember that television pilot we auditioned for a couple of months ago--the one the director said was going to be better than Miami Vice?"

"Yeah." Lila thought of protesting the abrupt change of subject, but Deeana hurried on.

"Well, he should have hired Mr. Malavesi for the part. I've never been so frightened in my life."

Lila's patience was being tested in the extreme. Ever since Deeana had moved into to the apartment Lila'd had to endure her chatterbox conversations. Mention a simple thing like sex and Deeana would go on and on about 'love' and 'commitment' and stuff like that. Suggest making a few quick bucks on an X-rated video and she'd be in for a two-day lecture on 'morality' and 'media responsibility'. The kid wasn't stupid by any means, but she was boringly idealistic, and interminably long-winded. "What'd he say?"

"It's not what he *said*. It's what he *implied*. Or maybe it's what I inferred."

Lila let a little of her impatience show. "Cut to the climax, kid. Gimmie the bottom line."

Deeana stopped pacing again, regarded her own twisting fingers for a moment, then lifted her blue-eyed gaze to Lila's face. "I think he wants me to become his mistress or something, but I also think he thinks I know something about his business I shouldn't and he figures that's an easy way to keep me quiet."

"Ah-h-h." Lila snubbed out her cigarette and reached for her drink as she settled back into the cushions. She worked at keeping her face a mask while she furiously tried to figure an advantage for herself. The kid had stumbled onto something good. It was obvious Deeana was either too innocent, or too dumb, to take advantage of it. The question was, what was in it for Lila? "So what are you going to do?"

"I don't know." Deeana sank into the armchair as though someone had let all her air out. "I didn't come to Hollywood for this. Even if I knew as much about his business as he seems to think I do, Rico Malavesi doesn't even come close to what I would call appealing." She made a sour face. "I think I'd rather do one of those videos you keep talking about..."

Lila let the silence linger for a long moment while she made up her mind. Then she leaned forward. "Kid, I feel a little responsible for your dilemma since I'm the one who got you the job.

Because of that I'm going to give you a little motherly advice. I'd say you have two choices--go along with Rico all the way or do the best disappearing act since Jimmy Hoffa."

She had already decided which of the two alternatives she'd rather see her young roommate choose. If Deeana left town Lila would not only be in a good position to get her old job back, she stood a good chance of making a lot more money than before. She could feed Rico little bits of information about the blonde, stretching out the revelations so that by the time Rico caught up with Deeana he'd see Lila as an indispensable part of his team.

At the very least, if Deeana decided to tough it out for the sake of her budding acting career her job would be up for grabs again. Either way little Lila was going to come out of this smelling like the proverbial.

"Isn't there some way I could--?"

"Hold it right there. I know just what you're thinking, and before you go any further let me remind you of that rising young starlet, Sandy-what's-her-name, they found floating off Santa Monica Pier some time back."

"Sandy Rose? The girl who died in that sailing accident?"

"Except she hadn't been sailing and her death was no accident."

"You don't mean--?"

Lila nodded. "What the newspapers didn't report was that at the time of her demise Sandy was working as a cocktail waitress in one of Rico's clubs--moonlighting it just like me and you. Rumor has it Rico took a shine to her and she turned him down."

Lila thought about adding more details, but she noticed Deeana had squeezed her eyes shut and was trembling. She could barely hear Deeana's whispered comment a moment later.

"So that's what he meant by 'taking the blush off the rose'..."

"Like I said, kid. If I was you I'd high-tail it pronto. And I don't mean back home to Mommy and that kid sister you phone all the time--that's one of the first places he'd look. I'd head for Mexico myself, but you'd stick out like a sore thumb down there. You'd be better off in Canada or maybe Oregon, a nowhere place where you'd fit right in."

"Oh, God. I'm really scared." Deeana's eyes opened wide and filled with tears.

"Better you stay smart instead of scared. Drive your Cougar till it drops, then take a bus or hike into the woods. Rico's got real long arms. I got a few bucks if you need traveling money."

"No. I have some cash." The blonde seemed to take a grip on herself, sit a little straighter. "I'll change back to my own name, start over somewhere. Maybe I could even sell the Cougar..."

"Now you're talking. C'mon, I'll help you stuff your things into the trunk of your car. No point wasting time packing."

Lila convinced herself she had Deeana's best interests in mind while covering her own ass as well. The sooner the dumb little blonde got out of town the better head start she'd have. From what Deeana had just told her, it was obvious Rico thought the kid had learned about his protection racket or maybe one of the other pies he had his thumbs stuck into. That meant he would be sure to come looking for her sooner or later. It also meant either Rico or one of his goons would be questioning her.

So little Lila might as well make it easy on herself. She'd give the blonde a few hours to get clear of L.A. and then she'd call Rico. She knew a few things about Deeana Jones--like her real name and where she came from--that Rico probably didn't know, and that information should be worth something.

And if Miss Goody-Two-Shoes was smart enough to stay hidden until Rico lost interest in her, then they'd both come out ahead.

CHAPTER ONE

Deeana Jones fought her way back to consciousness, gagging on the smell and taste of oil, smoke and dust. She felt cramped and disoriented, and a cold, hard object dug into her cheek. She turned her head, sending another explosion of pain through her body. 'Window crank', she thought. Wrong. Her Cougar had electric windows.

She tried for a more comfortable position but only succeeded in plunging herself back into unconsciousness as another wave of pain engulfed her. Memory surfaced. These cramped quarters belonged to the Toyota she had traded her Cougar for near San Francisco. She'd made the swap to throw Rico off her trail. If the evidence of her senses could be trusted the Toyota now lay on its side.

The frantic drive along a winding mountain road came back to her. If there'd been a warning about the pavement coming to an end she'd missed it, and the tires which had been squealing in protest around curves suddenly slid on gravel. There'd been that one sickening moment as she lost control of the car, then it sailed off the road and slammed in to the gulley.

She appeared to be trapped inside the wreckage of this car, too bruised and weak to get out. Maybe it made more sense to stay put, to rest, perhaps sleep a little, gain strength. At least the bears or wolves or whatever manner of beast roamed these Oregon mountains couldn't get to her in here.

A beast lurked outside right now. She could hear it breathing heavily in its effort to get at her. She forced her eyes to open, wondering if the beast could be frightened away by the sound of her voice, and also wondering if she had the strength to speak above a whisper. She could see it none too clearly because the windshield was spider-webbed with cracks. She squeezed her eyes closed, then opened them for another look. Red and black squares appeared in a corner of the window. Only birds and snakes wore bright colors like that, she told herself, and this beast seemed much too large to be either.

"You okay in there?"

The sound of a human voice brought tears to her eyes and a grateful whimper to her lips. She tried to speak but strength failed her, as did consciousness.

Harsh sounds of screeching metal and breaking glass penetrated her dream and mixed with the incongruous sensation of floating through space. Was she dead? Had she just passed through 'the pearly gates'? Someone--or something--gripped her tightly, pinning one arm to her side. Strong hands pulled at her back and thighs. She formed a fist with her free hand and struck out blindly.

The grip that held her did not weaken, the sensation of floating through space did not alter. As she raised her fist for another blow a surprisingly gentle voice spoke close to her ear. "It's okay. You're all right."

She relaxed, reached out for the shoulder she

had been beating against, felt the scratch of rough cloth beneath her fingers. She opened her eyes briefly and saw the red and black squares again. Maybe they dressed angels that way in Oregon. She succumbed to sleep once again.

* * * * *

Rico Malavesi stepped from the shower, wrapped himself in a towel and reached for another just as the phone began to ring. He kicked at the door to open it, stepped into the bedroom. The redhead was still asleep, her mouth hanging open. He draped the towel over his dripping hair and stepped to the side of the bed, then slapped her shoulder with enough force to turn her onto her back.

"Answer the phone!"

He faintly heard her mumblings as he dried and fluffed his curls, pointedly ignored her as he twisted corners of the towel to dig the water out of his ears. He didn't need to ask who it was--there was only one person who would dare to call him here--but he made a point of waiting for her to tell him before he took the phone.

"It's your secretary, Rico."

He took the phone from her, ignoring her ingratiating smile. "What?"

"The Jones woman sold her car in Daly City. She's driving a Toyota now. We have a trace on it."

"So call me when you have real news. I told you to find the blonde, not her droppings." He tossed the handset in the general direction of the redhead, dried his back. "Thought you told me she was headed for Michigan."

The redhead waffled, her eyes betraying her fear. Good, he liked them scared. They were more useful that way. "Well?"

"I don't know what to say, Rico. She did say she was thinking of going home to visit her mother and sister. Of course, she also mentioned Mexico and even Canada, but I didn't pay much attention to it. Where is she?"

He ignored her question. "What about those papers? Tell me about the papers she ripped off."

"I didn't actually see them. She just talked about them, said they were...you know, like, insurance."

"So how come she didn't just go straight to the cops?"

"I don't know. Maybe she knew you have too many good--I mean, you have good connections here in L.A.. Maybe..."

"Maybe, maybe, maybe! If maybe's the best you can do, then what good are you?"

"What about last night?"

"What about it?"

* * * * *

Deanna returned to consciousness once again, feeling far more comfortable than she had before. The first sight that greeted her eyes--a green forest outside the window--made her think she still dreamed about being home with her mother and sister in White Cloud, Michigan. She liked dreams where she could think of herself as Dee Johansen instead of Deeana Jones, liked dwelling on the simple pleasures of life in the country rather than the fast life she'd carved out for herself in Los

Angeles.

This clean, soft bed she lay in could be her bed in White Cloud, but further inspection brought her back to the present with a shock. If the sparse furnishings, bare wood walls, and timbered ceilings weren't enough, the collection of cobwebs that marked the many corners of the slanted ceiling were a dead giveaway. Her mother would never have tolerated cobwebs.

She sat up, then had to wait until the room stopped spinning before she reached for the glass of water on the dresser beside the bed. She gulped greedily, feeling the welcome liquid penetrate well beyond her mouth and throat. She placed one hand against her belly, sighed, then realized she felt bare flesh. Looking down at herself brought the return of dizziness, but she shook it off. Whoever had undressed her had left her with lacy wisps of modesty but the sight of her bare midriff and bruised arms brought back a sense of vulnerability.

She clutched the sheet to her neck, then wrapped her arms around raised knees and, steeling herself against whoever might answer, called out, "Hello?"

No response. No sounds of anyone moving about or approaching the room in which she waited. She called out again in a firmer voice and strained to hear the slightest noise.

She scanned the room, saw only the bed, the dresser next to it and what appeared to be a closet opening covered by a green army blanket--twin to the wool one on the bed. A terrycloth robe hung from a post at the foot of the bed. She scrunched down, keeping the sheet wrapped around her bare legs, and reached for the robe. It was extra large and she fumbled impatiently with the sleeves but managed to knot the tie around her waist.

Fear of the unknown and anxiety over the all-too-well remembered quickened her pulse and shortened her breath. She forced herself to take deep breaths as she rolled up the sleeves of the robe and continued to orient herself, trying to separate reality from fantasy.

Leaving Los Angeles in a hurry had been real, though some of the events surrounding it now seemed wholly impossible. She was not sure, despite Lila's predictions and her own paranoia, if the threat from Rico was real or imagined.

Trading her Cougar for the cranky old Toyota south of San Francisco as a way to throw Rico off her trail had been real. The decision to head for the secluded Silver Falls State Park had been real, though she hadn't found the park--that treacherous mountain road had ended her flight.

Everything that had happened since the accident seemed entirely too fanciful to be real. An angel dressed in red and black checks, a bear about to eat her for dinner, that floating sensation, a well-muscled shoulder cradling her head, a soothing voice. None of it squared with reality.

She tried the bedroom door. It wasn't locked. There wasn't even a decent door knob attached to it, just a latch. She looked around for something to prop against the door in case she wanted to keep it closed. Only the bed and the dresser presented themselves, there wasn't even a chair in the small room, and moving either of the large pieces of furniture seemed out of the question.

She pulled back the blanket covering the closet and peered inside. The clothes there could not belong to one of Rico's henchmen. The collection of jeans and plaid shirts did not equate with ruffled shirts and silk suits. She dropped the blanket and walked back to the door.

The living room of the cabin looked as sparsely furnished as the bedroom. An upholstered chair sat beside a wood stove at one side of the room and a small desk with a wooden chair pushed into the knee hole decorated the other end of the room. A large window beside the desk showed more of the forest view the small bedroom window had provided.

She called another greeting but did not wait for a response. She crossed the worn, braided rug that covered the center of the floor and tried the cabin's exterior door. It opened easily after she thumbed the latch. A rush of warm, dry air smelling of pine needles and dust washed over her. If she was being held prisoner her captors must assume she would be incapacitated for much longer. She closed the door and crossed to the desk. Her need for more information overrode the guilty feeling that nagged at her for prying.

Like the rest of the cabin, the desk contained little. In the top right-hand drawer she found a collection of yellow slips of paper which proved to be time sheets from Manpower Temporary Services. The 'customer name' spaces varied with each slip, but they were all written in the same bold, neat hand and they all indicated the 'employee' was one Jeff Westman.

So much for the vacation cabin theory. The time slips indicated work assignments for Jeff Westman spanning a period from early that year through the present--nearly eight months. This only led to an even greater puzzle. If Mr. Westman lived here why did the place seem so barren? No books, no television, no newspapers. Nothing except the braided rug on the floor even came close to decor. The black telephone on the desk with its rotary dial almost qualified as an antique.

She was about to investigate further when a noise from outside startled her. She quickly stuffed the time sheets back in the drawer but could not get it closed before she heard a door opening. She whirled to face the door but found it still closed. Only then did she realize the sound had come from another room--the kitchen.

"You're up," she heard.

Turning back the other way after her sudden movement did damage to her equilibrium. She closed her eyes to keep the room from spinning and clenched her teeth against the pain that threatened to drive her to her knees.

"You okay?"

She remembered that voice. His voice had spoken to her in her dream about the wreck and floating through space. This man was her "angel".

"Barely." She opened her eyes again and tried to focus on him. The red-and-black pattern from her dream turned out to be a plaid shirt--cousin to those in the closet. The man wearing it must be the owner of the robe she had found--the size was right. He stood a full head taller than her, his unruly shock of jet-black hair an extreme contrast to her blonde curls. His dark brown eyes regarded her steadily with a look she hoped was sympathetic. His nose looked 'wrong' but the rest of his features presented a pleasant picture: firm jaw line, prominent cheek bones, well-muscled neck. A hint of beard darkened his chin, as though he had forgotten to shave that morning.

Morning? It dawned on her she didn't even know the time of day. She'd seen no clocks, her watch was missing in action.

"What time is it?" she asked, aware that she must sound muddleheaded.

"Noon."

"You mean I slept through the night?"

"Two nights. Noon Wednesday."

Shaking her head in disbelief proved to be a mistake. The room started spinning again, but then she felt his strong arms supporting her. He smelled of dust and pine needles, of damp wool and something else faintly musky and quite pleasant. They seemed to be moving...dancing?

"You better eat."

"Yes," she agreed as he deposited her in the single wood chair at his kitchen table. "I could eat a horse."

"Sorry. Beef stew."

He glanced down at her while reaching into a cupboard and she detected a twinkle in his eye, a slight upward curl of his mouth. Dee tried for an answering smile, but couldn't be sure she'd succeeded. She wished things would slow down a bit, give her a chance to clear up one mystery before presenting her with a new one.

"Where am I?"

"My house." He turned from the stove and opened the refrigerator.

He took bread and milk out of the fridge and placed them on the table, poured generous glasses of milk, then left the room. Clearly he must feel he had answered her but she was a long way from satisfied. The idea of playing 'twenty questions' didn't appeal to her, but after two healthy gulps of the milk she decided to give it a try.

He returned with the chair from his desk, and her glance confirmed his having closed the recalcitrant desk drawer without comment. Flushing slightly at the memory of having snooped, she decided to pursue knowledge of her situation by more conventional means.

"I'm Dee Johansen. I guess I owe you a debt of gratitude for rescuing me."

"License says 'Deeana Jones'."

Uh-oh. Apparently he'd done some snooping of his own and had put her at a disadvantage. Time to come clean.

"Dee Johansen is my real name. I started calling myself Deeana Jones when I moved to Hollywood. Thought it sounded cute. You know, like a female Indiana Jones."

He made no response--just kept stirring the stew which was beginning to smell wonderful.

"I had to leave L.A. in a hurry because I...got in with the wrong crowd. Didn't have time to change my papers back to my real name. What's yours?"

"Jeff Westman." He ladled generous portions of stew into two bowls.

"I'm glad to meet you Jeff. I guess I owe you my life."

He made no comment.

She devoted the next few minutes to listening to the happy gurgling of her stomach and the occasional call of a bird outside the kitchen window. "It's peaceful here...but where exactly is 'here'? Are we near Silver Falls State Park?"

"Near. Maybe two miles."

"I was headed for the lodge there. I think I got lost."

"You'd have made it...if you'd kept going up the road."

"How did you find me?"

"Out walking. Heard you go over."

"I seem to remember something about being carried. Did you carry me here?"

"Yes."

"Was it far?"

"About a mile."

In which direction, she wondered. She could see only forest from the kitchen window, as with the bedroom and living room windows. The road could be just a few feet beyond the clearing in which the house sat, or it might be all of that mile away.

He scooted back his chair and reached for her bowl. "More?"

"Please. You're a good cook."

Again no response.

The Silent Type. Then she gave herself a mental kick, reminded herself she was no longer in L.A. where keeping men off-balance with compliments and body postures was *de rigueur*. She didn't have to play those games now. And besides, this man didn't seem to respond to them. "How long have you lived here, Jeff?"

He turned from the stove, about to place her bowl of stew on the table in front of her, and stumbled. She hadn't given much thought to the way he moved before that moment, but she immediately realized that until he stumbled he'd seemed surprisingly graceful for a tall man. She glanced up at him and saw a deep frown creasing his brow. He placed the bowl of stew on the table with an obvious effort and clutched the back of his own chair for support. She started to reach for him, concerned that he was having a heart attack or something like that, but halted in mid-motion.

In a voice not much above a whisper, marked by a sing-song cadence, he seemed to be reciting a list of events. "...took a walk, saw a squirrel, put oil in the van, sharpened the splitting maul..."

"Mr. Westman? Jeff?"

He looked at her, initially unfocused, then seemed genuinely surprised to find her sitting at his kitchen table. He let go of the chair, straightened, and rubbed his forehead and eyes as though trying to relieve the pressure of a headache.

"Are you all right?" she asked.

"Fine. Eat."

"You looked pretty bad for a moment. Do you have a headache?"

"No. Eat."

The spoonful of stew she put into her mouth tasted like cardboard. What have I gotten myself into, she wondered. She had simply asked him how long he had lived here and he went sappy on her. He seemed fine now, in his own close-mouthed way, but a moment ago...

Swiftly she changed the subject, hoping to put their conversation back on an even keel. The possibility of facing Rico had been bad, but at least she knew something about how to handle men like Rico. This was entirely new territory for her.

"What happened to my dress? I didn't see it

in the bedroom."

"Ruined. Went back to your car. Couldn't find anything else."

He returned to the table, looking as friendly and as open as he had before. She felt a stirring of hope that whatever had been wrong with him momentarily would not recur.

"You want to hear something really dumb? In San Francisco I traded my Cougar for that old Toyota. I was in such a hurry I drove the Toyota off the lot without bothering to take my clothes out of the trunk of the Cougar. I didn't realize my mistake until I got a hundred miles north of the city at a rest stop on the freeway. Dumb, huh?"

"Why the hurry?"

"I was working for a man I knew was into a few shady sidelines, but I was just doing clerical work for him between auditions. I overheard a conversation I shouldn't have. Evidently he's some kind of gangster. He sort of made me an offer that didn't appeal to me, and my roommate suggested I get out of town fast. That was about a week ago."

Jeff seemed to be following her, though his face betrayed no strong emotion one way or the other. It felt good to have someone to talk to, but she cautioned herself against telling him too much-- at least until she found out a little more about Jeff Westman.

"Once I made up my mind I didn't look back. Then I made that stupid mistake in San Francisco and followed it up by going off the road into that ravine."

"You're an actress?"

"Was. I'm through with that life and I'd just as soon forget it, though I'm not sure what I'm going to do next. I'd planned to get a room at the lodge, but...

She trailed off, half hoping he'd offer her continued refuge here in his cabin. She had already convinced herself the headache incident had been a fluke and reminded herself of his evident humor and curiosity. Hard as it was for her to explain, even to herself, she felt attracted to him. She waited a few more heartbeats, but he said nothing to her rather obvious lead. With a shrug, she tried for more casual conversation. "What do you do for a living?"

"I work for Manpower."

"What kind of jobs?

"Last week I unloaded boxcars in Dallas."

"Dallas, Texas?"

"Dallas, Oregon. Just across the river from Salem---Oregon, not Massachusetts." The hint of a smile dimpled one cheek.

"And what did you do before that?"

"Cleaned apartments for the City Housing Authority. Dirty places. They used a lot of chemicals, like they wanted to kill everything in sight. Probably why they use temps--breathe in that stuff long enough you burn out some brain cells."

He gazed out the window, seemingly lost in thought, and she wondered if he was thinking about his own brain cells. As the silence stretched on she remembered the stack of time slips in his desk drawer. He had worked at quite few places, and that should provide her with a great deal of 'safe' conversation.

"How long have you worked for Manpower?"

The instant the question left her lips she knew she had made a mistake. She reached out toward him, ready to withdraw the question, ready to tell him she realized her mistake--but she was too late.

His face turned ashen, making the frown lines on his brow stand out even more prominently than before. Pain distorted his features so markedly it made her catch her breath. Suddenly he leapt to his feet, sending his chair clattering to the floor behind him, and turned on her.

"Don't ask questions!" he ordered through clenched teeth. Then he stumbled from the room, hands pressed against his temples.

CHAPTER TWO

Dee felt surprisingly calm, considering her situation. Barefoot and dressed in the man's robe, she faced an unknown distance of forest floor or gravel road to traverse should she think of leaving to find other help. She was also bruised and sore and barely able to walk after her accident. She was--damnit--trapped. But it could be worse.

This man was not Rico. With Rico her options, if Lila could be believed, had been limited to total capitulation or flight. There might have been a third option--facing him down and trying to convince him she posed no threat to him--but she didn't have that much confidence in herself so that idea had died even as she had thought of it.

Unlike Rico, Jeff Westman had not threatened her. He was certainly no gangster and he had already displayed a quality of mercy and concern, at least for her physical well-being, she had not witnessed in any of the men she'd met in Los Angeles. His clipped conversational style might be due to nothing more sinister than the fact he lived alone in these mountains.

The headaches or temporary black-outs or whatever they might be called were another matter, though she decided that peculiarity might be easily explained. Maybe Jeff's past frightened him, too--if that was the right word for it. In that, they were two of a kind.

It wasn't the first time she'd seen a man storm out of a room, either. Memories of her own father came to her as she sat alone in Jeff's kitchen. Her father had frequently shouted at her mother and stomped out of the house. Oddly enough, some of her fondest memories involved moments like those because her mother had a single, unvarying, response to such outbursts. *Dee*, Mama would say, *let's bake some cookies*.

Dee would help her mother prepare the kitchen while a pot of fresh, strong coffee was brewed and then the two of them--and later, little sister Inga as well--would powder themselves from head to toe with flour as they measured and mixed ingredients and baked enough cookies to last a week. Long before the last batch was out of the oven they'd be sitting at the kitchen table enjoying the comforting smells, eating the fruits of their labor and chatting. Sometimes her father would return to the house before they were done and, usually, he'd pour himself a cup of coffee, join them at the table and start eating cookies as though he'd never been part of the ugly scene that had sparked the baking party.

The memory gave her inspiration. A coffee maker sat on Jeff's kitchen counter and a two-pound tin of Folgers sat next to it. She got up from the table quietly, took her uneaten stew to the sink, and made a pot of coffee.

The coffee machine made a pleasant gurgling sound and the smell of the coffee lifted her spirits. She took her first sip of a suitably strong brew just as Jeff reappeared in the kitchen doorway. She did her best to emulate the calm exterior she had witnessed her mother assume at such moments and hoped he would do the same.

"You'd better go," he said, his usual economy of words cutting into her hopeful expectations.

She returned her coffee cup to the table with a deliberate motion and looked up at him. The sight of his puffy eyelids and hang-dog look made her want to rush to him, wrap her arms around him, and tell him everything would be all right. His shoulders were hunched forward and his hands kept forming and re-forming fists--not like a man getting ready to fight but with the thumbs wrapped inside his fingers like a little boy with something to hide.

"I thought you might like a cup of good, strong coffee," she offered.

He said nothing, continued to stand in the doorway. She took another sip from her cup and kept her eyes on the steaming brown liquid as she placed it back on the table. Then she looked directly into his eyes. "I'm sorry about upsetting you. I think I understand now that my questions caused you pain. Do you mind if we talk about it?"

His shoulders relaxed and some of the frown lines eased, but he didn't sit nor did he stop the nervous movement of his hands. She pressed ahead.

"You don't like to think about your past, either, and I asked some foolish questions that made you think about it, right?"

He took one step into the kitchen, leaned far forward and pulled the chair toward him, then sat in it--in the middle of the room. She worked at keeping her face impassive and reminded herself to go slowly.

"I *promise* not to ask any more questions

like that. I won't ask *any* questions at all, if you like. I'm trying to escape my past, too."

He leaned forward in his chair, rested his elbows on his knees, clasped his hands together in front of him. He remained that way for a long moment, studying his hands, then looked at her briefly and sighed as his gaze fell again. "There's something wrong with me."

She was tempted to object, or maybe offer some lame assurances, but stopped herself. Better to wait, give him time to say whatever was on his mind.

Moments later he sighed heavily again, then spoke without lifting his head. "It's not the same. You don't want to think about your past--I *can't* think about mine. I've tried. It's always the same. If I think about my past I get a helluva headache."

Another long silence stretched between them, but the air seemed less charged, more relaxed.

He continued, seeming to choose his words carefully. "I hear other people talk about last week, or last year, but...I can't talk about those things. I can't even think about them."

Again she felt the urge to reach out to him, hold him, comfort him; but he was too far away from her. She would have to stand, leave the safety of her chair, and she felt it would be unwise. Questions flooded her mind but she knew she would have to tread very, very carefully lest she bring on another incident like the last.

"You talked about the last two jobs you worked without any problem. Is it safe for you to think about other jobs?"

"Yes." He frowned, a faint echo of his tortured look. "I think about some of them. About the people I met."

She might be onto something here. She could picture the stack of time sheets in his desk drawer, knew if he could just identify something beyond a few weeks in his past they could pin down a date. "What's the oldest...uh, which of the jobs that you can think about seems to be the first?" She held her breath and watched his face carefully while she waited for his answer.

"I remember Bob. A driver. His helper was sick. I worked with him and we moved furniture. He didn't talk much. Played the radio all the time."

"Do you remember the name of the company?"

"Something with two letters. Ess-something Moving."

"How--damn! Sorry, I almost goofed. Do you have any records that would show when that was?"

His head snapped up and he gave her a sharp look. Now the fat's in the fire, she thought. If he's thinking about that open drawer I may have just cooked my goose.

Instead of the storm she feared his face lit up like a klieg light. "Yes, I do. I'll show you."

She followed him into the living room, not bothering to hide her eagerness as he pulled open the drawer and took out the stack of time sheets she had flipped through earlier. He divided the slips into two batches, handed her one. "Here. You look through those and I'll look at the others."

She took the small sheaf of papers he handed her and then the two of them hunched over the desk, flipping through the yellow carbon copies, scanning the 'customer' lines. Near the bottom of her stack she found a promising entry. S & L Moving and Storage.

"This must be it." She handed the slip to him, then almost clapped her hands with glee as he exulted.

"See? There's his name--Bob Finlay. And there's the date, February 17, 1983."

"That's over six months ago...seven. So you can remember seven months without a problem?"

"Seven months."

The awe with which he said the two words brought tears to her eyes and without a conscious thought she filled her arms with his lean, hard body. She pulled herself close, ignoring the small pain in her left arm, and laid her head against his chest. She filled her senses with the feel and the smell of him, gave no thought to the consequences of her actions.

When his hands began caressing her back through the thick robe with long, gentle strokes, she sighed.

"Seven months," he repeated.

"Seven months," she agreed.

A warmth spread within her and she knew it had nothing to do with the seven months' worth of 'past' she had just given Jeff. Her feeling came from the immediate present. Being in his arms, feeling him touch her like this was all she cared about at that moment. She lifted her head from his chest, looked up at him, expecting him to kiss her. She wet her lips in anticipation and the action told her what she had not allowed herself to think consciously--she *wanted* him to kiss her.

Then he broke the spell his embrace had woven. "I don't even know if I've ever touched a woman like this before. It feels good."

"I'm happy you now have a past, even if it's only seven months worth." She moved her hands to his waist, leaned away from him, away from the heat and the desire.

She wanted him, and she suspected that with very little effort she could make Jeff want her. She also sensed that, in his present condition it would be like making love to a child. She relinquished her hold on him, turned back toward the desk, tried to ignore the hand that remained on her shoulder.

"C'mon, I'll pour us a fresh cup of coffee and we can talk."

Back at the kitchen table Jeff brightened noticeably as he flipped through the records and related his memories of the people and events associated with some of the temporary jobs he'd held in the past seven months. A few of the time slips apparently meant nothing to him but others brought forth a flood of stories. Dee found herself enthralled with his strongly positive attitude toward the people he'd encountered, and shared his delight at remembered successes--like the day he'd managed to hold his own in a conversation about the Super Bowl even though he had no idea what it was and only a vague concept of the game of football with which it was apparently associated.

"I just said things like, 'Yeah, that was great!' or 'You're right, they shouldn't have run that play' and the guys all thought I was one of the regulars."

During his occasional pauses Dee forced herself to think about his 'problem' rather than allow herself to feel the growing closeness between them. She formulated, then discarded, one theory after another. She knew nothing about amnesia beyond the 'bump on the head' episodes she'd seen in movies and she realized now that far too many of these had been played for comedic effect to be of any use in understanding Jeff.

When he answered her questions about the existence of other records in the negative she was forced to conclude she'd learned nothing beyond the fact that he was a gentle and patient man. Even the 'blow to the head' theory didn't fit his present circumstances without further assuming he'd suffered his accident here rather than somewhere else, before moving to this secluded cabin. If it had happened elsewhere, before he came to live here, he'd surely remember events from his previous residence and the move to this cabin, wouldn't he?

Her senses told her many other things about him but she tried to ignore that information--his attractiveness and desirability had nothing to do with solving his headache problem.

Dee reminded herself to remain firm in her resolve, and as she did so the phrase 'New Year's Resolution' popped into her head. Inspired, she broke his reverie. "Jeff! I have an idea. A couple of times you mentioned events that had nothing to do with the job you were on. Those men talking about the Super Bowl, things like that. Suppose I talk about current events, but not exactly current. Events from more than seven months ago. It wouldn't be about *your* past, but maybe you'd recognize something. Maybe we could stretch that seven months out to eight months, or more. What do you think?"

Jeff reached across the table, took her hand in his and held it for a moment, melting some of her resolve. Then, sadly, a little bit of the light went out of his eyes and he regarded her with a sober expression. "It might work...but it might give me a headache."

"If you don't want to try it, that's okay. Just because I thought of it doesn't mean it's a good idea."

They had been having such a good time talking about his jobs, and she'd taken the edge off the good feelings. The puzzle his forgotten past presented, however, could not be ignored. More than simple curiosity motivated her. Perhaps, if he regained his memory, she wouldn't view him as such a child. And there was another, more selfish reason she had to admit to herself. As long as he allowed her to help him, he would be providing her with a convenient hideout. She wasn't too proud of herself at that moment, but Rico's implied threat and Lila's warning made it imperative that pride would have to take a back seat to matters of life and death.

"Let me think about it," he said at last.

He placed his hands against the table's edge and the action drew her attention to his strong hands, his well-muscled forearms. Those arms had carried her to safety, and she found she could not reward his kindness with lies.

"Jeff, wait. I haven't been completely honest about why I want to help you. There's more to it. I've been thinking that if you let me help you, you'll also let me stay here, where *I'm* safe. I guess you could say I'm trying to use you. If you'd rather I didn't hang around and upset you, just say so. Take me someplace where I can buy new clothes and find a bus, or a train, or whatever out of here. I'll go away and let you have your own life back."

"Okay."

What did 'okay' mean? She found she didn't have the courage to ask. She'd used up all of her store of forthrightness for the time being and felt cold, and grubby, inside and out. "Do you have a shower or a bath tub?" she asked abruptly.

"I'll show you."

* * * * *

"Hi, Sammy. How are things in Portland?"

"Hot, Brian. Not a day to be standing in a phone booth. I'd rather be in my air-conditioned office using the scrambler line."

"If it's any consolation my phone booth is not only hot but muggy to boot. Chicago breezes don't hold a candle to your ocean. How's our boy?"

"He's doing fine. In fact, he's made such a good impression on the ladies in the Manpower office down in Salem they're beginning to show signs of questioning my cover story. Seems they find it hard to believe he was once a 'hardened criminal'."

"They wouldn't do anything foolish, would they?"

"No sweat. They don't even see him any more--they handle everything by phone. But they keep getting these glowing reports from the supervisors on his jobs. You making any progress?"

"Not enough to satisfy me. I've talked to dozens of people he had contact with and so far I've only managed to confirm what I already knew. I still don't have anything to fight Hobart with. Damn! I wish we hadn't had to do it this way."

"Look, we've been over this ground a

hundred times in the last seven months. The only other choice you had was to do what Ashton Hobart ordered--cancel his ticket."

"I know. Still, if I'd had time to discuss alternatives with that shrink of yours instead of---"

"Neuro surgeon, Brian. Now knock it off, willya! It's too damn hot in this box for this crap. Our boy is going to thank you for this when we bring him out of it, so why don't you get back to the job of clearing him and let me get back to my air conditioner."

"Sorry, Sam. Give my love to Cindy and the kids. I'll talk to you next week."

* * * * *

Jeff sat in his armchair and listened to the water running. He couldn't help thinking about the beautiful blonde lying in that tub, though it was difficult for him to picture her completely nude. In his mind's eye she still wore her under things, but that made little difference. For the first time he could remember, he understood why other men made those groaning sounds when a pretty woman walked by. Dee, or Deeana, or whatever her name was, made him feel like groaning. He still didn't quite understand why, but he was beginning to get concrete ideas.

He had been content with his life until two days ago when he had found her in the wrecked Toyota. At first he'd considered walking away, not getting involved. His decision to act had only been the first of the many disturbing changes she had caused. When he took her torn and bloody dress off before putting her in his bed he felt emotions that upset him almost as much as his headaches.

He had lied to Rosemarie at Manpower the morning after the accident. She'd called to offer him a new job and he told her he was sick. It was the first time he could remember lying to anyone-- especially someone as nice as Rosemarie.

The thing Dee suggested about current events sounded like a good idea. When she talked about the man she was running from he felt a familiar chord being struck. Not exactly a memory, more like *seeing* something from his own past while she talked about hers. And it hadn't given him a headache. But did he really want to find out about his past? Did he want her to stay badly enough to put up with all the upset she caused? It wasn't just the headaches, but all the other feelings too. He just didn't know enough about any of it to make any kind of informed decision and there seemed to be no way around the dilemma.

* * * * *

Dee rejoined Jeff in his living room, toweling her hair. "That was the best bath I've had in years. I feel almost human."

He smiled up at her in an absent way. "If you like, I'll take you to town tomorrow so you can buy some clothes. You can try wearing some of my things for now."

If they handed out Oscars for ambiguity Jeff would be nominated on the first ballot. His statement did indicate she was welcome to spend another night in his cabin, but she was still left with nothing but 'okay' to explain what would happen tomorrow, after the clothes shopping. One day at a time worked for some, but with this guy it was more like one *hour* at a time. She'd just have to make do with that, though. "Did my shoes survive?"

"They're on the porch with your purse. I'll get them."

"May I just help myself to anything I find in your closet?

"Sure."

The sight of the rumpled bed where she had spent her convalescence took some of the buoyancy out of her step. She straightened the bed linens, fluffed the pillow, and tucked in the blanket before going to the closet. A short time later she emerged from the bedroom dressed in rolled-up jeans and a flannel shirt long enough to be a mini-dress. She'd had to turn up the cuffs three times to free her hands.

She slipped into the flats she usually wore for driving, amazed at how a simple thing like an old pair of shoes could make one feel so complete, and sat on the rug in front of the wood stove to go through her purse. But before she could open it, the air was pierced by a sound so alien in that peaceful environment both she and Jeff sat bolt upright.

Jeff leapt to his feet and looked out the window. "A Sheriff's patrol car," he announced.

Another burst of sound--the amplified voice of a police dispatcher--rent the air. Compared to the siren's growl it sounded familiar and even friendly to her, but Jeff apparently didn't agree with her assessment.

"Go back to the bedroom. Stay there."

She moved without hesitation, taking her purse with her. Not even his earlier demand about not asking questions had carried the force of command that now rang clear. Once behind the closed door of the bedroom she had time to ponder this latest change in him. Being in his presence was one heck of a wild ride, roller-coaster in style but with even more abrupt changes, and she found herself wondering what new surprises might be in store for her. She faintly heard the front door opening before any knock sounded.

"Yes sir. What can I do for you?" Jeff said in a voice loud enough for her to hear clearly.

She strained to hear the sheriff's words and thought about opening the door just a crack, but decided against it. She pressed her ear to the door and breathed through her mouth as evenly as she could.

"Yes, I saw it," she heard Jeff say.

"...anything...where they went..." she heard faintly.

"No. Just the car."

What little she could hear of the conversation was driving her nuts with curiosity, and she wished Jeff were more wordy with his answers. She couldn't tell from his clipped way of speaking exactly what had been asked. She knew he had, for reasons not completely clear to her, decided to deny having seen her. She lost track of the conversation as she considered this display of deviousness in him. Was he steeling himself against the possibility of being asked a headache-inducing question, or did he have other motives for avoiding the police?

"...investigate further..." the sheriff said.

"The car can stay there until you're done. If you want to have it towed away, that's okay too.

"Mind if I look around?

"In my *house*? Yes, I do mind."

"Now look, fella." An unmistakable tone of authority laced the words as the volume of the officer's voice raised. "I don't want to get highhanded with you."

"That's right. You don't."

"I might have to insist."

"Not without a warrant. And not without giving me your name and badge number. I'll want to call headquarters and verify your rights."

She missed the sheriff's reply but got a good sense of what had been said from Jeff's next remarks.

"I *am* cooperating, deputy. I've given you permission to come onto my land to investigate an accident. However, it did not happen in my living room, and there's nothing further I can tell you about it. If you get a warrant, I'll honor it. If not, I insist on my right to privacy."

The next sounds she heard were of two doors closing. A car door slammed shut and the big wooden door of the cabin closed with a soft thud. She waited until she heard the sounds of gravel crunching under the tires of the patrol car as it climbed the drive away from the house and then ventured a peek through the bedroom door.

Jeff leaned against the closed front door, breathing heavily, his fists working but his face held impassive. She opened the bedroom door and stepped into the living room.

"Did you tell me everything?" he asked.

His abrupt manner startled her. She'd thought, given the way he dealt with the deputy, he had chosen to side with her. Now she wasn't so sure. "Well, no. I left out some details, like I said."

"Have you done anything illegal?"

"No!"

"Did you pay for the Toyota?"

Righteous anger replaced her disappointment. "Of course I did! I traded my Cougar for it. They gave me the Toyota and a check for nine hundred dollars, which I cashed at the bank across the street from the car lot. The stub is still in my purse."

"Who is the man you ran from?"

"Rico Malavesi. He runs some gambling operations in southern California. And he's into some other things, too. Why?"

"That deputy claimed there's an advisory out on your car. That means someone in authority--he wouldn't say who--wanted it found."

"Rico!" I chill raced through her like ice water in her veins.

"Possibly."

"He always bragged about his connections. Lila told me he had the cops in his pocket. Oh, God!" She slumped into the armchair as she imagined Rico peeling bills off his wad and handing them to a cop. She had never stood a chance. If he could find her in this Oregon wilderness, he could find her anywhere.

"We're getting out of here," Jeff announced.

"What?" She couldn't believe she had heard him correctly, but he spelled it out for her.

"I said, we're getting out of here. Now. You're not safe here any more."

"You mean you're going to help me? But that could put you in danger, too."

"What do I have to lose? Seven months? Come on."

CHAPTER THREE

"We found the car, Mr. Malavesi."

"The woman too?"

"No sir. The car was wrecked somewhere in Oregon."

"Oregon!"

"Yes sir. The locals noticed the advisory on the C.I.C. and informed our people. They filed a report and requested follow-up instructions. Shall I fax them a description of the Jones woman?"

"Just a minute. Let me think..." So she was still headed north, and maybe she'd run to ground. If they found the car and not her maybe she'd wrecked it on purpose, to throw him off the trail. Nice try.

"No. Tell them nothing. Send the usual thanks to our people and tell them to let the yokels up there think we've lost interest because of the wreck. I'll stop by the office and pick up the report on my way to the air strip. I'm going to handle this myself."

Rico didn't wait for a reply before disconnecting and hitting the speed dial for the air strip. When they answered he barked an order to have his plane made ready, hung up, then told the boy to pack him a bag. His hands were already itching with anticipation. It was going to be a pleasure to wring that blonde bitch's neck himself. But first he'd give her a long time to think about the mistake she'd made.

* * * * *

"I can't get over the change in you," Dee remarked when Jeff handed her into his van. "Before that sheriff came to the house you...well, you were quiet and gentle, and---"

"And now I'm loud and mean?"

"That's not what I meant. You seem so much more self-assured. In charge."

"I know what I have to do and I'm doing it. Just because I don't talk much doesn't mean I'm some kind of simpleton. I steer clear of conversation because it's a good way to avoid being asked questions that might bring on one of my headaches."

"I didn't mean to imply..."

"I know you didn't. But I've heard it before." He fastened his seat belt. "This might be a bumpy ride. I've walked this old logging road a few times, but I never planned to drive it--especially in this van--so I haven't paid close attention to the terrain. If my plan works we'll come out on Malden's farm near the park. Then we'll head through the park and down to Salem. They'll never expect us to go that way."

"Do you really think they'll be watching for us?"

"I don't know, but I'm not going to trust my luck to some redneck deputy sheriff bucking for a promotion."

Conversation became nearly impossible at

that point. Jeff concentrated on his driving and Dee was forced to try to find hand-holds. As she was jostled and slammed back and forth she did her best to believe he knew what he was doing, but it wasn't easy. The 'road' he spoke of with such conviction looked like nothing more than a barely passable space between trees. Apart from an occasional low branch that whipped the windshield she saw nothing but weeds, and judging by the way they bounced and jolted from side to side the weeds hid more rocks than roadbed.

Long after she had given up hope of coming through the experience without additional bruises the trees gave way to an open field and Jeff braked the van. He threw off his seat belt, opened his door, and got out.

She was too busy catching her breath and checking for bruises to object to being left alone, but a moment later she noticed the fence directly in front of them. He bent over, pulled at a part of it.

"Can I help?" she called through his open door, hoping he would say no, and welcoming his lack of response. A moment later he returned to the van, put it into gear, and drove a few yards. He got out again and disappeared in the other direction. It came to her then that he must have driven through some kind of gate and was now closing it behind them.

"They'll play hell following us in anything but a four-wheeler, even if they do come looking for you in the morning," he said as he put them in motion again.

She had forgotten about time during the past day. The forest around his cabin was so dense there had been no direct sunlight even at noon--or what he had claimed was noon. Now they were out in the open she looked around for some sign of the sun but saw only a slate-gray sky that defeated her efforts to guess the time.

She glanced at her wrist, then immediately remembered she hadn't worn her watch since waking earlier that day. Earlier that day? It was hard to believe all this had happened in the space of a single afternoon.

"What time is it?"

"'Bout seven."

His eyes remained glued to the road ahead. She began to see traces of real tracks between the weeds now, though the ride was still bone-bruising.

"What happened to my watch?"

"Smashed. I threw it out, like your dr--- damn!"

"What?"

"Your dress. It's lying in plain sight on the washtub out back. If they come back with a warrant they'll know you were there, for sure. Guess I am simple, after all."

"Don't say that. There are probably lots of other ways they could find out, like following your tracks from the Toyota, or finding long blonde hairs in your bathtub."

"Yeah, but no point in making it easy for them. Damn!"

"How long will it take us to get to Salem?"

"Never went this way before. Why?"

"Just wondering if we'll get there before the stores close. I could buy something that fits. Not that I'm not grateful for what I'm wearing."

He smiled broadly and she decided she liked the way his face looked with that smile. In fact, she liked the way his face looked most of the time.

"One thing about that outfit, nobody would mistake you for Deeana Jones, the actress."

The sound of his laughter lifted her spirits.

"From now on it's Dee Johansen, simple country girl from the hills of western Michigan. Forget the shopping spree. These clothes suit her just fine."

"We'll get you stuff that fits. Why don't you start talking about current events, like you suggested."

"I don't think current events would be a good idea right now. If you get one of your headaches while you're driving..."

"Right. Tell me about your home."

She thought about her little sister, Inga, still living at home in White Cloud with her mother and wondered when she'd ever see them again. A yawn escaped her and she closed her eyes, leaned her head against the window beside her.

* * * * *

A feeling of *deja vu* came over her as she felt herself being lifted from the van by strong arms. She felt no panic, though, because she knew it was Jeff who carried her. She pressed the side of her face against his shoulder, kept her eyes shut, and relished the feeling of being cared for so completely.

The faintly disinfectant smell of a freshly cleaned motel room told her where they were. The cool, crisp feel of washed cotton replaced the warm, rough texture of his shirt against her face and she burrowed into the pillow as his arms slipped from beneath her. His hand brushed her shoulder a moment later and she thought he would begin undressing her, but then she realized he had simply placed the cover of the bed over her.

She reached out, captured a handful of his sleeve. "Please don't leave me," she murmured.

She felt the bed take his weight and when his arm settled across her waist she allowed sleep to take her fully.

* * * * *

For the second day in a row Dee woke up in a strange bed. She turned to reach for Jeff and discovered she was alone, still dressed in his clothes. The other bed in the room looked undisturbed so he must have slept through the night with her, she thought. Too bad she missed it all. She got out of bed and checked the bathroom, found it empty but with signs he'd been there. The tiled shower beckoned her and she hurriedly stripped. No telling when, or even if, Jeff would return but that shower came first.

She wrapped one towel around her after her long, hot shower and began drying her hair with another. She needed a decent shampoo, wasn't even sure if she had a comb or brush in her purse. The sheriff had interrupted her inspection last night. She opened the bathroom door, trying to remember if she had seen her purse in the room anywhere, and saw Jeff depositing a large paper bag on the unused bed.

"Jeff!"

Without thinking, she threw herself into his arms. Maybe it was his confronting the sheriff on

47

her behalf, or his decision to leave his home to help her--heedless of danger to himself. Maybe it was the tender way he held her while she slept, still not taking advantage of her. Maybe she just decided she'd practiced enough restraint. Whatever the reason, she just did it and she was glad she had.

She reached up, took his face between her hands, and kissed him on the lips.

He stood rock still for a moment, but she felt his lips soften, felt an answering pressure against her mouth. She thought he responded elsewhere, too, although it was hard to tell for sure through the heavy jeans he wore. When his hands gripped her shoulders a low moan started somewhere inside her throat and her breathing grew ragged. He moved them apart and she waited for him to strip the towel from her, put his hands on her. But the waiting stretched beyond a reasonable limit and she opened her eyes.

He trembled and his eyes were squeezed shut. Oh no! Was he having another of his attacks? Or was he simply turned off by her? Then something he'd said, something about not being sure if he had ever held a woman in his arms, came to her. How could she had forgotten so quickly? In a number of ways he was still a seven-month-old. She felt like a dolt.

With a visible effort he calmed himself, opened his eyes and dropped his hands to his sides. "Let's eat breakfast," he said, avoiding her eyes.

"I'll get dressed." She took her clothes into the bathroom, brushing aside the ache of unanswered passion, and tried to put cheerfulness into her voice as she called, "What's for breakfast?"

"Scrambled eggs, bacon, muffins, and

coffee."

"Sounds wonderful, smells even better. Guess I conked out on you last night, eh?"

"Yeah."

The eggs tasted like rubber and the bacon was far too greasy but she didn't care. She ate it all, then took her time with the coffee.

Jeff toyed with his food. She watched him stir his scrambled eggs for a while, then pointedly ignored him. He seemed lost in thought and she had a feeling he would not appreciate any interruption, even for a little mothering reminder that he needed to eat. She focused her thoughts on what kind of wardrobe she would begin building for herself later that morning.

"I've been thinking," he said abruptly, startling her. "When you kissed me, it reminded me. Last night when you were...when we were sleeping together I kept getting...pictures, I guess. Like when you talked about Hollywood."

She couldn't see what sleeping together and her abbreviated confession about Los Angeles had to do with each other, but he seemed to think it made sense, so she decided to wait him out. He didn't continue.

After a long wait she tried coaxing him. "Was it like what happened when the sheriff showed up?"

"No. That was different--made me mad. I knew what to do, but there weren't any pictures."

"Do you know what to do now?" Her question could be taken as an invitation, if he so chose. She was slightly disappointed, but not surprised, when he elected to give it a broader interpretation.

"I'm not sure, but...we have to stay together. We...we need each other."

He looked into her eyes and she knew she might be able to make it on her own, but she'd rather have his help. Impulsively, she said, "Sometimes you scare me, when you go away into another world like you did a minute ago. But I think I understand that you're remembering, aren't you? You're getting flashes from your past--from beyond seven months ago, right?" She thought she detected just the hint of a nod from him and hurried on. "I'll try to control my fear if you'll try to tell me what's going on with you."

"You'll stay with me?"

"Yes, Jeff. I'll stay with you. And the first thing we need to do is break out the Visa and do some shopping." She dug out her favorite credit card and waved it.

He looked at it curiously, as though he'd never seen one before. She asked, "Have you been paying cash for everything? Your rent and utilities and everything?"

"The bank pays the utilities," he said slowly, as though the point had just registered. "And I own the house. I pay cash for groceries and things like that."

"Wait a minute. You own your house and land? Where do you keep the papers?"

"At the bank."

"Bingo! That means we hit the jackpot. You have all your papers in a safe deposit box at the bank, right?"

"Um...yes. That's my key there," he said, pointing to the keys on the ring in the van's ignition.

"Great. All we need to do is drop by the

bank, open your box, and we should find out
everything we need to know about you. Bank
records, titles, whatever else you have in there. If
you can stand to hear me talking about the past,
maybe I can tell you about what's in your papers, a
little at a time. You know, stretch it out and give it
to you in small doses so the shock won't give you a
killer headache."

Jeff stared at her, open-mouthed and wide-
eyed. Then his face turned cloudy. "No. We have
to get out of here. They may be looking for you."

"We have time," she said with a wave of her
hand. "You said yourself the sheriff won't be able
to get a warrant until this morning. They'll waste a
lot of time going up to your place, then they'll have
to check with DMV, or whatever it's called in this
state, and find out what you're driving, and that
could take time. We have a few hours, at least.
Let's go shopping, find me some clothes, maybe
even get you something a little less conspicuous.
Then we'll go to the bank, pick up the papers, and
get out of town."

He looked doubtful, but surrendered.
"Okay, let's go."

* * * * *

When they carried their purchases to the
cashier at Nordstrom's Jeff suggested she put away
her Visa card. She was about to protest with a
comment about holding her own, but he grabbed her
elbow and pulled her away from the cashier. "That
card has your name on it. Your old name. If you
use it someone may find out your were here, know
when you were here and what kind of clothes you'll

51

be wearing."

She stuffed the card back into her purse. Maybe he was a seven-month-old in some ways, but at other times he was smarter than her by double. "Good thinking. I'll use my cash."

"I'll pay half," he insisted "I have cash, too."

When they arrived at the bank Jeff insisted on her accompanying him into the vault. In less than ten minutes they were back in the van, a sheaf of papers tucked into her new purse.

"Yesterday, when we were talking about your jobs, I thought it might be helpful to visit some of those places and see if anyone remembered anything about you. Now I'm not so sure that would be a good idea, especially since all those time slips are sitting out on your desk at home. The cops might get the same idea and be waiting for us. Let's just get out of town. Is Portland a big city?"

Jeff chuckled, and she flashed him an answering grin. Neither of them needed to say 'Portland Oregon, not Portland Maine' for the joke to be appreciated and recognized as a statement of their growing camaraderie.

"I got lost there once," Jeff admitted, sobering.

"Wonderful. Maybe we can 'get lost' there again."

Jeff headed for the entrance to the northbound freeway. Dee let out a low whistle as he eased the van into the flow of freeway traffic. "I should have let you pay for these clothes yourself," she said, glancing up from her inspection of his papers. "You're a rich man."

The van swerved slightly. "I am?"

"Definitely. That wad of cash we found in

your box was nothing compared to this. These are certificates of deposit. According to them you have well over a hundred thousand dollars in various C. D.s. with your bank. Here's the really interesting part. Are you ready? They're all dated January 20th of this year. That's a little over seven months ago."

"Seven months."

"Exactly."

"I don't feel so good."

She sat bolt upright, immediately alert, and checked the nearby traffic. "Do you want me to drive?"

"No. No headache. I feel..."

"Sick at heart?"

"Yeah, I guess that's it. Someone's been playing games with me. I feel like a puppet. What else can you figure from the papers?"

"Are you sure you want to hear?"

Tires hummed against the surface of the freeway, the van's engine purred between them. He straightened, put both hands on the wheel. "Tell me."

"The title to your land and house has the same date."

"So my whole life started at the age of thirty-seven."

"That's how old you are?"

"That's what my driver's license reads. Thirty-eight next month. But why should I believe that? Everything else about me seems fake."

"You look thirty-seven," she said, giving him a critical squint, "which that makes you about eight years older than me. And there's a lot about you that's very genuine," she added, leaning over to trail her hand reassuringly down his arm.

"Thanks."

She glanced back at the papers in her lap. "There's something else. The seller is a corporation in Seattle, and there's a title insurance policy written by a company there. Maybe Seattle holds the answer."

"I'm not sure I want the answers. What do *you* think?"

"You might have been in some kind of accident. The money could be from a settlement, though there's nothing in any of these papers to support that theory. Or maybe your condition is congenital and some rich relative wanted to take care of you without..."

"Without having me around to embarrass the family, right? There's just one thing wrong with both ideas. The headaches. If I've suffered some kind of brain damage, why would it hurt *only* when I try to remember? No other time. Always then. The only conclusion that makes sense is that someone played games with my mind on purpose."

She looked at his hands gripping the steering wheel, his knuckles white from the pressure. It was her turn to feel 'sick at heart'. "But who would do such a thing? And why?"

A few more miles of concrete passed beneath the wheels of the van before either of them spoke again. When Jeff broke the silence his words made it clear they had been thinking the same thoughts.

"You told me, back at the house, that I might be putting myself in danger if I helped you. It's beginning to look like the same might be true for you. It would take someone with a lot of power to do what's been done to me. If we start rattling the cage..."

"I know." Dee managed a brave smile, then added a few brave words--more to convince herself, she realized, than him. "In for a penny, in for a pound."

"In this case it's probably more like 'in for a ton', " Jeff predicted.

CHAPTER FOUR

Dee preceded Jeff into the restaurant, then turned and laid her hand on his arm. "Order me a steak dinner, medium rare, with all the trimmings. I have to make a phone call."

He nodded and followed the hostess to a table, noting how closely the decor and layout of the Portland restaurant duplicated the Elmer's he frequented in Salem. The mental and physical shocks he'd endured lately made him all the more grateful for familiar surroundings. He felt comfortable here. Thanks to Dee's suggestion they stop for lunch, he would soon add to that comfort.

"Coffee?" the hostess asked.

"Please."

The restaurant held few patrons other than Dee and himself. Jeff settled back in his chair and continued his thinking about January 20th--his apparent birthday--trying to find something significant about the date. Whoever had done this to him must be a very strange individual. On the drive from Salem he had deliberately tried to remember every possible event since January 20 and had succeeded in spending a large portion of the time thinking about things as mundane as buying a new shirt or as significant as the time he almost crushed his hand in a near-accident. Not one of those thoughts caused him pain.

Now the time had come to start thinking

about January 19th, to find out of it was possible for him to extend his recall of the past beyond that date.

"Did you order my steak?" Dee asked as she rejoined him.

"No. Who were you calling?"

"Hi Folks!" The waitress interrupted. "Are you ready to order?"

"Two steak dinners, please. All the trimmings." Jeff turned back to Dee but the waitress persisted with questions about their steaks, choice of potato, soup or salad. He felt annoyed, unsure if it was the delay the waitress caused or just her overly cheerful manner. Dee ordered salad and he nodded an assent to that idea. Then he had to put up with the dressing choices. Finally the waitress left them, promising to be 'back in a jiff'.

"Who were you calling?" he asked again.

"The police," she said. Before he could express his shock she added, "My roommate in L.A. had a friend on the police force who checked out all her new boyfriends for her. She'd give him the guy's name, description, and license number of his car. She told me it took her friend less than ten minutes to let her know if the guy was wanted or had a record. Come to think of it, she seemed to know a lot about criminals and cops. Anyway, the cops have some kind of computer called Leads or something like that..."

"LEDS."

"Yes. That's---"

She stared at him, open-mouthed, but it took him a few seconds to comprehend. When it finally hit him, he added his own puzzled look to hers. "Now how in the hell did I know about the Law Enforcement Data System, LEDS?"

"Good question. Got an answer?"

He closed his eyes, concentrated on the only picture of a computer he could bring to mind--the one he'd seen in the Manpower office--but came up with nothing. Annoyed, he shook his head, muttered an exasperated curse, and asked Dee to continue.

"I tried a variation on Lila's technique. I called the State Police here in Portland and told them I'd seen a van engaged in some suspicious activity. I made a pest of myself, came off like some lonely old woman, and got the guy to admit the only vans they are currently looking for are both white--a Chevy and a Ford. That leaves your blue Dodge in the clear. And that means they're not looking for us. At least not yet."

"Very clever. And if I may add, surprising in a woman who flew out of L.A. like a scared rabbit and managed to leave her clothes behind in the trunk of her car."

"I've thought about that myself," she admitted. "I never thought of myself as especially clever or resourceful, but somehow since we teamed up I seem to have found new strengths. Must be your good influence."

Jeff watched her eat while he picked at his salad. He decided he liked most everything about her. Just yesterday he had fervently wished she had never come into his life, but now he was beginning to hope she'd never leave.

* * * * *

"She's been here. I can smell her. And this is probably her dress. Okay, get on the phone and

58

have a couple of guys sent up here--I'm not going to wait around in this hole. You and me will go back to that burg we just left and I'll see what I can find out about this Westman character. Not that phone, stupid! Use the one in the car. And be sure to tell 'em I want the girl alive and unharmed. I want to deal with her personally."

"Yes, Mr. Malavesi."

"I'm gonna take a leak, then we'll get the hell out of here. Tell them I want one of them here and alert at all times. And no noise. Don't want to scare them off when they come back."

"Yes sir."

* * * * *

Dee pushed her plate away with a satisfied groan. She didn't have room for dessert after all. "Looks like we have a few more options now. We could go on to Seattle, stay here, or go back to your cabin. It all depends. If you really want to know why this was done to you, we first have to find out what was done, and maybe by whom. Are you listening to me?"

"Sorry. Thinking about January 19th."

"January...oh! No headache?"

"No headache."

"Well, that's a start. So do we stay here in Portland, go south to your cabin, or north to Seattle?"

"Staying in Portland is pointless. If they're not looking for us there's no need to 'get lost'; but now that we've started this I'd like to get some answers that mean something, so I say we go north."

"Then let's go."

Jeff paid for lunch while Dee went to the restroom. She'd put the decision in his hands but now he'd made the choice she wondered if it had been wise. He had said 'looking for *us*' even though they had no reason to suspect anyone was looking for him--a sign he too considered them a team. On the other hand, going to Seattle was purely a matter of his problem, not hers.

Before he'd whisked her away from his cabin he had been little more than a convenience to her--a way to hide from Rico. She'd been intrigued by Jeff's special problem, but her own problem had been foremost in her mind.

"And now?" she asked her reflection. Did the implied commitments they'd made somehow change all those feelings? Perhaps. Even discounting physical attraction, a new element had entered her life. But she wasn't ready to put a label on it just yet.

When she got outside to the van she saw Jeff sitting in the right-hand seat, his head tilted back and his eyes closed in repose, so she climbed in behind the wheel and familiarized herself with the controls. The van handled more like her Cougar than had the Toyota and by the time she reentered northbound I-5 she felt at ease behind the wheel.

"Try me on current events," he suggested.

They were passing through Centralia, Washington--halfway to Seattle--before he evinced even the slightest reaction to her recall of major news events from the past four or five years. When he muttered a drawn-out, "Ah-h-h-h-h," she stopped talking and looked carefully at him. No furrowed brow, no hands clutching his temples.

"What were you talking about?"

"One of the favoritism scandals targeting the White House, I think."

"Tell me about it again."

"Okay." She repeated what she could remember, watching him as closely as driving conditions would permit, hopeful her words would stir a memory, fearful the reaction would not be positive. As she completed her re-cap she trailed off, waiting for a reaction.

"You can quit now," he finally said after a long sigh. "This isn't getting us anywhere."

"It got us somewhere," she argued. "We now know that your problem has nothing to do with the past in general, just your own personal history."

"I suppose...but I still don't see any connections."

"Don't be so impatient." She reached over and stroked his shoulder, felt a responsive flexing of his muscles beneath her fingers. "Look at all we've learned in just over a day."

"A great deal," he agreed. "Especially considering the nothing I learned in seven months. I owe you a lot already. I'm glad you came into my life, Dee. I'm not very good at showing it, but I hope you understand how much it means to me."

"Oh great! You wait until we're hurtling down the freeway at sixty-five miles an hour to turn mushy on me. If you really want to show how much you care, just try talking that way the next time we're in a motel room--with or without towel."

He flashed her an answering grin. The way his eyes lit up did funny things to her insides and she wondered how he would react if she pulled the van onto the shoulder right now.

"I really shouldn't distract you from your

driving," he teased, the grin still lighting up his face. "Your record isn't all that good."

"Ouch!" Despite the shared humor Dee's mind reeled with a number of sobering thoughts. She had actually suggested he 'turn mushy on her' the next time they were in a motel together; and had even thought of taking action along those same lines herself. It wasn't like her to be so bold, even considering her life-long reputation as a Chatty Cathy. Perhaps the feelings she'd chosen not to label back at the restaurant in Portland bore closer scrutiny.

They spotted Seattle in the distance as they topped a rise near Boeing Field. Dee let out a long sigh of relief. "Now that's a city. I was beginning to think there wasn't anything but trees and fast-food restaurants in this part of the country. How do you feel about treating ourselves to a luxury hotel with all the services?"

The cityscape had disappeared behind another hill before he replied. "Let's find a motel where we can keep the van handy."

Dee took the Madison exit and turned east, away from the city center. In less than five minutes she pulled the van into the parking lot of a small but clean-looking motel. She was about to offer to get their room, then remembered he had checked them into the motel the night before without her assistance. She once again reminded herself to stop treating him like a child.

He emerged from the office a few minutes later. "We have number six, next to that hallway. You can back the van in right there."

She was about to protest his somewhat paranoid instructions, but then remembered the bumpy flight from his cabin and changed her mind. If he wanted to be able to leave the motel in a hurry, it was fine by her. She backed the van into the parking space he'd indicated.

Jeff was inspecting the bathroom when she entered the room. The single king-size bed caught her attention, reminded her of her earlier flirtation.

"This is the only room he had on the ground floor," Jeff said, as though reading her mind.

"Fine with me. Mind if I use the bathroom first?"

"Go ahead. I'll get our things from the van."

When she emerged from the bathroom she saw that Jeff had dumped their 'things' onto the bed. The pitiful pile on the large bed made her realize how woefully inadequate their hurried shopping spree had been.

"We need to go shopping again. I need a few more items--toiletries, make-up, things like that. And we'll both need coats or jackets. It's colder here than in Oregon. You'll need shaving stuff--you can't go walking into banks or wherever looking like that."

Jeff took over the driving chores on their shopping trip, but the frenzied Seattle traffic--worse in some ways than even L.A.--wore her out even though she wasn't driving. She sighed with relief as they let themselves back into the motel room armed with their purchases.

"I'm tired, but I need to organize all this stuff before I can use it. Why don't you take your shower first?"

Jeff hung up their coats then carried his new shaving kit into the bathroom. She watched him out of the corner of her eye, wondering if he was simply overwhelmed by the extent of their purchases or if something else ate at him. He had suggested finding a branch of his bank and cashing in one of his CDs when their cash dwindled, had easily admitted his ignorance of traveler's checks to the teller and listened patiently to her explanation. He'd taken a thousand dollars in traveler's checks, but had insisted on having the rest in cash. When Dee questioned him about his decision later, he answered with a cryptic remark about preferring cash.

He had seemed as interested in the process of shopping as she had been; but somewhere along the way his attention had begun to wander.

She had been the one to suggest coming to Seattle initially, to follow the slim lead offered by his papers, and even though he had made the final decision she now wondered if it had been a good idea. Jeff seemed restless and unaccountably moody--in some ways even more so than he had been that day back in his cabin.

She tried to shake off the feeling of concern while she busied herself with their purchases. After she'd hung their clothes on the few hangers the motel supplied she sat on the edge of the bed and went through her purse. Jeff emerged from the bathroom and she turned to him, was surprised to see him fully clothed. "You got dressed again."

"No bathrobe. What are you doing?"

She grew puzzled at the look of discomfort on his face, but just then the credit card she had been bending back and forth snapped. "Destroying my credit cards. Since I'm not going to use them again I might as well relieve myself of the burden. Besides, it's fun."

And no sooner had the words left her mouth than she felt the heat rise up her neck and flush her face with what she was sure must be a lovely shade of shocking pink. She gave herself a mental kick, with hob-nailed boots. The foggy Seattle air must have clogged up her brain for her to have missed the obvious. Of course Jeff was uneasy. She was sitting on the one and only bed in the room and the hour for retiring was near.

Little more than twenty-four hours before Jeff had confessed to being unsure if he'd ever kissed a woman, yet she had been acting as though the two of them sharing the same bed was as natural as sharing a table at a restaurant. It was true that Jeff had begun to assert himself in some ways, taking charge of their escape, insisting on cash in return for his certificate. It was also true that in most other ways he still displayed the innocence of a child.

Guilt fueled her embarrassment further as she realized she had been behaving with as little regard for his feelings as Rico had with her. She picked up another of her cards and began bending it as she had the others, and launched into a rambling explanation of her activity. Jeff sat on the opposite edge of the bed and watched her, but she avoided looking at him. When she finished with the last of the credit cards she went directly to the bathroom, cutting off her own nonsensical spiel in mid-sentence as she closed the door between them.

The shampoo-and-cream-rinse treatment she gave her hair matched the most enjoyable hair salon experience in memory. Five or six days without a decently clean head of hair was an experience she did not care to repeat. Unbidden, a song from her high school production of South Pacific ran through her mind. She did not want to 'wash that man right out of her hair'--she wanted, rather, to treat him with the same degree of respect she expected for herself.

The heat lamp hurried along the drying process and she happily noted the return of her natural curl as she brushed and fluffed. Most of her bruises had abated except for the one on her left shoulder. That large area of blue-black skin still pained her when she touched it and it looked awful. She applied a light coat of cover-up, checked herself in the mirror, and decided against using anything else.

She also rejected the idea of getting back into her dirty clothes despite having worn them only that one day, and wrapped herself in the largest of the towels. Jeff would probably be in bed, his back to her, maybe even feigning sleep. It would be quicker, easier, and possibly even less seductive to simply drop the towel and slip into her side of the large bed. She promised herself she'd stay on her own side, wait for him to make the first move, avoid confronting him with her own naked desire.

She checked the towel again to make sure it was secure, opened the bathroom door and stepped into the room. Jeff was sitting on the edge of the bed, right where she had left him. "You're not in bed?"

"Been thinking. Going to be an important day, tomorrow. Wonder what we'll find."

She went to the other side of the bed, noted the tense way he held himself. "Come to bed, Jeff. Worry about tomorrow when it gets here."

He stood and turned to face her. Suddenly she felt very undressed. If she were fully dressed in street clothes and heavy winter coat and boots she would probably still feel undressed. It had nothing to do with the towel she wore, it had more to do with the moment. Surprisingly, it was Jeff who finally broached The Subject.

"I lied about the room. There were others. With more than one bed. I wanted to sleep with you."

The tension in the room was thick enough to cut with a knife. She wanted to laugh, or shout for joy, or simply throw herself across the wide expanse of bed into his arms; but she did none of those. She was acutely aware of what the admission must have cost him and remained determined to be sensitive about the encounter. "Thank you for telling me."

She held his gaze as she pulled down the covers on her side of the bed, dropped the towel to the floor, then slid between the sheets. "Turn off the light, take off your clothes, and come to bed. I need you to hold me. You don't have to do anything else. Just come to bed and hold me. Please."

She moved closer to the center of the bed, then turned on her side, her back toward him, closed her eyes, and held her breath.

A moment later the light went out and she heard the rustle of clothing, the scratch of zipper. She felt the bed take his weight, felt the covers settle again.

It seemed like an eternity before she felt him touch her ankle with his foot, but the rest of his body quickly followed--as though after dipping his toe into the pool he had simply dived in headlong. He formed himself to her and draped an arm over her side without allowing his hand to touch her.

She let out the breath she had been holding,

then waited, unmoving, until her heartbeat slowed. The heat of his body against hers soothed and excited her. She tried her best to ignore the excitement.

Slowly, very slowly, she found his hand with hers, wrapped her fingers around his palm, and gave it a gentle squeeze.

"Thank you for holding me, Jeff."

"You feel good."

She could feel his heart thumping against her back. She wanted to pull his hand to her, press it to her breast, feel him respond.

She didn't move.

She wanted to reach behind her, pull him even closer, press herself against his hardness, feel the manliness of him, see if his need was as great as hers.

She didn't move.

Her body began to respond to the touch and the smell of him lying behind her. A moist heat began spreading within her and she squeezed thighs and knees together in an effort to hold it back. She swallowed hard to ease a constriction in her throat, refused to let it come out as a sob or a gasp. She forced her breathing into a steady rhythm, kept her mouth closed.

And still she didn't move.

Moments later his steady breathing told her he had relaxed, possibly fallen asleep. She bit her lip in an effort to hold back the tears, to keep them from wetting her pillow. *It isn't fair!* And the moment the thought formed she chastised herself. She was lying in a warm bed with a loving man beside her--a man who had saved her life and who now represented her brightest hope for a better future, assuming such a thing was possible in light of the disasters she'd managed to stumble into these past few days.

And that future would be better for a gentle, measured development. Wouldn't it?

CHAPTER FIVE

Dee felt rested, safe, and secure. She decided to snuggle into her pillow and enjoy the feeling a while longer. Then she realized her 'pillow' was Jeff's shoulder.

He lay on his back, softly snoring, and her head rested in the crook of his shoulder. That arm was wrapped around her, his hand lightly pressed against the small of her back.

She snuggled closer, sliding her leg a little higher up his thighs. He was still wearing his shorts.

When she felt him stir beneath her she planted a kiss on his chin. "Did you sleep well?"

"Very."

"We should think about getting up in four or five hours."

"Bladder won't hold out that long."

"Drat! Well, I'm going to keep you pinned here until you cry 'Uncle'."

He said nothing. She gave him another peck on his chin and then snuggled back into her sleeping position.

They hadn't made love, hadn't even been very sensual with each other. So why did she feel so good? What was it about being with this man-- just being with him--that made her feel relaxed and complete and...loved?

She kissed him lightly on the shoulder. "Have I told you I...I like you very much?"

"Don't!" He rolled her off of him, propped himself up on one elbow and looked into her face.

"Don't talk about...us. Not until we find out who, or what, I am. You don't know me. I don't know me. What if I turn out to be like you said-- some kind of idiot who somebody decided to get rid of? What if I never remember anything of those thirty-seven years? What if---"

"What I feel for you---"

"Don't feel for me, Dee! Not yet. Excuse me, I have to go to the bathroom."

As the bathroom door closed she leapt out of bed, fighting back tears of frustration and anger, and quickly slipped into new panties and bra, slacks and a blouse. She ignored the raspy feeling of the new, unwashed, fabric against her skin, avoided looking at herself in the mirror above the dresser.

It had seemed so perfect, just being with him. Never in her life had she slept with a man without sex. She had always assumed the two went together like...like love and marriage. Hah! Last night she had experienced something completely new, discovered feelings she hadn't known existed, and the man who was the cause of it all had just rejected her--again.

Maybe he thought he had a good reason. Maybe he thought he was protecting her against some awful mistake. But maybe he was just a coward, like all the rest of man-un-kind. Maybe he was just using her, taking advantage of her. He probably wanted to be free to dump her when she'd outlived her usefulness, damn him!

He reentered the room and broke into her

thoughts. "I'm sorry."

She was still too angry and frustrated to be polite. She took possession of the bathroom and closed and locked the door behind her. A stinging cool-water shower reduced her physical frustration below the boiling point; but it took a long, self-imposed lecture featuring reminders of her resolve to allow him to make the first move, and suggestions that Jeff was not responsible for her feelings before she felt composed enough to face him again. She dressed, then took a couple of deep breaths before opening the bathroom door.

Jeff was reading a tourist brochure. She flashed him the biggest smile she could manage. "The Spoiled Brat is ready to go to work when you are."

* * * * *

Their trek through Seattle's financial district left them with little to show for their efforts. The company name shown on the title to his property turned out to be a 'holding company'. The only woman in their office who would talk to them claimed none of the company's records indicated the seller of the property. The title company told them little more. The land had been part of an estate, according to their title search, and had been divided by a realty firm and sold off as parcels. The local office in Salem had actually done the search, but nothing in the papers filed with the main office indicated that anyone knew how, or when, or by whom Jeff's cabin had been built--it simply turned out to be on the parcel. The holding company had requested a title search when an offer had been made. There was, however, no record of Jeff's offer even though his signature appeared on all the requisite papers.

Jeff remembered none of it.

Their annoyance at being thus frustrated in their search did not help with the emotional tension between them.

Dee got into bed that night still dressed in panties and bra, huddled close to the edge of the bed, and tried to will herself to sleep.

Jeff sat in the chair, reading and re-reading his title papers. For all Dee knew, he might have passed the entire night there. When she awoke late the next morning he was in the bathroom, shaving, and fully dressed. The crumpled and scattered bed linens were a mute testimony to the way she felt.

When Jeff emerged from the bathroom he groused that they might as well have stayed in Salem.

"I'm afraid you're right," Dee agreed, just as frustrated as he sounded. "We might learn more by talking to your neighbors than we've managed to pry out of these people."

"I don't have many neighbors. I think a couple of tree-farming families own most of the land outside the state park, and I don't know any of them."

"You didn't exactly get on the good side of the most likely source of information--the County Sheriff."

He shrugged. "Guess I'll head back. You want to come?"

The question caught her by surprise. She'd been expecting his announcement for more than a day, but the question changed everything. With his usual flair for ambiguity he'd managed to dump the decision about what she would do squarely in her lap. And she couldn't decide. She had no particular fondness for Seattle, but the thought of returning to his tiny cabin with its tiny bed didn't exactly appeal to her, either.

Against all of these negatives there was another consideration. He'd rescued her twice, helped her get farther away from Rico; while she'd done little for him beyond stirring up his settled existence, and would be leaving him with a lot of unanswered questions. In spite of the sexual tension between them, she felt she owed him something more; but she'd need time to think about the prospect of returning to Oregon with him.

"As long as we're here, why don't we spend the rest of the day playing tourist? We could see some of the sights I've noticed on these maps and make the trip count for *something*."

It would also give her a chance to think things over, consider all of her options, and maybe even ease some of the tension between them. His somewhat reluctant "okay" was good enough.

They started at the waterfront on Elliot Bay, visited shops and the aquarium. Jeff vetoed a harbor tour on the grounds he didn't know if he was prone to seasickness, but the shops and museums along the waterfront kept them occupied through the morning. In the afternoon they climbed the stories-tall staircase up the side of the hill to join the throng around Pike's Market--which the brochure they'd picked up touted as the country's oldest, continuously operating, open-air market.

They'd passed by the market the day before on their fact-finding tour and Dee now suggested they skip it, but Jeff seemed adamant in his desire to walk through the shops and stalls at a leisurely pace. Dee shrugged off his streak of perversity, returned to her own thoughts as she climbed and then walked with him.

She bought a long skinny loaf of French bread, broke it in half and munched on her half of the tasty sourdough while they strolled. The tensions between them had eased somewhat but she had not quite made up her mind to stay with him for the return trip. She watched him carefully out of the corner of her eye, hoping to catch a smile, or even a friendly look, as a sign he was coming out of his funk.

Her alertness to his mood proved fortunate. In mid-stride, about to pop the last crumb of his share of the bread into his mouth, Jeff froze.

"What's wrong?"

He turned pale and stared straight ahead, his hand with the small piece of bread poised near his chin. She followed his gaze, trying to pick out whatever had shaken him. She could see nothing but a milling crowd of shoppers and gawkers in front of a fish merchant's stall at one corner of the market.

"Jeff! Tell me what you see that upsets you."

Still he said nothing.

"Do you see something you recognize?"

He turned his head from side to side with a jerky motion.

"A person you think you know?

A curt nod.

"The man in the dark suit?"

He shook his head.

"Someone buying fish?"

An abrupt nod.

Half a dozen people were being waited on at the fish counter. It was difficult to scan the crowd because many people gathered to watch the entertaining process--a man with a deep voice kept up a sing-song cadence describing his wares laid out on the iced table out front, and then, when one had been selected by a customer, would pick it up and toss it behind him to one of the countermen who would then weigh it and complete the transaction. A nice orderly line of people with numbered tickets would have made the process much easier to follow, though less fun to watch. She moved behind Jeff and went up on her toes so she could watch the crowd and the movements of his head at the same time. She dropped her bread, wishing her mouth weren't so dry. "Woman in blue?"

No.

"Man with green sweater."

No.

"Pregnant woman with--"

A vigorous nod told her she'd hit pay dirt.

"The pregnant woman is someone you know?"

Again the nod.

"Want me to get her?"

A whimper escaped him as he shook his head violently.

"Follow her?"

The woman was already moving away from the counter with her package of fish and Dee wasted no time waiting for Jeff's response. She grabbed his hand and began to follow the woman, then was jerked backward as Jeff refused to move.

"Come on!" She shook his arm.

His feet started moving, but slowly. She tugged at him, pulling him along like a recalcitrant toddler. Back to childhood again, she thought as she tried to keep up with the woman who was about to be lost in the crowd. Luck played a role when the woman began descending the stairs outside the market. Her distended abdomen slowed her down on the stairs and Dee could keep pace.

Please let her be headed for the parking lot, Dee prayed as she continued to tug at Jeff. Jeff's van waited under the freeway in the waterfront parking lot. If the woman's car was there, there was a slim chance Dee could get Jeff into the van in time to trail the woman by car. If the woman headed for the trolley or some other form of mass transportation, they would probably lose her. She began calculating at what point she would let go of Jeff and forcibly stop the woman, who was clearly far too valuable to Jeff to just let her get away.

They were only two cars away from the van when the women stopped at a white station wagon and began looking through her purse. Dee whirled and thrust her hand into Jeff's pocket, came up with the keys to the van, and managed to get the side door open. She shoved him inside, climbed in after him, and slammed the door behind her. Jeff huddled in a ball on the floor of the van but she paid him little attention. He was safe for the moment. All of her thoughts focused on the white station wagon two aisles over.

She ignored the scraping metal sound as she backed the van out of its small space and spun the wheel to the left, racing the engine to keep it from stalling while she held it back with her left foot on the brake pedal.

The station wagon turned right across the trolley tracks and onto the busy street that served the waterfront shops she and Jeff had visited that morning. *Don't let a policeman be watching!* Dee prayed silently, cutting off a vehicle which had the right-of-way, then cutting off another when she moved into the left lane and raced ahead to draw nearer to the station wagon. Had she known Seattle's streets better, she would have been content to follow the car at a distance; but her only hope of not losing the quarry was to stay on her back bumper as if she were being towed.

"Jeff! Are you alright?"

No response. Damn! She could use him right now, to write down the station wagon's license number, which might come in handy if she lost the vehicle.

She ran a yellow light with the station wagon as they climbed a hill away from the waterfront, then had to slam on the brakes before she was clear of the intersection as construction backed up traffic on the already crowded city streets. She ignored glares and blares from drivers on the crossing street as they were forced to merge into one lane to get around her.

Dee couldn't see the woman in the car--she sat too high in the van--but she could imagine what must be going through the other's head. She hated putting another woman--especially a pregnant one-- through this, but right now her loyalty was to Jeff.

The thought made Dee realize she had made her decision. The commitment stood.

A number of other items began falling into place as well. Ever since their arrival in Seattle Jeff had been moody and out of sorts, with none of the humor or good-natured bantering that had marked their first two days together. She had chosen to put a personal interpretation on the change, had chalked it up to sexual tension between them. She'd been wrong.

Jeff's strange behavior had less to do with the two of them than with the city itself. Seattle must be his home, and he must have been feeling that, sensing it without knowing it. She tried to imagine being caught up in that odd sensation of deja vu for hours or days on end rather than for just a brief instant. Just thinking about it sent an involuntary shudder through her body.

They began to inch forward, coming close to a freeway entrance ramp. The woman hadn't turned on her signals, but Dee wasn't relying on courtesy. She kept her gaze glued to the front of the station wagon, alert for any movement indicating a turn in either direction. And she didn't bother checking her side mirrors for other traffic. The bulk of the van would, she hoped, intimidate anyone into allowing her to do things she would have considered unthinkable under ordinary circumstances.

Yes, the station wagon was heading onto the freeway! At least they'd be out of this city snarl, but tailgating at the higher freeway speeds would be a little more dangerous. If the woman made a sudden stop for any reason...Dee tried to ignore the possibilities for disaster.

A scant car length between them, they sped along the freeway and Dee kept repeating the license plate number to herself in an effort to memorize it. If only Jeff would snap out of it, get a pencil and paper out of her purse... Her purse! It

was still hanging from her left shoulder. The short straps were not designed to be worn from the shoulder and the soft bag was jammed into her armpit. She stripped it down, put it in her lap, and fished around for a lipstick--all without taking her eyes from the station wagon.

Dumping both purse and the top of her lipstick onto the floor between the seats, she wrote the license number of the station wagon on the dashboard in front of her, then let the lipstick join the other things on the floor.

The station wagon veered at the last second onto an exit ramp, without signaling. The woman must know she was behind followed. Three blocks later, the car pulled into a new subdivision and Dee decided to give its driver a little room, backed off to eight or ten car lengths as they slowed to twenty-five miles an hour.

In the middle of an intersection the car turned abruptly then shot forward, disappearing down a side street. The van's engine coughed once before catching as Dee jammed the accelerator to the floor, and by the time she got to the corner the car was out of sight around a curve in the street. She felt a grudging admiration for the woman's skill as she raced ahead in the direction the station wagon had gone.

Just around the curve another street intersected the one she was traveling. Dee turned right and drove slowly down the street, looking for the white station wagon. The street ended in a cul-de-sac so she returned to the intersection and continued down the street in the other direction.

She spotted the station wagon in a driveway three houses from the next corner. She noted the house number but continued driving on by to the next corner. She turned left after stopping and drove half a block before pulling the van to the curb. Retrieving her lipstick she wrote the address, 1309 Tamarack, on the dashboard under the license plate number. Then she continued down the street until they were out of the subdivision, pulled off the road in front of a small business complex. Time to see about Jeff.

He was still huddled on the floor of the van, his arms wrapped around himself as though chilled. He lips were moving, but no sound issued from his mouth.

"I found her house," Dee reported. "Who is she?"

He lifted his head, and she tried to remain calm when she saw the look on his face. She had seen him in pain, caught in the grip of one of his headaches, but that had been a trifle compared to what she now witnessed. She thought again about the deja vu he must have been experiencing, thought about the Herculean strength it must be taking to keep him from cracking. She wondered if that strength would fail him, if he'd remain in the grip of the malaise brought on by the encounter with the pregnant woman.

She got down on the floor of the van with him and cradled his head with her arms. She prayed it would be enough, because she didn't know what else to do.

After what seemed like an eternity he stirred.

"Are you feeling better?" she whispered, stroking the back of his head.

"What happened?"

"You saw someone and went into a state of

shock. I managed to follow her. I found her house."

"Where are we?"

"Near there. I'm going to drive back to the motel now. Will you be okay?"

"Yes."

She drove slowly, frequently consulting both map and street signs to be sure she could find her way back. When she reached their motel, Jeff was barely able to get himself out of the van and into their room. He went straight to the bathroom. When she heard the toilet flush she knocked on the door, then entered.

"Are you okay now?"

"Yeah. Just need a cigarette."

"You don't smoke. I'll go get you some coffee."

He gave her a look of disbelief, then turned on the tap and splashed water in his face. She left him, went to the machines in the hallway next to their room and got two cups of black coffee.

He took the paper cup from her with a weak smile, gulped down half, then sat down heavily on the edge of the bed. "Tell me what happened."

"Do you remember being at Pike's Place and seeing the pregnant woman?"

"I remember the waterfront."

"Okay." She related the sequence of events as well as she could remember them. "She must be important to you. And from the way you insisted earlier on our doing a second tour of the market, I'd bet that place is, or was, important to the two of you. So think, Jeff. Who is she?"

"I haven't the foggiest idea. I can't even remember what she looks like now. I guess I'll just have to confront--"

"No you don't. I'm not going to go through another session with you in a state of shock. I've been developing a plan, and this is how it's going to work. First of all, you stay here and rest. I'm going to visit the local chamber of commerce or whatever I can find open on a Saturday where I can get the materials I need, then I'm going back to her house alone. I'll find out who she is and then we can talk about it when I get back here."

"I don't get it. How..."

"Leave that to me. Up till now I haven't done much to keep up my end of this partnership. You rescued me from that wreck and kept me away from the cops--which I suspect was the same thing as keeping me away from Rico. That means you've probably saved my life twice, and I've done little except come along for the ride. Now it's my turn."

CHAPTER SIX

Jeff paced the floor of the motel room, worried about more things than he could cope with at once. He didn't like being here, didn't like the thought of Dee out there alone with his van, facing problems that were his. He didn't like not knowing, and he didn't particularly care for the process of finding out. There was, in short, little to nothing about his situation he did like.

Dee herself was too big a problem for him to resolve, even without all the rest. She aroused him in ways, both physically and mentally, he had not even thought possible; and he had no experience to guide him in how to respond.

Her uncanny habit of asking exactly the wrong question, of getting right to the heart of a matter, of forcing him to face things he didn't want to face, had led him to hide a small part of the truth from her. He had lied when she asked him if he remembered seeing the woman at the market. He did remember that woman, and he remembered his reaction. What he had experienced when he caught sight of her had been beyond the kind of pain his headaches brought him, but he had known from the first instant they were connected somehow.

He didn't know the woman's identity, but he knew they had been close--possibly even related in some way. The woman might very well be a part of the family who had tried to banish him. He should have told Dee, but he feared she would question him further, stir up more of the past. To avoid potential pain for himself, he had hidden the truth from her. Doing so, he now realized, might have placed her in greater jeopardy. It was a helluva way to treat a woman who meant so much to him.

* * * * *

Dee had little trouble putting together her "road show". Her first job in L.A. had been as a Welcome Wagon Hostess and she had enjoyed the work. It paid almost as well as waitressing and the hours were more flexible, freeing her for auditions. That experience, even without her acting talents, gave her the gimmick she needed to get her through the pregnant woman's front door.

She stuffed the brochures she'd found at the motel office and a nearby Visitor's Center into the pocket of the plastic folder she'd bought, clipped it to her new clipboard, and headed north. She parked down the street from the woman's home, walked briskly up Tamarack Lane to 1309 and rang the bell.

"Good Morning! I'm from Welcome Wagon and we're visiting all the families in your neighborhood. May I come in?"

The haggard-looking pregnant woman invited her in, offered coffee, and brightened up a little as Dee heaped compliments upon her attractive home. They talked decorating for a few minutes before Dee turned the conversation to more informative subjects.

She dutifully noted "Walter and Sondra Culver" on her pad, added their address and phone number, then eased off to inquire about the new

85

baby--their first. In a short time she learned Sondra had been married to Walter a little over a year and that Walter was a programmer who worked in the IT department at Boeing. The first sign of resistance from the woman came when Dee asked if she had been married before.

"Actually, I just need the information for our files. You'd be surprised at how much money we waste sending mailings to couples who have divorced and moved away. It really cuts down on the services we can provide to people like you."

"Well, my former husband is dead."

"Oh. I'm terribly sorry. All the more important we correct our records, though. What was your late husband's name?"

"Eastman. Gerald Eastman."

It took all of Dee's reserve strength, and more acting ability than she knew she had to avoid reacting to the name. She quickly changed the subject. "Oh! I forgot to ask if you and Walter enjoy the theater. We have two mailings we send to couples. One is basically a restaurant premium, but the other is more oriented to the fine arts."

"We don't get out much these days," the homemaker suggested, stroking her abdomen, "but we do enjoy the arts."

Dee's hand shook as she scribbled a cryptic note in her pad, and decided it was time to make a graceful, but hurried, exit. She thanked the woman for her time, excused herself on the grounds she had a lot of other families to see. It took all of her willpower to walk, not run, away from the house and back to the van.

Taken alone, the name of the woman's late husband would have meant nothing to her. But given Jeff's extreme reaction to seeing the women in the market, she felt the similarity between Eastman and Westman must be more than coincidence. And that meant Jeff's prediction had been accurate-- someone was playing with him like a puppet. Given the evident emotion with which Mrs. Walter Culver had spoken her former husband's name, the whole business was taking a rather sinister turn.

As she climbed into the van and buckled up she realized she should have asked a few follow-up questions: like how Gerald Eastman had died, what kind of work he had done, how long they had been married. It would have been easy to work in questions like that if she hadn't lost her equanimity, but it was too late now. She'd just have to make do with what she had. And now she had to decide what, or even if, she would tell Jeff about the woman.

* * * * *

Sondra Culver watched the Welcome Wagon woman walk down the driveway, then turned away from the window. She carried their coffee cups to the kitchen but did not bother to rinse them out. Something about the woman bothered her, and she decided to see which of her new neighbors the woman would visit next. She returned to the front window just in time to see a dark blue van drive past the house, the blonde at the wheel. She was almost certain it was the same van that had followed her earlier.

She slumped into Walter's chair and cradled herself, rocking her baby and herself as she composed her thoughts. Then she reached for the phone and entered eleven digits. It did not help her peace of mind to discover she still knew the number by heart.

The phone whirred and clicked as the switching connected her with Chicago. She heard the phone ring twice and then an all-too-familiar voice answered by repeating the last four digits.

"Brian, this is Sondra."

"Sondra! What a pleasant surprise. How are things in Seattle? Did the baby arrive?"

"No, Brian. The baby isn't due for another month. That's not why I'm calling."

"What can I do for you?"

"Brian, do you have someone keeping an eye on me and Walter?"

"Good Heavens no! Why would I do that?"

"Because a woman followed me home from downtown and then showed up at my door later pretending to be a Welcome Wagon Hostess. She seemed inordinately curious about my past."

"Well, salespeople can be pushy at times, Sondra. What makes you so sure she wasn't just a busy-body?"

"Brian, listen to me! I said she followed me home. She was driving a dark blue van, dirty and banged-up. It was not the kind of vehicle that fit her, or her line of work, at all."

She could hear the line hissing and crackling in the silence. "Brian?"

"I'm here, Sondra. Just thinking. Did the van have commercial plates, or anything else distinctive about it?"

"I didn't notice, Brian. I've tried to forget the habit of looking over my shoulder every minute of the day. Six years was enough."

"Okay, it's probably not important. Did you call the local Welcome Wagon people to check her out?"

"No. I don't think she even gave her name. She left some brochures. Wait a moment."

She put the phone down and pushed herself out of the chair with an effort. She brought the papers from the dining room table back to the phone, sat again, a cradled the phone against her shoulder.

"There are no names on any of these brochures."

"Okay. I don't want you to worry about anything. Stay calm and relaxed and welcome that baby of yours into this world in a happy frame of mind. I'll arrange for some protection, just as a precaution. They'll be discreet--you won't even know they're there. Secondly, I'll check with the Welcome Wagon people myself, try to track this woman down and find out what she's up to. I'll let you know the minute I find out anything."

Sondra sighed, succumbing as usual to his soothing manner, his charm.

"Meanwhile, you just relax. No need to tell Walter about any of this, if you'd rather not. I'll call you during the day, and if a man answers I'll hang up."

She smiled in spite of herself. "Thank you, Brian."

"Don't mention it. 'Bye now."

* * * * *

The phone nearly slipped from Brian Whipple's hand as he replaced it in its cradle. His hands were wet with perspiration. He wiped them on his vest, stood, and took two quick steps to the window of his 12th floor office. "Damn!"

He drew in two quick breaths, wiped his palms again, and returned to the desk. He entered a single digit, then waited impatiently. When he had satisfied himself as to the identity of the man in the Seattle office he issued orders regarding the protection of the Culver home.

"...Item number two. I want the area within a fifty-mile radius of Kirkland combed for a dark blue van. It's a Dodge and probably has Oregon plates. Number and description of occupants unknown, though one may be a blonde woman. Once the van is spotted it is to be kept under close surveillance, but the occupants are not to be approached. Notify me immediately but take no further action. Clear?"

"Yes sir."

"There is one exception. If the van attempts to entered the Culver neighborhood, stop it. Wreck a car or whatever seems appropriate without blowing your cover."

"I take it the two items are connected?"

"Yes, but forget the connection. And make sure you use operatives who will act as instructed without asking a lot of useless questions."

"I'll put my best men on it, sir."

"Good. I may be en route before anything breaks. I'll advise you."

Brian broke the connection, then entered another number. He had to wait for Sammy to be located, then wait again for a scrambled line to be established.

"Sam. I want you to hot-foot it up to our

boy's cabin and check on things. There may be some unusual activity, so use extreme caution. Advise me soonest."

"Got it. Anything else?"

"No. Just hurry."

His hands were dry now. Action always cooled him down. He'd like to believe it was all a mistake, but one didn't get far in this business acting on fantasies. He could guess accurately what Sammy, and the others in Seattle, would find. And that left him with two decisions to make. Should he go to Seattle and confront Gerald head-on or should he wait for Gerald to come to him? Either way, his life probably wasn't worth a plug nickel.

His other dilemma involved equally drastic consequences and was no easier to contemplate. What to do about Ashton Hobart? There was no question of telling him anything, but if he left Chicago in a hurry, Ash might have him followed and all of Brian's efforts would go for nothing. Of course, if what he suspected was true, he might soon be in no condition to care about Ash's reaction.

He decided he needed a drink. Badly.

* * * * *

"You're back." The relief that flooded through him did not completely dispel the negative feelings he had been suffering, but it helped.

"Yes. But to be completely honest with you, I'm not altogether happy about it."

"What happened? What did you find out?"

"Let me go to the bathroom first."

Dee was being frustratingly evasive after all the hours he had spent worrying about her. He had a mind to grab her by the shoulders and shake the information out of her when she came out of the bathroom. Boy, did he need a cigarette!

There it was again...that cigarette thing. He didn't smoke. Of course, he also didn't think about grabbing women by the shoulders and shaking information out of them.

"Okay, I'm going to tell you everything," Dee assured him as she came out of the bathroom. "But I'm going to do it my way--in small doses. I want to go easy on your because I don't want you going into shock again. So just bear with me, okay?"

"Would you like to tie me down and put a stick in my mouth so I don't bite my tongue?"

"Sarcasm doesn't become you, Jeff. Maybe *you* can forget your headaches and the rest of it, but I can't. I've watched your face screw up in pain too many times."

Her intensity struck him like a physical force. "I'm sorry. I don't know what's happening to me."

"It's all right. I'm a little edgy myself. The woman's name is Mrs. Walter Culver. Mean anything?"

She might as well have said Mrs. George Smith. "No."

She fidgeted with the clipboard she was holding, ran her finger around the edge. "Her first name is Sondra."

"Sandra?"

"No, Sondra. Sondra Culver."

He ran the name through his mind a few times, savoring it. The name didn't mean anything to him, nor could he picture a sister or cousin named

Sondra. "Go on."

"Okay. She was a widow, but she's been married to Walter Culver for a little over a year." Dee paused again, as though expecting a response.

He tried to not show his impatience.

"Her late husband's name was Gerald Eastman."

The pain hit him like someone had driven a white-hot poker into the back of his neck, then was immediately washed away as he felt himself engulfed in a flood of memories. He staggered, was vaguely aware of the blonde helping him to sit on the edge of the bed. Then he closed his eyes, and remembered.

CHAPTER SEVEN

He shook his head to clear away the fog and registered his presence in an unlighted motel room. Early evening lights and noise drifted through the half-open window, and there was a woman with him. He sensed no danger--but had no idea who this woman was or why either one of them were here.

There should be nothing unusual about the present circumstances. He frequently met with men and women in places like this, but his inability to define the exact roles being played at the moment alerted him. He not only didn't know the roles being played, he also had no idea exactly where he was or even what day it was.

And he wasn't wearing his gun, not even his holster. A quick scan of the room revealed no familiar clothing, and the woman's clothing shared the space on the open clothes rack with a man's. Where was his jacket, which was the logical place for him to have left his gun? *Where was his holster?*

More than a little disoriented, he took a minute to calm himself with a few measured breaths, eyes closed. Gun and holster must be under one of the pillows on the bed. The woman seemed alert and watched him with a frown, possibly of puzzlement.

Pretty, he thought. Too pretty to be one of

the call girls he usually used as a source of information. Something about her felt familiar. Maybe she'd say something that would jog his memory. Cautiously, so as not to telegraph his confusion until he learned enough to regain control of the situation, he prompted her to say something. "You were saying...?"

"Wha--! I haven't said anything for hours, Jeff. How do *you* feel?"

No help. The name she used should have clued him in to their relationship, but it didn't. What did she mean about not talking for hours? He stood and wobbled into the bathroom. When his eyes adjusted to the light he did a double-take. Who was that "hick" in the mirror? He was either wearing an expensive wig or at least two or three months had passed since he last looked at himself in a mirror. He ran his hands through the thick hair, tugged here and there and confirmed it was no wig. Then he looked down. Jeans and an off-the-rack sport shirt must be some sort of disguise, but the fog of confusion did not disperse.

He returned to the motel's bedroom. The woman still sat on the edge of the bed. Now was the time to get his gun from under the pillow, walk out of the motel room, hail a taxi back to his apartment, and figure out this amnesia alone; but curiosity kept him rooted. "No more games," he said. "Tell me who you are and what you want."

* * * * *

Stunned by his abrasive manner, Dee gaped at him. The hours she had waited quietly for some reaction from him had lulled her into a state of near sleep. At no time during the long wait had he shown any sign of headache pain, so she had not attempted to move him or disturb him in any other way. His first words, so completely out of context with anything she knew about him, startled her and she answered without thinking. "I'm Dee Johansen and I'm trying to help you..."

His response suggested he had forgotten everything rather than remembered more. He must be disoriented. Listening to her quick re-cap of events, he paced back and forth like a caged animal, at times pausing near the bed or dresser to shove his hand under a pillow or into a drawer as though looking for something before resuming his pacing.

"...then I told you about Sondra, Gerald Eastman's widow, and you went into that stupor."

"My *what?*"

His face turned pale again and she wondered if he would collapse where he stood. But before she could move to support him his color returned and he regarded her with a wide-eyed look. "You're Dee!"

His unexpected acknowledgement gave her a great sense of relief. "Yes! I'm Dee. Remember now?"

"My mind tells me I should be in Philly, not Seattle. Or at least just outside D.C. That's where the hospital--just a minute. Exactly who are you? How did you find me, and why? And where is this cabin you mentioned?"

She fought her impulse to cry, or laugh, or make a mad dash for the door. Patiently she related additional details of her flight from Rico in L.A., his rescue of her from her wrecked Toyota, and the events that had transpired since then. She did this even as she thought he should be as aware of these details as she was, and that the exercise was as futile as fumbling though the multiplication tables in front of the class.

The way he held himself, as though prepared to leap at her--or away from her, and the way his gaze fixed on her, like he could see into her soul, also unnerved her. This man now standing in front of her bore too close a resemblance to the kind of men she was running from, and a part of her urged her to run, to disappear from his life...if she could.

Only the faint hope she could somehow bring back the gentle, considerate man she had called Jeff Westman kept her going. But even that hope was dashed against the cold, emotionless words of his response.

"And you expect me to believe you had no idea who I was?"

"I don't even know who Jeff Westman was, let alone this other person--this Gerald Eastman you seem to have become. If you don't believe me, then I guess our partnership is dissolved. I'll just pack my things and be on my way."

"Not so fast. How is it you knew what to do and where to go, to 'recover my past', as you put it?"

"I *didn't* know! We were just fishing. When we got the papers from the bank and noticed the coincidence of the dates we agreed to see what we could find here."

"What papers?"

"Your bank statements. Your title. They're in my purse. I'll show you."

"Mind if I look for myself?" He grabbed her purse from the dresser so fast the movement was a blur. She sat back down on the edge of the bed, fighting anger and frustration, furiously blinking back tears. Apparently, knowing who she was wasn't enough for him, and it hurt her more than she wanted to admit.

He went through her purse, stirring up the contents as though he were looking for a bomb, then dumped it back on the dresser, the packet of papers in his hand. He leafed through them, and she thought she saw a glimmer of recognition, or maybe surprise, cross his guarded features. "Okay, so somebody has a sense of humor."

"Pardon?"

"The dates. They're all January 20th."

"That was the last date you could remember without getting headaches. It's close to the date of your first job with Manpower. I don't see what's humorous about it."

"Inauguration Day."

It took her a moment to make any sense of that. "Does that mean someone in the government had something to do with all this?"

He took a few steps closer, looked down at her. "You really *don't* know what's going on here, do you?"

She wanted to stand up and decrease the effect of his imposing figure towering over her, but she couldn't do so without either scuttling away from him like a crab or standing on his toes. "I guess not. I did think we were friends--more than friends. By your present attitude I guess I was wrong."

"You weren't wrong."

He took her by the elbows, helped her to stand, then took her in his arms. She went willingly, wrapped her arms around him. It felt good to have him holding her again, the way he had that first night in this room. She drank in the smell of him and felt the firm muscles of his back beneath her hands. She told herself the questioning and the suspicion didn't matter as long as they were together.

"The situation has changed. I need to be cautious."

His hands moved over her body. She liked his touch, liked the way he molded his fingers into every little--hot anger flared as she realized what he was doing, and she tried to pull away from him. "I'll say things have changed! Do you always frisk your friends? What are you looking for, the machine gun I keep strapped to my back?"

"Relax. My gun is missing and I just had to make sure..."

"You have no gun! At least you haven't had one since I met you. There were no guns in your cabin, none in your van, and you certainly weren't wearing one the night we slept in each other's arms. Unless that lump in your shorts was your gun. Let go of me!" Dee tried to free herself from him but she couldn't break his grip.

"Easy. Easy. Just sit back down there while I check the rest of the room. Then we'll talk."

She considered telling him she was through talking. She had enough money in her purse to keep her going for a while, and she could easily find work in this city and remain anonymous enough to hide out from Rico. She didn't need another minute of this aggravation from Mr. Jeff Westman, or Gerald Eastman, or whoever he was.

He dropped to the floor and searched the underside of the bed. Then he pulled out each of the dresser drawers in turn, checking all surfaces of each drawer and the space it occupied, and then the back wall of the dresser, inside and out. Then he went into the bathroom. Fascinated in spite of herself, she wanted to tell him he'd make a great cleaning lady--he didn't miss a spot in either of the two rooms--but thought better of the impulse.

"Okay, let's talk." He joined her on the bed. "Start from the beginning and tell me everything."

"I've already *told* you everything."

"Tell me again. Please."

She considered for a minute. Tired, hungry and frustrated, she wasn't sure she wanted to bother. The look in his eyes, though, reminded her of the "old" Jeff and the promise she'd made to stay with him. She took a deep breath and began, making sure to leave out no details regardless of how insignificant they might seem, trying her best to make him see she was telling the truth--the whole truth.

He listened without encouragement or acknowledgement, until she came to the part about their sharing the bed on which they now sat. She hesitated, a small warning voice in the back of her mind suggesting things about the male ego. In his present state it seemed unlikely he'd believe the truth--that they'd shared the same bed three nights in a row and not made love. She decided to gloss over the details. "...The next morning we..."

"Wait. Are you shy, or are you suggesting we didn't make love that night?"

She certainly couldn't fault his perceptiveness, but there still seemed little point in attempting to convince the abrasive man she now faced of his own reluctance, or of his tenderness. "We didn't. I...I guess we were both pretty tired."

She ignored his skeptical look and pressed on. When she got to the part about her "interview" with Sondra Culver he stopped her again.

"Did she seem upset by any of this?"

"I don't think so."

"Think. It could be important."

"It's hard to tell. She's eight months pregnant and women in that condition sometimes act a bit...I just don't know. She walked me to the door and seemed pleasant enough. No, I don't think I upset her."

"Did she watch you get into the van?"

"No. I had parked it down the street from her house, so I'm sure she didn't see me. She would have had to come down the front walk and I'm sure she stayed in the house."

"Good. That gives us a little time, then."

"I don't understand."

"She probably married Brian the moment I was disposed of," he said. "He always was sweet on her."

How Brian, whoever he was, being sweet on Sondra explained their having "a little time" mystified her. This New Jeff was certainly more verbal than the Old Jeff, but his tendency to go off on tangents made his conversation far more confusing. She tried to keep up. "She told me her husband's name is Walter."

"Names don't mean anything. We change names and phony occupations like other people change shirts. Brian did this to me, then took Sondra. She's probably carrying his baby."

Dee felt the tension in his voice, saw it mirrored in the muscles of his neck and arms. A part of her wanted to comfort him, assure him things would work out somehow; but a tension of her own was growing within. His strong reaction to this Brian/Walter/Whoever and what he had done did not hide the fact that the woman she had admired earlier that very day was far more important to him than she could ever hope to be.

Unbidden, one of her mother's bitter observations on the male gender came to her. Most men, Mama maintained, saw women as nothing more than bearers of their offspring. She'd never have thought to characterize Jeff Westman with her mother's words, but the man now sharing this room with her certainly came close to fitting the description. In spite these thoughts her nurturing side won out. "I'm sorry about all this. It makes me wish I hadn't brought your past back to you."

His look reflected the warring emotions within her. "It's not your fault. It seems I asked for your help."

"Yes. Thank you. Should I call you Gerald now?"

"Makes no difference. Jeff is fine. Brian and Sondra were the only ones who called me Gerald." He took in and then expelled a deep breath. "I'm gonna get that bastard."

His single-mindedness annoyed her. The most positive thing she could think of at the moment was that they finally seemed to be talking *with* each other instead of *at* each other, though he wasn't exactly a font of information. She decided to press the advantage. "Fine, but isn't it about time you filled me in?"

He went back to pacing the room. "You don't know what you're asking. If I tell you anything--anything at all--your life won't be worth a dime. You have no idea what you're dealing with, and believe me you'll be better off not knowing."

He stopped directly in front of her, feet planted, fists on hips. "Best thing for you to do right now is to take a hike. Forget you ever knew me or had anything to do with me."

"Forget? Just a darn minute *Mister* Westman."

Walking out was one thing, but being thrown out was quite another. She'd probably be out of his life in less than five minutes, but she wasn't going to get pushed out.

She shoved him out of the way and stood. "'Forget' is a very interesting choice of words. I'm not looking for a pat on the back, but if it wasn't for me your life wouldn't be about anything *but* 'forget'. You seem to have gone back to your old life in a big way, so I'll assume you're glad you got it back. And who gave it to you? Me, that's who."

She imitated his hands-on-hips stance, facing him. "You were happy enough to use me when you needed my help. Hell, you practically begged me to stay with you. Now you have what you want and it's 'So long Sweetheart', eh? Well, that's fine with me. You can just go off and face your dangerous friends on your own.

"And speaking of danger, she added, shaking a finger in his face, "you seem to have conveniently forgotten the other side of our bargain. Rico and his thugs are still looking for me, and if you think *your* friends are dangerous, you just try tackling Rico Malavesi and his crowd--with or without your precious gun."

His suspicion of her had been hard to swallow, but his chauvinism was even worse. He'd turned out to be just like every other man--thinking his own problems were the only important thing in the world and hers were insignificant. "Sure, I'll get out of your life, and I'll do my darndest to forget you. In fact, given the choice between facing Rico on my own and having to deal with you, I think I'll choose Rico. At least I know where he stands, the rat!"

Jeff reached for her, but she slapped his hand aside, moved past him, scooped up her purse and walked to the closet. She began to pull things from hangers, the ball of white-hot anger crowding out all thoughts. She wanted only to collect the clothing she had bought for herself and get away from him before she started crying.

"Dee, wait. Will you please stop?"

She ignored him as she draped her slacks and blouses over her arm, then turned toward the bathroom door, but found him barring her way.

"Look, I'm sorry. Will you give me a minute to explain? Please?"

His tone almost matched his conciliatory words, but her anger still raged. She tried for a calm, or at least indifferent, tone as she said, "I don't see there's anything more to explain. You've made your position clear."

"No I haven't. If you stay with me you'll be in very grave danger, and you'll---"

"Slow you down?"

"That's not what I was going to say. Look, this guy Rico may be real to you, but to me he's only a phantom. Maybe he's still on your trail, maybe not. Brian, and whoever else is in this with him, are very real to me. Don't you see it would be more dangerous for you to be involved with me?"

Couldn't *he* see they had been on the verge of meaning something special to each other? "No, I don't see. I've told you about Rico, told you what he's capable of, what he does to people who cross him. If you choose not to believe me, that's your prerogative. But you've told me nothing. I don't know who this Brian is, or what he means to you other than your suspicion he's the one who did whatever it was to you so he could take your wife. You've haven't even told me who *you* are. Just how do you expect me to understand *any*thing?"

They were starting to talk in circles, saying the same useless things over again to each other. The only thing that kept her from really telling him off was the fact he'd saved her life. "Just get out of my way and let me go. You don't need me, and I guess I don't need you."

He nodded, then stood aside to let her enter the bathroom. She tossed her things into the bag, fighting back bitter tears all the while, then walked to the door of the motel room without looking at him.

"Wait."

What now, she wondered. One last plea on his part for her to absolve him from any guilt he might feel for throwing her out? Or was he going to offer to drive her to the bus depot or call her a cab? She stopped with her hand on the doorknob.

"At least let me check outside before you go."

Before she could form an appropriately sarcastic remark about watching him in action, he moved the curtain away from the window a scant inch, then quickly dropped it back in place. The look in his eyes as he turned from the window made her catch her breath.   The parting words she had been forming died on her lips.

"Looks like you didn't buy us enough time, after all," he intoned.   "We're being watched."

CHAPTER EIGHT

"Rico's caught up with me." She leaned against the door for support, her anger and frustration forgotten in the face of this renewed threat.

Jeff put a hand on her shoulder, but quickly withdrew it, walked to the bed. He sat down and let out a long sigh. "I guess I owe you an apology. I thought this Rico character was just some two-bit hood who'd be satisfied you'd left town. But given that Deputy Snoop back at the cabin and now this..."

It would have been easy for her to crow, to score a few points in the verbal battle they had been waging. But those things didn't seem to matter any more. He was talking in terms of "we" again and that fact, like a handful of baking soda spread on a hot grease fire, made the bitterness and the anger seem like a momentary error.

He startled her by leaping to his feat, but she was too drained to react beyond a blinking of her eyes. He measured the length of the room with his pacing. "No time to worry about details," he said, more to himself than to her. "We need to get out of here." He stopped pacing and turned to face her. "If I remember correctly, we're next to a hallway that leads out back."

"Yes. And you had me back the van into the parking space, so we could..."

"Forget the van. Whoever those two are, my

guess is they're not going to let us just drive away from here. Get rid of those things, wrap a towel around your head. Take the ice bucket..."

Dee had almost forgotten the clothes draped over her arm, the bag stuffed with toiletries in her hand. She placed them on the bed. "What do you mean, wrap a towel around my head?"

He made motions in the air around his own head, seemed at a loss for words.

"Like I just stepped out of the shower?"

"Exactly. Take off your coat. Try to look casual. Take the ice bucket and go to the ice machine in the hallway. Take your time, as though you have nothing to do but fix a drink when you get back."

She stopped herself from reminding him she had been an actress. "Yes, but..."

"Just do it. When you get to the ice machine, put some ice in the bucket, but be quiet about it. Listen carefully. If you hear anything-- someone running, or a shout, or sounds of scuffling- -run like hell and don't look back. Go through the parking lot behind the motel and keep going. Find a cop, tell him your story, insist on protective custody."

The sudden change in him from combative to cooperative made her light-headed. "What about you?"

"If you can keep them from following you down the hallway, I'll join you. If not, just do as I say."

"What about my clothes? My purse?"

"What's more important, your purse or your life?"

"At least let me take your papers."

"Forget it. No time for debate. Get moving before they decide they've waited long enough."

With trembling fingers she wrapped a towel around her head. It was hard to keep in place without wet hair to hold it, but time would be wasted searching for a bobby pin or wetting her hair. Jeff handed her the ice bucket when she emerged from the bathroom. She took it, opened the outer door and then improvised, "Okay, Honey. I'm just going to get some ice," she called over her shoulder in a lilting voice.

"Leave the door ajar, like you're coming right back. I'll be able to watch them from here."

She avoided searching the parking lot for the watching men, despite her curiosity about them. It probably wasn't Rico himself. He wouldn't have bothered to wait. More likely a couple of his henchmen had been ordered to keep an eye on her until he arrived. She kept her eyes on the hallway entry, then focused on the ice machine as she strolled along, swinging the ice bucket beside her in what she hoped was a casual manner.

The hard part would come when she started filling the bucket. Jeff's insistence that she listen carefully made the usual noise of ice cubes rattling around in a paper bucket inadvisable. She decided pretending she didn't know how to get the machine opened was better than picking up ice cubes one-by-one. If only he had told her where the men were. She'd know if they could see her in this hallway, know just how careful she had to be.

She decided she'd spent enough time ignoring the handle on the metal door of the ice machine, even with the "time out" she'd given herself to readjust the towel on her head. She

109

opened the door, then made a show of trying to decide if she should use the plastic scoop provided or just dip the bucket into the mound of cubes.

Suddenly, almost magically, she was grabbed by the wrist and yanked to the side, bucket and towel sent flying. She almost lost her footing, her mind filled with wonder at where Jeff had come from.

They ran into the darkened parking lot behind the motel. Jeff tried a few car doors, finally found one unlocked. He jerked it open, then shoved her inside. "Get on the floor," he ordered as she scrambled across the seat.

She tried to curl herself into a ball on the floor as he followed her into the car and began fumbling under the dash. The interior light went out and for a moment she heard nothing but the sound of their labored breathing. The engine suddenly came to life, hesitated, then raced as he placed a hand on the gas pedal. He straightened, gunned the engine a few times with his foot, and was reaching for the shift lever when she heard a muffled thumping sound that felt like a heavy door being slammed on an air-tight room.

She looked past his profile out the window just in time to see the back window of their motel room bursting outward in a shower of glass shards. A split-second later, the car was rocked by the force of the explosion.

She didn't have time to watch. She was slammed sideways against the seat of the big car as Jeff sent it racing forward. Then she was bounced and jostled as they went over curbs and into tight turns with a squeal of tires and the sound of the engine racing in her ears. She grabbed for the dash, tried to pull herself into the seat.

"Stay down!" he ordered tersely without taking his eyes off the road.

Braced between the floorboard and the seat, she realized her present position was probably more secure than a flimsy seat belt anyway. And it turned out she didn't have to endure it for long. When he stopped turning corners on two wheels and slowed the car to a more reasonable pace, she pulled herself off the floor. They were on a freeway. "What happened?"

"I'm not sure." He glanced at her with a pained, but companionate, look.

* * * * *

Jeff's reply wasn't exactly a lie. He did have a few clues, but they would have taken more explanation than he was prepared to give her at the moment, and they were only clues--not surety.

The two men in the sedan could have been Rico's henchmen, as they had initially assumed. Though he hadn't been able to see their faces clearly, their attitudes were of men prepared to watch and wait for an indefinite period. His training and experience told him that much was certain.

The explosion put a different light on things. A grenade rifle had been used. There was no mistaking the characteristic double-thump sound. That meant Ashton Hobart, his former boss, was likely involved. The grenade rifle was a special favorite of Ash's. It could, of course, be mere coincidence--this Rico could be fond of the same instrument--but Jeff doubted it.

He did his best to keep his speed within acceptable limits as he drove, and tried to analyze the situation as they headed south out of the city.

If Ash was involved, Brian was also involved. Dee had probably been wrong about Sondra's level of suspicion. Sondra would have called Brian immediately. Then Brian and Ash arranged for an assassination team to finish the job they'd bungled in Philly. He saw at least three holes in that theory, but for the moment it was all he had.

"Where are we going?"

"Sea-Tac. We're getting out of this city as fast as we can." Even if that hadn't been Rico's men back there, Dee was now identified with him and he owed it to her to get her safely away. There were a few other reasons he wanted her with him, but he didn't allow himself the luxury of dwelling on them now. They'd grab the first flight out of the Seattle-Tacoma airport and...well, he could decide the rest later. "Do you have a pocket in those slacks?"

She wrinkled her nose in a puzzled frown. "Why?"

He released the lower button of his shirt, reached inside and fished around until he found the compact and lipstick he'd taken from her purse. He handed them to her. "Thought you might want to have these. I brought the papers, too. I'll keep them in here."

"You *are* full of surprises."

"Never a dull moment with me," he quipped, covering his sudden embarrassment at the warm look in her eyes. "Look, I'm sorry about the way I was acting."

"Don't apologize. I wasn't being very understanding of your situation, either. We seemed to have a good thing going and all of a sudden everything changed. I was a little shook up, though that's too mild a term for it. The way my insides feel, I could churn butter without even trying."

"You handled yourself pretty well back there. I've seen agents who didn't do as good a job at keeping their heads."

"Is that what you are, Jeff? A government agent?"

The airport exit gave him the opportunity to side-step her question. He pulled his wallet from his back pocket and passed it to her, asked her to check the cash content while he drove through the light traffic toward the airport entrance. In other circumstances he wouldn't have worried about cash, but this was "Jeff Westman's" wallet and held no credit cards. He could take care of that problem easily enough with time, but right now they had none.

He left the car idling at the curb, steered her by the elbow toward the ticket counters. The departure listings showed two United Airlines flights about to leave: one for Portland, the other for Denver. They had enough cash for either, but going back to Portland was out of the question at the moment. He asked for two tickets to Denver.

"I'm sorry, sir. It's too late to get you on that flight. I can book you on the..."

He was about to pull Dee away from the counter toward one of the other airlines, but she spoke to the ticket agent with a confidential, woman-to-woman, air. "Linda, we have a small problem. If my ex-boyfriend catches up to us here, there's going to be one heck of a messy brawl in front of your counter. If we promise to run all the way, couldn't you call the gate and ask them to wait for us. Please?"

"Well, I guess I could get them to wait for two first-class passengers." The woman punched her keyboard.

"Thank you, Linda. We'll hurry."

They couldn't hurry while they rode the subway to Concourse C, but Dee matched him stride for stride every other step of the journey from ticket counter to gate. As he had expected, they hadn't had to hold the flight anyway. More than thirty seconds passed after they had settled into their seats before the door was closed.

"Pretty slick," he said. Her quick thinking had probably resulted in their making a clean getaway. Even if they had been seen leaving the motel, no one would expect them to get on board a plane that quickly.

He longed to put his seat back and go into alpha state for the duration of the flight, but he knew there would be little chance for rest. Dee's obvious intelligence and curiosity would drive her to question him unrelentingly. He'd have to tell her some of it, of course, but he'd also have to be careful not to tell her too much about the agency's operations. If they were to part company when they reached Denver, which would be the best way to insure her safety, the less she knew the better--for her and for him.

* * * * *

Dee gave him a long, appraising look while she waited for her heartbeat to return to a more reasonable pace. He didn't *look* different, but his actions, voice, and manner were those of a man other than the one she'd known. Freed from her anger at his earlier rejection of her, curiosity became dominant. He hadn't told her much but a careful examination of the scant clues on hand made it obvious that the money behind him was government, not family, money. It was also obvious that the people who'd wanted him out of the way had both good resources and a positive regard for him to have handled him in such a careful and complex manner instead of simply killing him. Now was a good time to fill in the gaps. In a voice barely above a whisper she took up the conversation where they'd left it. "I don't believe you answered my question. Are you an agent?"

He gained points by setting aside his earlier evasiveness. "Yes. Brian and I were working the same case from different angles, and I thought we were close to cracking it. Then Brian flew into Philadelphia with the news I had somehow blown my cover. I couldn't see how, but he knew about aspects of my end of things he shouldn't have, so I believed his story about a leak."

"Had you two been close?"

"Brian and I met in Cambodia. We were a good team there, and we made a good team with the agency..."

He drifted into a reverie and Dee allowed him his memories for a moment, despite her desire to learn enough to enable her to connect the present self-assured man with the shy "hermit" she had encountered in the Oregon Cascades.

"This is August, right?" he asked abruptly.

She nodded.

"Those bastards tore out ten months of my

life, not counting the time from when my *new life* started on January 20. I went into the hospital in March, of *last year.*"

"You lost me. What hospital? Were you injured?"

"No. When Brian told me about my having blown my cover he said Ash--Ashton Hobart, our immediate superior--recommended an identity change and reassignment. Brian told me he would relocate Sondra for me while I was undergoing the treatment. I should have realized something was wrong. He kept telling me over and over how he would 'take care of Sondra' for me. I fell for it hook, line, and sinker. It's just like that cocky bastard to leave her right where she was. He's probably sleeping in my bed these days."

"So Seattle *is* your home. I realized after we encountered Sondra at Pike's Market that you must have been experiencing a sense of deja vu all the time we were there--you were moody and out of sorts."

Jeff grunted an acknowledgement and she was tempted to add that the home Sondra was living in was too new to have been "their" home, but decided to avoid any hint of argument. She wanted information, not confrontation. "You were telling me about the hospital," she prompted.

"The first few days in the hospital was routine tests and work-ups. I did a lot of reading, studying my proposed new identity. Then they wheeled me into surgery one day for what was supposed to be a minor face-job. My next conscious thought as Gerald Eastman was in that motel room with you."

Dee felt stunned. Her early attempts to

understand his memory loss had started with the assumption there was a rational explanation. This tale, however, was far from rational. "This is too weird," she said after digesting the story. "Why would anyone go to all that effort just to give you a new identity, and then not tell you about it?"

He drew a hand across the stubble of beard on his face. "I don't have an answer...yet."

Compassion and tender concern flooded her. She laid a comforting hand on his arm. "At least you got back your thirty-seven years."

He turned toward her, brown eyes searching her face. "Thanks to you. If you hadn't had that car accident...I owe you more than I can hope to pay." He took her hand in his. "Listen, I..."

"Can I get either of you a cocktail?" the attendant asked.

"Coffee for me," Dee told her, trying to hide her annoyance at the untimely interruption. Jeff just nodded without looking at her and Dee added, "What we need more than anything right now is just to talk with each other, though we're both ravenously hungry."

The woman was good at her job. She looked directly at Dee, flashed her a friendly smile, nodded, and walked away.

Dee turned back to Jeff, surprised to see one corner of his mouth turned up in a wry grin. His eyebrows arched and a twinkle lit his eyes. The twinkle reminded her of the way he had looked when he joked about beef stew as a substitute for horse. "You handle people amazingly well," he said.

The compliment warmed her for personal reasons but she chose to respond on a more professional level. "That was nothing. A director once told me most people, not just actors, are waiting to be told exactly what they have to do to play their chosen role in the best possible way. I told her."

"All the world's a stage, eh?"

Dee nodded. "You were saying?"

"I was about to apologize for the way I treated you back there." He hooked a thumb over his shoulder. "It was all a bit of a shock to me. I'm sorry."

"Forget it. And about the debt you mentioned. The way I figure it you've saved my life three times. I'd say the debt's been paid. With interest."

"I'm not so sure that grenade was meant for you, Dee. I suspect Brian had a watch on my place, or on Sondra's, and knows I re-surfaced. He probably told Ash, and Ash ordered his special goons to finish the job on me. The grenade rifle used at the motel is one of Ashton Hobart's trademarks."

Steaming cups of coffee were placed on their trays at that moment, but the service was so swift and efficient it hardly caused a pause in their conversation.

"Whoever the grenade was meant for," she told him, "your quick action saved us both from being blown to bits. Debt paid. If you're right about it not being Rico back there, maybe he's written me off. *That* puts me in *your* debt. In any case, there's still a problem to be solved, and as far as I'm concerned we're still a team."

He had started to reach for his coffee, but arrested his movement to give her a sidelong glance.

His brow knitted into a frown.

Alert, she chose her next words with care. "I told you back at that motel in Salem you frighten me sometimes. It's still true, though for different reasons now. I agreed to stick with you until this is over and I haven't changed my mind."

He lifted his coffee cup, took a sip, then replaced it in its saucer with deliberate care. She listened to the throb of the plane's engines while she watched his eyes and waited for his reply.

"Once this is resolved, I'm going to have to do a little...soul-searching. I'll need your support. I can't promise you anything but danger and more uncertainty in return." He lifted his cup again.

She lifted her own cup, raised and lowered it once in a silent salute before bringing it to her lips. The words which formed in her mind were far too melodramatic to voice; and for the moment at least she preferred to focus on the commitment rather than on the danger.

CHAPTER NINE

Dee was distracted from her desire to learn more about Jeff's past by the arrival of a meal that smelled surprisingly delicious for airline food. Jeff immediately attacked his roast beef and she realized she wasn't likely to get a word out of him so she put her curiosity on hold in favor of satisfying her own hunger.

Her first bite of roast beef with horseradish sauce was such a shock to her taste buds it was actually painful. The sharp jab of pain reminded her of that "other" Jeff--the one with the headaches, the defensiveness, the vulnerability. She had agreed to stay with that Jeff and help him find his past, and now that that had been accomplished she found herself questioning her desire to remain with him. She told herself with an attempt at the bravado she had so often employed in L.A. that she was just a sucker for a handsome face.

Until he asked, "What's that?" around a mouthful of beef she was unaware she had laughed out loud at herself.

"I was just thinking how far I've come from...from the person I was in Hollywood."

"Me too. Thinking about me, I mean. I guess we've both gone through a lot of changes. Hard to reconcile the two people I've been. They seem very different."

"What was your childhood like?"

"Pretty ordinary. I grew up in New Jersey, hung out after high school a while, went to college in Montana to escape the draft. I wanted to be close to the Canadian border just in case. I guess you could say I got hooked on college. Wound up majoring in Forestry, of all things."

"That doesn't seem so unusual. I mean given where you were living when we met."

"Huh. You're right about that. That cabin in Oregon was a kind of a throw-back to my college days, I guess." He paused long enough to cut another slice of beef, scoop some potato onto his fork, insert it into his mouth and chew lustily. "Anyway, the Army finally caught up with me and shipped me out. They gave me a commission, which didn't mean diddly-squat in those days. I did all right. Met Brian when they sent me for extra training in Special Forces--we became a team. They dropped us into...I shouldn't be telling you about this, it could still be classified."

"After all this time?"

"You know the government." He dismissed the federal bureaucracy with a wave. "Anyway, Brian talked me into going into the agency when our tour was up, and they kept us as a team. You know the rest."

There was a great deal about "the rest" that she didn't know, but she decided she wanted to know more about his personal life as well so she let it go. "Are your parents still living?"

"Dad was, last I knew. Mom died when I was twelve. What about you?"

Dee stifled a pulse of sympathetic anger before responding. His missing ten months--or eighteen, counting the time he had spent in the mountain cabin--had cost him more than she had realized until that moment. But she put aside her initial reaction and answered his question.

"My folks are still alive, but Dad left home about five years ago. The usual--a younger woman. Mama didn't seem to mind all that much. She and my baby sister, Inga, are still in White Cloud. That's western Michigan, where I grew up."

Their empty plates were removed and fresh cups of coffee served by their unobtrusive attendant while Dee thought about home and realized just how much she missed her mother and sister. "Where are we headed after Denver?"

"Chicago. I'll pick up some supplies in Denver before we head out. I've got to figure a way to get to Ash. That business back at the motel puzzles me. At first I thought it was all Brian's doing, but now I'm not so sure. I'll get answers out of Ashton Hobart and then..."

She wondered if he would be as attracted by the idea of finding some quiet place to think things over as she had been when she left Rico and Hollywood behind. "Maybe when this is all over we can drive up to White Cloud from Chicago. It's nice country up there. I'll bake us a batch of cookies and we can sort things out."

His broad grin did not match the pained and haunted look in his eyes. She was glad she had been able to ease the tension a little, wondered idly how she might further relax him.

As the plane taxied to the gate at Stapleton International Jeff suggested she spend the time while he was in town replacing her lost purse.

His decisive manner rankled, but she did her best to keep her voice even. She was not ready for a reprise of the motel room confrontation. "I take it you've decided I won't be accompanying you to town."

"Not on this trip. I'll be moving fast and dealing with people you shouldn't know about."

So she was still an *outsider* to him. She wondered if there was any chance she'd be able to change that attitude before they parted company for good.

"I didn't mean it the way it sounded," he quickly added. "I know you've seen society's underbelly. What I mean is, it would be a breach of security to let you see these people. So I'd have to leave you somewhere..."

"I'd slow you down," she put in. And I don't mean *that* the way I meant it back at the motel. I'd just be adding more work to your load." She wasn't going to let him see how hurt she was. "No problem. I can replace the things I really need right here in the airport shops, and I'll also get you some new shaving things, too. We'll save time, save energy, and get on with this business sooner. Want me to get our tickets to Chicago while you're gone?"

He hesitated. "I'm not sure how long this will take me. Eighteen months is a long time in this business. Things might have changed. Keep tabs on the Chicago departures--just in case we have to leave in a hurry the way we did in Seattle." He took out his wallet and handed her three crisp hundred dollar bills.

Relief washed through her. Despite the feeling of conviviality brought on by his more relaxed attitude and the shared secrets, she was acutely aware of the fact he might choose to dump her at any time. He'd probably be more gentle about it than he'd been in the Seattle motel room, coat the pill with honeyed rationalities and piecrust promises; but the possibility nagged at the back of her consciousness nonetheless. At the moment, though, that did not seem to be his intent.

She stuffed the bills into the pocket of her slacks with her lipstick and compact, then leaned over to run her finger along a jagged tear in the side of his shirt. "With this much I can buy you a new shirt, too."

"Bathroom window back at the motel," he explained.

"I wondered how you got out of there." She followed him into the aisle, allowed him to link her arm in his. He thanked the attendant for her thoughtfulness and they headed up the ramp to the terminal.

As they turned the corner onto the concourse he pulled up abruptly, causing a minor collision with someone following close behind them. He pulled her back around the corner, wrapped his arms around her shoulders, and held her in an embrace, the side of his face pressed against hers.

Dee started to protest, then decided she liked it. He had certainly picked a strange time to get physical with her, but beggars couldn't be choosers.

"Damn!" he hissed in her ear. "They're here already."

So much for getting physical. "What will we do?" she whispered back, molding herself to him for safety's sake. She put aside questions of how he'd detected the danger, and who "they" were, exactly. Memories of the explosion in Seattle led her to trust his instincts.

"Let's head for those phone booths behind you. I'll go in, you stand in front of me."

He set a casual pace across the wide aisle,

his arm around her shoulder, he head pressed against hers. She rested a hand on his hip, tried to relax against him as they walked. She had a moment to wonder if he would have invited such intimacy without the threat of danger, then he broke the embrace and slipped into the open phone stall.

"It looks like they're a little unsure of who they're looking for. But there's no way we're going to get past them. Damn!"

Dee feigned a hair adjustment so she could look over her shoulder. She spotted the two men outside a snack bar at the entry to the concourse. The moment she saw them, she knew. Their drab suits, close-cropped hair, even their plain brown oxfords looked like they'd been issued from wardrobe on a B-movie set. Cops.

The thought of movies and typecast roles gave her an idea. "I don't know this airport at all, but it looks to me like all the United flights leave from this concourse. I could go get us a couple of tickets out of here and you wouldn't have to go past those men."

"Too risky." He resumed his study of the men, his scowl deepening.

"No more risky than standing here, waiting for them to come to us. And a lot less than the two of us trying to get past them. Tear me a strip of cloth off that shirt of yours. Six inches will do."

Decisiveness worked two ways, evidently. Jeff wasted no more time with futile arguments, but simply tugged his shirt out of his waistband. She dug out her lipstick, touched the tip of her finger to the stick and quickly rubbed it into her cheeks. Then she applied a thick coat to her lips. A quick check in her compact's mirror confirmed the harsh look she had achieved.

The strip he had torn from his shirt was wider than she needed, but it would do. She folded it lengthwise then held it between her teeth while she gathered her loose hair into a pony--high and a little to the side. She tied it with the strip of fabric, then smiled at him. She wished she had a large wad of gum to chew, but she could fake that. Putting on her best nasal whine, she said flirtatiously, "You'd better give me some more money, Sugar. I got real 'spensive tastes."

He stared, open-mouthed and wide-eyed. "That's amazing!"

"Thanks for the applause, but I really will need more money. You can wait for me in the restroom right behind you. I'll knock twice. Like: knock-knock, knock-knock."

"No need. I'll be watching for you."

She stuffed the new bills into the pocket with the three he had given her earlier and gave him a broad wink as she turned and sauntered up the concourse, feeling nowhere near as brave as she had led him to believe. She tried to not think of what might happen if the watching men decided to stop her. She chewed her imaginary wad of gum and watched the men around her as though sizing up potential customers.

The taller of the two waiting men eyed her with open interest, and she could tell his interest was not "official". She reached the end of the concourse without being stopped and allowed herself the luxury of breathing again.

The departures screen at the ticket counter showed a flight for Minneapolis-St. Paul due to leave in twenty minutes, a Seattle flight in thirty, and one for Dallas in a little less than forty. She decided on the Dallas flight purely on the basis of timing, and bought two first-class tickets. Dallas was not exactly the right direction, but maybe that would be a plus--the people who were looking for Jeff probably wouldn't expect them to go that way. And she still had time to make a few more purchases.

The bored clerk in the gift shop rang up her odd collection: two cheap plastic flight bags, one billed cap with a Broncos patch, matching long-sleeved sweatshirts with "HERS" written on the larger size, "HIS" on the smaller, a plastic clutch purse, a man's travel kit complete with disposable razor, and a pack of sugarless gum. She distributed the items into the two bags as the woman rang them up, popped two sticks of gum into her mouth while the clerk counted out the change from a hundred, and headed back toward the United concourse.

She passed a beauty salon on her way, then retraced her steps, entered, and approached two idle operators. She asked the young one for coloring mousse. The woman went into a sales pitch, but Dee cut her off. "I just want a quick fix, Honey. My boyfriend ogled a redhead a few minutes ago and I thought I'd shake him up a little, y'know what I mean?"

The woman grinned and pointed to a small display. Dee allowed her to pick out the most expensive can of red foam on the shelf while she took out her pony tail. A few seconds later her hair was the color of pink cotton candy--and just about as stiff. She tipped the woman generously and left the shop with a jaunty wave.

She slowed her pace to a hip-swinging stroll

as she approached the concourse, but a quick scan of the area showed no sign of the two waiting men. Her pulse began to race as she considered the portents, but slowed when she noticed a thin wisp of cigarette smoke being blown through the slightly opened door of the men's room. She stopped in front of the door. It opened a little wider and Jeff's hand reached for the bag she was holding out.

"Plane leaves in twenty minutes. See you at the gate," she called as she headed for the Women's restroom.

"Right," his disembodied voice acknowledged.

In the act of pulling on her new sweatshirt in the restroom, the impressions registered. His arm had been bare, as though he'd already taken off his shirt, and he had been smoking. It was impossible to keep up with the changes in him, she mused, trying to work her stiffened hair into some reasonable style.

Jeff was waiting for her near the departure gate. He crushed his cigarette, glanced up at her, then did a double-take. "So I wasn't seeing things. How'd you do that to your hair so quickly?"

"Magic." She grinned. "When did you start smoking?"

"When I took the smokes off the guy in the restroom. I think I used to smoke..."

"What guy?"

"Let's get on board. I'll tell you about it when we're alone. I like the shirts."

They were "alone" in less than twenty minutes because the three other first class passengers on the late-night flight to Dallas appeared to be asleep even before the plane left the

128

ground. "Tell me! What guy?"

"Right after you got past those two, one of them headed down the concourse toward the restroom. He was about half way when the other glanced at his watch, then took off--my guess is to check on another airline's flight coming in from Seattle. It's a good thing I didn't think about that factor before you left, or I might have been tempted to try to wait them out."

Jeff pulled off the cap and stuffed it into the bag at his feet. "Carter--that's the name on his I. D.--came into the restroom and seemed in no particular hurry, so I figured no one would look for him right away. I watched from one of the stalls and when he bent over to tie a shoelace, I hit him before he knew I was there. Took his wallet to make it look like robbery, stuffed his gun into the bottom of a waste bin. He's one of us so we not only have a little extra cash, I might be able to use his I. D. to open some doors I wouldn't want to try without papers of some kind. I tore up the rest of my shirt and tied him in a stall. With luck, it will be hours before anyone finds him."

"My God, Jeff! What if..."

"But me no buts. Even if Carter's partner decides to check every stall in the every restroom near that concourse, we'll be long gone before he raises an alarm. And my guess is a lot of time will pass while his partner assumes he's gone off to some other concourse to watch another incoming flight and like that. Even when they do realize he's missing in action the clear robbery will deflect attention away from us...it could have been any junkie or whatever. Top that off with your clever ploy of taking us to Dallas....Texas, not Oregon.

We make a good team."

He talked about the encounter as though it were a walk in the park. She decided against telling him how frightened she'd been, or how she'd chosen Dallas solely on the basis of departure time. His comment about "teamwork" and the reference to their running joke about city names tipped her emotional scales out of kilter and she suddenly felt an overpowering need to sleep. She put her seat back and closed her eyes while he rambled on.

"I've been thinking about how to get to Hobart. I know his favorite restaurant, so since we've thrown them off the trail we can slip into Chicago and just wait for him to show up there. I may need you to drive for me when we take him somewhere quiet to sweat the truth out of him. Then I'll tackle Brian. We won't have to hurry things that way, we'll be able to take our time..."

Either he'd stopped talking or she'd stopped listening. She heard no more.

* * * * *

"No, sir," the young Seattle operative admitted. "I don't know if he was in the room. The woman went to the ice machine a few minutes before and we didn't see her go back into the room. The man didn't leave, as far as we know, but I can't be completely certain."

Brian scratched his scalp with both hands, tried to shake off the tiredness. He was not familiar with this agent, didn't know how reliable he was. "Are you positive it was a grenade rifle?"

"Almost certain, sir. Fired from a light blue sedan. I couldn't read the plates."

It didn't compute. A grenade rifle smelled like Ashton Hobart, but if the blonde was working with Ash, why had she questioned Sondra? If Ash knew about Gerald he wouldn't have waited--he would have ordered everyone involved, including the blonde, executed immediately. The only possible explanation was that the blonde was an agent for another power. It made sense in a twisted sort of way. She had been with Gerald. She had been the one to question Sondra. Could Hobart have been right about Gerald after all? If the blonde was working for the other side, they might have some plans to exploit the whole affair to their advantage. Maybe they'd found "Jeff Westman", tried to turn him, and when that didn't work..."What did you tell the locals?"

"Nothing, sir. Just said we were checking in case it turned out to be terrorist activity."

"Good. Anyone been near the van yet?"

"No, sir."

"Get it out of here before the locals figure out it's connected. You've taken care of the motel records?"

"Yes, sir."

"I'll be at our room at the Hilton. Let me know the minute there's some positive word on bodies. And tell the team at Tamarack to tighten up. They'll have to watch every vehicle entering the neighborhood for a while. Christ!"

Brian let himself into the company's room at the Hilton, glanced longingly at the bed, then cursed when he saw the blinking light on the phone. The operator gave him the message that "Sammy" had called, so he immediately placed a call through the mobile operator to Oregon.

"I'm at the cabin now, Brian," Sam announced through light static. "Our boy and the woman he's traveling with left here a couple of days ago. Sorry I missed them."

"Never mind, Sam. What's the situation there?"

"There were two men here. The one inside insisted on doing things the hard way--he's no longer with us. The other one is sitting on the floor now, nursing a lump on his head. Apparently the woman is connected to a character named Malavesi, out of L.A., though this guy isn't clear about the relationship and seems to know the woman only as 'The Blonde'."

"What do we know about this Malavesi?"

"First name, Rico. Family man. Runs gaming houses in the L.A. area and seems well connected. I'm having someone scour the files now. One other thing--I guess you'd have to call it a hunch rather than a fact--I get the distinct impression our friend with the lump is more afraid of this Malavesi than he is of my forty-five. My guess is Malavesi doesn't have both oars in the water."

Brian checked his assumptions against these new facts. An L.A. hood, even a "crazed" one, didn't exactly qualify as an "unfriendly power", but if the connections Sam hinted at were extensive enough, the labels might not matter. The results were still the same--the woman had somehow found the cabin and soon thereafter "Gerald Eastman" had emerged, apparently having overcome the post-hypnotic orders against remembering his past.

"Sam, put your friend with the lump on ice. Make sure he won't talk to anyone about anything, and start working your way up through this Malavesi's organization. Of primary importance is information about the woman, but if you happen to put Malavesi out of business along that way, it won't hurt. I'll need every scrap of information about the woman as soon as you get it, so I'll keep my mobile phone with me. Use as many operatives as you can trust--seconds could count if I'm going to be effective on this end. Got it?"

* * * * *

The bumpy carnival ride Dee was on shook her even more than before.

"Wake up, Sleepy Head. We're coming into Dallas."

"Can't I just cuddle up here for another few days?" Dee snuggled closer to him.

"Sounds good to me, but the crew might object." Jeff brushed her forehead with his lips, gave her shoulder a squeeze, then gently pushed her away. "We have to be on the alert. The Company Boys may not have been fooled by your maneuver, or they might have cast a much wider net just on general principles."

That brought her around. She straightened, rubbed the sleep from her eyes. Her hair felt stiff and sticky. She tried to remember where she put her flight bag, wondered if she'd have time to slip into the bathroom to freshen up before they landed.

"I like you better as a blonde," he remarked.

It came back to her then. "So that's why I was dreaming of pink cotton candy." She patted her hair, decided a quick trip to the restroom wouldn't help much, and tried to stretch without standing.

Jeff rubbed his eyes, looking more rested than she felt. "I did some thinking while you were asleep. I can't get over what a completely different person I was for those seven or eight months. Did I really feed you beef stew from a can?"

"Yes. It was delicious."

"I can't remember eating food like that since my college days, and I'm not even sure I ate that junk then. Yet my cupboards back at the cabin are full of stuff like that. I sure hope I get to find out just what they did to me before I beat Brian into a pulp." He smacked one fist into the palm of his other hand with a sound that startled her.

She could smell the fear and anger on him. She much preferred the cool, dispassionate, even aloof and suspicious man she had faced in the Seattle motel room to this angry and vindictive one, and she sought for a way to sidetrack his anger. "Have you given any more thought to why they did it? Maybe that case you were working on?"

"Hm-m...the Walburg case," he mumbled.

"Walburg?"

"Sh-h-h! Careful with that name," he continued in a near-whisper. "Don't you know who Walburg is?"

She shook her head. He scanned the other passengers, then leaned even closer and spoke the full name of the man he had been investigating.

"My God!" she hissed, trying to match is secretive tone. "*Senator* Walburg? What---"

"Later. I'll explain later," he promised.

CHAPTER TEN

Jeff adjusted the shower head to a stinging spray and let the steaming water pour over his body. For a long moment there was nothing but the cascade of water against his flesh, nothing but pure physical sensation. All too quickly, though, his worried thoughts kicked into gear again.

He felt like a damn computer. *Take a short break while we download information from Nexus Research, then get your ass back to work!* He'd love to take at least a week to orient himself, but he didn't have the luxury of that much time.

Bless Dee for buying them a little time by bringing them to Dallas, and he had saved a little more time by dispatching a bellman to buy fresh clothing for them; but he needed days, not hours. Their pursuers wouldn't be thrown off the trail indefinitely. The Seattle motel incident had made that clear, even though questions about exactly who those pursuers were remained unanswered. It might have been Dee's Rico Malavesi, or Ash, or even Brian working in collusion with Sondra.

Sondra was another puzzle he needed time to think through. Did she really think he was dead, or had she simply given Dee the cover story Brian had provided her with? Her advanced state of pregnancy clearly indicated she hadn't wasted much time after his "death" before finding a new husband. It was damn near impossible to assimilate that piece of information--he still felt married to her himself.

True, it hadn't been much of a marriage the

last few years. On the few occasions he'd managed to get back to Seattle they'd been cordial toward each other; but they'd spent more time strolling through Pike's Market or the waterfront parks, smiling at strangers, than they'd spent smiling at each other in their own apartment. Sondra had been frightened of his lifestyle, and maybe even frightened of him.

Come to think of it, hadn't Dee said something about being afraid of him? At least she'd been up front about it, and she clearly hadn't let it bother her. She didn't shy away from danger. Beauty, brains, and guts. One helluva combination.

He slammed the side of his fist against the tiled shower wall and felt an agreeable pain wash up his arm, wiping out that train of thought. A second later a change in air pressure told him Dee had opened the bathroom door.

"You okay?"

"Yeah. Just dropped the soap." The door closed again but the smell of her perfume lingered, bringing back memories of Dee lying in his bed at the cabin, sharing a bed with him at the motel. The perfume-induced memories overcame the pain in his hand, caused an involuntary response. "Damn!"

He wrenched the temp control knob hard to the right, gasped as the cold spray hit him. He forced himself to stay under the sobering stream until he started to shiver involuntarily.

A brisk toweling brought the blood back to the surface of his skin, quieted his twitching muscles. He wrapped himself in the hotel's robe, then lit the last of his pilfered cigarettes.

Voices from the outer room told him either breakfast or their new clothing had arrived. A moment later Dee announced the former.

"Start without me if you like. I'm going to finish shaving," he called.

When he emerged moments later he saw that Dee had poured coffee for them but had left the covers on their plates. She was waiting for him at the table, one of the newspapers he had brought up from the lobby opened on her lap. "I don't think I've read a newspaper in years. I mean, really read one."

"I *know* I haven't." He joined her at the table, took a sip of his coffee. "They must have programmed a lack of interest in current affairs into me when they..."

He trailed off, realizing he'd begun to understand what had been done to him, though he still didn't understand *why* it had been done. The programming had probably included drugs and hypnotic suggestions against thinking about his past. That would explain the headaches. But if they'd wanted him out of the way, why hadn't they just killed him? "Accidents" were as commonplace as head colds within the agency. The only explanation that made sense suggested a plot he couldn't even guess at.

He discarded the Brian-wants-Sondra idea. That scenario would have fallen into the quick-and-painless death category, he now realized; but the conclusion left him no closer to understanding the mystery of why this had been done to him, or what their plans had been. Dee had made short work of their plans, that much was certain. But again, that only raised more questions than answers. Who exactly was she, and what were her real motives? Having only her word for this Rico person's existence did not satisfy him completely. He'd have to keep a watchful eye on her, be ready to capitalize on her least mistake and then force her to come clean.

She lifted her coffee up, pursed her lips as she sipped. The tip of her tongue flicked out to clean those lips. He reached for the stack of newspapers, but he couldn't take his eyes off her mouth.

"Here's something about Senator Walburg," she announced. "A story about an appropriations bill. Walburg is quoted as being in favor of it, of supporting the administration's position. It doesn't say why they quoted him--I guess you have to keep up with these things."

"Walburg is always supporting the--who *is* the administration these days?"

"Same as they were two years ago. I think a few people have resigned for various reasons. Tell me about Walburg."

He picked up another of the papers and scanned the front page. "Walburg was involved in an arms scandal a few years back...I mean a few years before I...well, you know. Anyway, he escaped censure because he had his flunkies do all the leg work and nothing could be traced directly to him. We uncovered connections he had that led us to suspect dealings of a far more serious nature."

"When you say 'we' do you mean you and Brian?"

"Yeah. Brian and his people in Chicago were supposed to make a lot of noise investigating a minor aspect of what we'd uncovered to provide a smokescreen for me. I penetrated Walburg's organization in Philly, hot on the trail of solid evidence."

"Now I know who's guarding the guardians," she remarked.

The attentive, trusting way Dee received this information raised a bittersweet feeling within him. If she was faking it, Hollywood had lost a star of some magnitude. If not, he was being an ass to suspect her.

"Brian and I got together for one of our infrequent meetings and he told me my cover had been blown. He said Ash ordered a change of identity and a brief cooling-off period. I didn't like the idea--I thought we were too close to pull back at that point. But Brian claimed Ash was adamant, so I went into the hospital."

A knock sounded at the door behind him. The bellman with their new clothes. Jeff signed for them, took a fifty from his wallet and passed it to the boy. "If we need anything else we'll call."

"Thank you Mr. Carter. I'll be on duty until four. Just ask for George."

"All this name-swapping makes me dizzy," Dee grumbled when he returned to the table. "I think I'll call my mother after breakfast, get myself in touch with who I really am."

He cut a bite of steak and quickly popped it into his mouth, holding back the bitter words about identities that came to mind, swallowing them with the tasty morsel. He raised his glass of juice in a small salute. "Here's hoping we can *both* get in touch with who we are soon. I need to do more research to put myself back in the picture. Let me know if you come across any more stories on Walburg. There are still holes in my memory."

The warm look she sent across the table erased a large portion of the bitterness he could not completely shake. They finished breakfast in silence, but the "noise" in his head was deafening. The phone call she mentioned might very well prove to be the misstep he had been waiting for. If she requested privacy for her little chat he'd simply make his exit from the room permanent. He'd head straight for the hotel operator, determine the true location of her call, and then be about his business. If she tried some kind of "code" he'd be far too alert to let it slip by him.

Dee perched on the edge of the bed, stared at the ceiling for a moment, then picked up the phone and gave the hotel operator a number--with a western Michigan 616 area code, he noted. He memorized the number for future reference, heard her mutter "Oh. Thanks," and watched her hang up and then dial the number herself. Score one for the kid from Michigan, he thought.

"Hello? Mama, it's Dee...Well, I thought you'd be glad to...Mama, is something wrong?"

Jeff had been in the process of remonstrating himself for doubting his forthright new partner when the evident fear in her tone brought him back to the alert.

"Mama, please don't cry. Tell me what happened...Oh my God! Are you sure?....Yes, I understand. When did this happen?..."

Jeff told himself it would be nothing--the family cat stuck up a tree or an ailing uncle rushed to the hospital--but he moved quickly anyway. He turned his back on her and pulled on a fresh pair of shorts from the package the bellman had delivered, lifted his new pants from their hangar and stepped into them. He was about to remove his robe when Dee started talking again.

"I'll be there as soon as I can, Mama....No, I'm not in California, I'm in..."

"No! Don't tell her where you are!," he cut in. "Tell her we're coming and hang up."

Adrenaline pumped through him. He had an image of Brian interrogating members of Dee's family to find out where they were. The bastard was probably listening with a wire tap at this very moment. If she didn't hang up, he'd have to rip the phone out of the wall.

He didn't have to. She shot him one stunned look, then acknowledged his command with a brief nod. By God, she was an impressive woman.

"...a friend, Mama. Look, I'm going to hang up. We'll be there as soon as we can. Just wait for us. Don't talk to anyone about our coming. I'll explain when we get there." She put the phone down and seemed to collapse into herself, head in hands.

Jeff took his time buttoning his shirt and gave her a moment to collect her thoughts. When she lifted her head, her eyes were red, her cheeks stained with tears. "They've kidnapped Inga."

His fingers fumbled with a button. Inga? He couldn't place the name immediately, but kidnapping was a word he had no difficulty understanding. He took a step closer, waited while she wiped at her tears.

"Inga..." The name came out like a gut-wrenching moan. "My baby sister. She's only sixteen."

All wrong, he thought. Why would they kidnap a teenaged girl? What could they hope to gain? "Give me the details."

"A man phoned Mama. It must be Rico. He

told her he would trade Inga for me. Said he'd know when I arrived. She's been trying to reach me..."

Embarrassment mingled with anger. He'd been so wrapped up in his own problems...

Her tears started again. He cursed himself for not finding out more about this Rico, for having dismissed him so easily. He lifted her to her feet and held her tightly for a moment. Then he gripped her by the shoulders and held her at arm's length. "Get dressed. We have no time to lose."

He found the phone book in the nightstand, opened it to the beginning of the yellow pages, ran his finger down the column of Aircraft Charters. He'd have to avoid the usual services--someone might recognize Carter's identification and stop them before they even got started. In the face of this new threat his business with Brian could take a back seat, but he wasn't going to be careless again.

He grabbed the phone, punched in a number and shortly heard "Bushwell Charter."

"I need a small, fast plane in a hurry. Two passengers."

"Destination?"

"Pennsylvania." That would get them started in the right direction. He'd be able to talk the pilot into a change of course once they were in the air. He glanced at Dee while the man talked to someone else, noted with satisfaction now nicely she was responding. If they got out of this mess, these messes, alive...

"I think we can accommodate you."

"Fine. The name's Carter. We'll be there in fifteen minutes. Have the plane ready." He hung up, finished dressing. Dee stuffed things into one of the flight bags while he tied his shoes. He slipped into his jacket, flexed to check it for fit, then grabbed Carter's wallet and his loose cash from the dresser.

* * * * *

Dee poured every ounce of concentration into the act of getting into her clothes, forced herself to ignore the frightening images of what might be happening to Inga that threatened to upset her. Mama had sounded on the verge of hysteria, and that fact alone spurred her forward. She remembered a scene from her childhood: Papa storming through the house, breaking things and shouting at the top of his voice. Through it all Mama had remained calm, following him at a leisurely pace, righting a table, picking up pieces of a broken lamp, her face impassive.

Hearing her mother blubber and sob as she tried to relay the message from the man who had kidnapped Inga had been more devastating than the news itself. She was grateful Jeff had not peppered her with questions. She only vaguely heard his conversation about a fast plane.

In the elevator she wondered how long it would take them to make the trip. She tried to picture a map of the country, tried to calculate the distance between their present location and home. When Jeff squeezed her hand she returned the grip and gave up her vain attempts to estimate the time of their arrival. "Shouldn't we check out?" she asked as he swept her through the lobby.

"They have the credit card number. They'll bill it." He walked to the first taxi waiting at the

143

curb, keeping her hand in his as the doorman hurried to open the cab door for them. "Bushwell Charter Service," he told the bearded cabbie, passing a bill over the seat. "And I'll pay the speeding fines."

The cab seemed to crawl forward, in spite of Jeff's suggestion, but when they reached the street it came to life with a squeal of tires. The smell of burning rubber and the roar of the cab's engine dominated Dee's senses for a moment, and then buildings seemed to fly past them in a blur. The cab driver had his microphone to his mouth and a burst of static added to the noise.

Beside her, Jeff lifted a hand to brush at her hair, gave her a look that threatened to bring fresh tears to her eyes. "You're doing just fine," he told her.

She couldn't imagine how she could be doing "just fine" with her insides churning away like a Kansas tornado. He smiled, gave her arm a squeeze, then took out his wallet. He flipped through the credit cards, selected one from the pack and placed it on top. He took out another bill, a fifty, then put the wallet back in his suit coat pocket. "When we get to the air park, you take the bags to the plane and I'll take care of the paperwork. Play dumb if anybody asks any questions."

Playing dumb would be easy. Numb and dumb, that was her. Inga, part of this mess...she couldn't bear it!

A man wearing greasy blue coveralls and a knit cap led her to the waiting plane The pilot was warming up the engines and the tinny whine of the jets jarred her, set her teeth on edge. The smell of aviation fuel and warm asphalt filled her nostrils. It gave her a sense of the reality of flying she had not experienced in the closed environment of commercial flights out of air-conditioned terminals.

Rico had talked about his private plane in his efforts to impress her with his assets. She had to fight tears again as she wondered if he had flown to Michigan in a plane like this one. The recurring thought of little Inga in his hands started her shaking, and once started she was unable to stop. She was quivering from head to toe by the time Jeff joined her in the small cabin.

"Okay, let's go!" he shouted to the pilot. Then he wrapped his arm around her and told her in a softer, quieter tone, "Go ahead, let it out."

She collapsed against him, let the tremors wrack her body like an earthquake, submitted fully. It took a surprisingly short time for the storm to pass. She would shed no more tears. The comfort of his arm around her helped. He said nothing until they were in the air, until she was resting, weak and spent, against him.

"Tell me exactly where White Cloud is. Nearest cities, things like that."

"It's about fifty miles north of Grand Rapids, thirty to thirty-five miles east of Muskegon on Lake Michigan." It was easier for her to picture the locations around White Cloud than to imagine the flight from Dallas. "I guess Muskegon is closer, and it would be faster to drive from there. There aren't any airports closer, that I know of."

"I could ask the pilot, but I don't want to let him know where we're headed. About the time we land the agency will know what I've done. They'll be watching for the Carter I.D. and the extra grease I spread back there won't keep mouths closed long.

The less the pilot can tell them about where we're headed, the better it will be. Did you say Muskegon's on Lake Michigan? That would cut their search area in half, make it too easy for them. We'll head for Grand Rapids. The fifteen minutes or so difference in driving time for us may mean additional hours before they figure out which way we've gone. They might even assume we're going to Chicago by a back door."

"Do you mean you think the agency kidnapped Inga?"

"No...no. That's not their style at all. I have no doubt it's your Rico..."

"He's not *my* Rico!

"Sorry, didn't mean it that way. I think it's far more likely to be him than Brian and his troops, but the fact remains the agency is probably still trying to track us. We have to accept the fact we have two separate groups after us and take appropriate measures. We'll get your little sister, but we have to make sure we don't fall into Brian's hands in the process, okay?"

"I understand."

He went forward to talk with the pilot. Dee took a moment to consider what he'd said, felt even worse than before. She brushed at her eyes before threatened tears could form, forced herself to think instead of feel.

Their problems had become intertwined. Just as she had taken on additional danger by being associated with him, he was taking on greater peril by exposing himself like this in helping her. For better or worse, they had become a team. And right now "worse" was definitely ahead of "better."

She could not hold back the wave of

recriminations pushing into her consciousness. If only she'd accepted her lot in the first place, knuckled under to Rico in L.A., or let him confront her after he'd traced her to Jeff's cabin, her baby sister wouldn't have been placed in jeopardy. If she'd ignored Jeff's confusion and frustration, not tried to help him find his past, he'd still be living a life of blissful ignorance in the Oregon mountains.

But no, she'd had to push it, hadn't she? She'd insisted on her right to make her own choices, to be in "command of her own destiny"--and she'd encouraged Jeff to do the same. And what had they gained? So far they'd been threatened, hunted, and bombed. They'd been forced to leave their few possessions behind twice while they'd gone scurrying across the country, skulking through airports like common criminals when they hadn't done anything wrong!

And now sleepy, humdrum little White Cloud was about to become the focus of new terrors.

CHAPTER ELEVEN

Jeff pulled more bills from his wallet, handed them to the pilot, then returned to the seat beside her and let out a heavy sigh. "Okay, that takes care of that little problem. We'll be in Grand Rapids in less than two hours. Now you'd better fill me in."

She took two deep breaths, tried to clear her mind of all the guilty reminiscences. "White Cloud isn't much more than a wide spot in the road. Just one street of shops off the highway, plus the county buildings. The high school's in Fremont, about fifteen miles to the west."

She warmed to her subject. With remembered affection she described the gently rolling hills, the farms and pine forests, the many small lakes with cottages occupied each summer by families escaping the crowds, noise, and filth of Detroit or Chicago.

When she started on the area's history, he cut her off. "Skip the tourist stuff. Tell me about your mother's house, your little sister's routine."

There it was again--the cool, dispassionate government agent. She remembered thinking she preferred this side of his new persona to the angry, vindictive one. *Careful what you wish for*, she told herself. "Our house is on the edge of town and sits back off the highway. There's a garden out back and I've mowed that front lawn more times than I care to remember."

She paused as memory dredged up the smell of fresh-cut grass, the feel of the smooth carpet of green beneath her bare feet.

"I don't know anything about Inga's routine. It's been too long since I was home. If she's anything like me she spends a lot of her time hanging out at Top's Pizzeria on the highway in town, or at a friend's house. But I don't even know who her friends are." She took a deep breath to calm herself but only succeeded in changing her sniffle into a wracking sob.

"Get a grip on yourself. I need information." He fixed her with a steely stare, his fingers beating an impatient tattoo on the seat arm between them.

She wiped at her eyes with the back of her hand. "Thanks. I'll remember your compassion the next time you get all choked up over what your friend Brian did to you."

His fingers stopped their annoying drum beat, but his eyes didn't change. "If I start blubbering when I should be giving you needed information, I'll deserve no quarter. If you really want to help your sister, use your intelligence. Give me the facts I need to do a better job when we get there, or you might have reason to shed tears."

She wasn't sure what angered her more: his unfeeling attitude, or his being right. She turned from him, looked out the window at the clouds passing swiftly beneath the wing, tried to focus her anger into a knot of determination. "Okay, what else do you want to know?"

"About Rico Malavesi. What does he want from you? Why is he afraid of you?"

She snapped her head around, expecting to see a look of sarcasm on his face, and was doubly confounded to find him regarding her steadily, expectantly. "I think you have that turned around. I'm the one who is afraid of Rico."

A sour look marred his features and he raised one hand, a finger pointed in her direction. She steeled herself for another "mini-lecture"; but he arrested both the motion and his look, and took her hand in his instead.

"Dee, listen to me. Please. I know you tend to think the best of people and I admire you for that. But the time has come for you to face some of the ugly realities of life. People like Rico are driven by greed. Their lust for power leads them to view other people in very simple, either-or, terms."

He gestured with his left hand, palm upward, as though weighing an object. "You either represent a chance for him to gain more power..." He released her hand and mimicked the gesture with his right hand, "...or you become a hindrance to that acquisition of power--an object to be feared."

Dee nibbled at her lower lip, wiped sweaty palms on her slacks.

"Someone--either you or someone connected with you--has convinced Rico that he has reason to fear you, that you represent a hindrance to him. Who is that, Dee?"

An objection came to mind but never made it to her lips. It was crowded out by her sudden recall of the conversation which had led to her departure from Los Angeles. "Lila."

Her one-word answer was met by a satisfied grunt from Jeff. "Your roommate."

"I just remembered something she said while she helped me stuff my clothes into the trunk of my car. It was something about my not having to be afraid of Rico once I left town. If he came looking for me at the apartment and questioned her..."

"Right. She feeds him a story that raises more questions--questions about how much you actually knew of his operations, what you planned to do with the information, and so forth. She feeds his fear."

Dee didn't care for the implications, but she had to admit they might be valid. Lila had never made any pretence about her own ambitions. She'd quit her job at Rico's club, offering Dee the position, because she'd landed a part in a television series. The series fizzled when the pilot got terrible reviews, and Lila found herself with nothing to fall back on. She went to work as a cocktail waitress-- and hated it. Maybe she'd told Rico a whopper, a big enough lie to start him searching for her.

And it was abundantly clear that Rico had been searching for her. There was no other explanation for the "advisory" on her little Toyota that deputy Sheriff at Jeff's cabin had mentioned.

"Jeff, there's someone else."

"Who's that?"

"You."

"Me? That's..." He muttered a curse and slapped himself on the forehead. "Of course! The red-neck deputy. Good thinking. If Rico followed up on their trace of your car, had someone check me out--the Jeff Westman who lived in that cabin, I mean--my all too brief past would have stirred his suspicions further, fed into his paranoia about what you were up to..."

Dee experienced scant satisfaction at having finally convinced him the threat from Rico was real. The pained look in his eyes spoke clearly of the self-recrimination he now experienced, and she felt guilty about adding that burden to his worries. She was about to remind him that she had been the one to ask for his help, that he was not responsible for Rico's action; but he spoke first--in that cool, dispassionate voice of his.

"You said he told your mother he'd know when you arrived. Could he watch her house from nearby?"

It took her a minute to adjust to the change of subject. Jeff waited for her answer, the muscles along his jaw line working rhythmically. She tried to picture the neighborhood, kept being distracted by those muscles, finally had to look away. "The house is on the highway, north of town, but there's a big yard and an old maple in the front. The nearby houses are spread out, some with gardens alongside. There might even be some corn rows here and there he could sneak into, but...no, nowhere he could hide for any long period. Someone would notice."

"He must have planted a bug in the house."

Her stomach did a flip-flop as she pictured Rico sneaking through the rooms of the house, looking for a place to plant a listening device. The thought disturbed her almost as much as her earlier pictures of Inga lying bound and gagged in some cold, dark room. "How? Mama walks the half mile to town once in a while, but she always locks the house."

"Locks," he sneered. With a wave of his hand he dismissed them. "He wouldn't have to get into the house. A small, nearly transparent piece of plastic glued to one corner of a window would do. Big picture windows make excellent transmitters."

"There are two big windows looking out

onto the front porch--one in the living room, the other in the parlor." Relief at the suggestion Rico might not have prowled through the house was overshadowed by her resentment at learning how easily one's privacy could be invaded.

A bubble of fear rose in her throat and turned into a wracking cough. "Is there anything to drink on this plane? My throat feels like sandpaper."

"I'll see." He went forward, talked to the pilot briefly, returned with a steel vacuum bottle. He handed it to her. "Coffee. We'll put down about three. Did you say it's an hour's drive?"

"Roughly." The steel bottle was hard to hold with sweaty hands. She spilled some of the coffee trying to pour it, then put the cup on the floor and used both hands on to fill it. The pungent aroma of the coffee was a welcome change from the faintly alcoholic smell of the plane's cabin. She hoped the caffeine would calm her nerves while it soothed her throat.

"It will still be light when we get there. We'll have to change the plan a little. Will your mother do what she's told?"

Dee swallowed the sip of coffee she had in her mouth, then deliberately took another sip, savored it, and swallowed before answering him. His willingness to help and his evident guilt at having put her in greater jeopardy notwithstanding, she had had enough of his high-handed attitude and wanted to think about her answer. She visualized throwing the remainder of the lukewarm brew into his face, but decided against it. Instead she rested the black plastic cup on the arm of the seat.

"What plan? And why do you want to

change it? Are you planning to order my mother around, too?"

He lifted both hands and, for a brief instant she thought he was going to reach for her, maybe hit her. Instead he pressed the heels of his hands against his eyes, made a rotating motion, then drug his hands downward until his fingertips reached his chin. He clasped his hands together and, with a loud sigh, dropped them to his lap.

"Okay, you take charge. You tell me what you want done, I'll do it."

"No!" She forgot she was holding the coffee cup in her left hand, but paid scant attention as her gesture sent it flying over the back of the seat between them. "Why does it have to be one or the other of us *in charge*? I thought we were partners. I thought we were going to work *together.*"

She had a few more choice words to say to him about how he'd been grilling her like a stoolie on the hot seat, but saw he was staring at her, open-mouthed, so she changed her tack, softened her voice a little. "Is that too much to ask?"

* * * * *

Jeff glanced down at his hands, studied how the months of manual labor had roughened them. It had been a pleasant, simple, uncomplicated life until this woman had dropped into it and turned him inside-out again.

The accusation she had just leveled at him had a familiar ring. Brian had used similar words on a number of occasions--especially that bit about "I thought we were partners". In ways he did not even begin to understand Dee managed to push all

154

the right buttons.

He considered covering himself by suggesting he had not wanted to discuss the plan within hearing of the pilot. He'd concocted similar stories for Brian and other colleagues in the past, and they'd worked. He couldn't even try with Dee, though. Her own forthrightness made it too difficult for him. Even when she was playing a role, as she'd done back in Denver, she'd managed to maintain her integrity.

"No....that's fair. I mean.... Uh, accept my apology. I've been a loner too long--and I don't mean just those seven or eight months in the cabin. But I won't make excuses. Let me sketch out the plan for you, and please feel free to interrupt if you see any holes in it."

If she had shown the least sign of gloating he might have regretted his decision, but she simply nodded and waited.

"I'm going to assume the worst--he's bugged the house and the phone as well. He may have traced you to my cabin, but he probably doesn't know who I am or that we're still together. That might give us an edge and we need to preserve it. Is there a motel in town?"

"Not in town. People mostly come to White Cloud for camping and hunting or fishing. There are two popular state parks just outside of town. Oh...and there's a motel on the highway about four miles south of town."

"Perfect. When we get to Grand Rapids, we'll rent two cars. I'll follow you to the motel. You'll go in alone, find out if Rico has checked in there. Seems unlikely, but we may get lucky. If he's there, I'll join you and we'll end the matter."

"How will you know..."

"You'll be carrying a radio with you. I'll hear everything you hear and say. If he's not there, you go on into town, to your mother's house, and I'll check into the motel. Now this is the tricky part. You can't talk about any of this inside your house. You can't speak of our plan, or even let your mother know I'm around. Rico might be listening. That's why I wanted to know how cooperative she'll be."

"Mama's pretty level headed, or at least she used to be. When I talked to her on the phone this morning she was pretty badly shaken, but she should be calmer now that she knows I'm coming. If not, I'll find a way to calm her down. I could bring her back to the motel..."

"No. That *was* my plan, but you've given me a better idea. If we let her know you've brought help, it may relax her, but it might also tip off Rico. And until we hear from him, there's really nothing for us to plan. Better to let her think you're alone. Just go home and tell her whatever you want about Rico, but play it a little dumb, like you can't figure out what he wants you for, like that. Don't let her see your radio, but keep it with you at all times. When Rico calls, play it straight. Don't try to tip me off by repeating what he says--you can tell me later when you're in your car."

"Right. Uh, what's this radio stuff?"

"We'll buy a set of two-ways when we get to Grand Rapids."

"And we'll be able to talk to each other when I'm out of the house--in my car or wherever?"

"Exactly." Her attitude encouraged him. She hadn't objected to keeping her mother in the dark, and seemed ready to play it by ear. He did a quick review, looking for holes. "Does Rico carry a gun?"

"I never saw him with one, but..."

"How about you? Can you shoot?"

"I've only handled a gun in front of a camera. I'm not sure I'd be able to shoot another person--even Rico."

"Okay. I'll buy a gun for myself in Grand Rapids assuming Carter's I. D. is still good. If you think..."

"No. I'll pass."

That was the A answer. Amateurs with guns in their hands usually found out, too late, that the cold steel had only made them foolishly brave. They invariably discovered that, unlike elk or deer or pheasants, other people shoot back. Without a gun she would be more inclined to run, or take some other defensive action that could keep her alive. "Good decision. You'll stay on the alert, act more defensively."

She brushed at a wisp of hair and, as she dropped her hand he caught it in his own. Then he sat back and closed his eyes, tried to relax in spite of the nagging feeling he had overlooked a crucial element of the plan.

One element he hadn't overlooked, and didn't dare share with Dee lest it destroy the little confidence she had in him, was the fact that he was operating well out of his depth. It wasn't just the muzziness of mangled memory. With a few notable exceptions most of his past now seemed to trail smoothly behind him like the wake of a slow-moving boat across a quiet pond. Unfortunately, this unfolding of his past only confirmed what he had suspected back in Seattle. He was *not* a man of action.

He'd probably never find the words to explain it to Dee, but in many ways their successful escape from that city was due in large part to the confidence he had drawn from her. Dee was a lot like Brian--able to launch into a course of action on the instant, able to handle people with a delicacy he admired.

Brian's baby-faced charm nicely disguised a veritable dynamo of action, a well-oiled machine capable of moving from dead stop to hyper-drive without visible effort.

His own tall, square-shouldered frame was also a disguise. His contribution to the team, whether in the jungles of Cambodia, the slums of Chicago, or the halls of Congress, had been about information, intelligence. His strength came from his ability to pull together scattered pieces of the puzzle and fit them into a comprehensive whole. One of his advisors in college had put it succinctly: *Stick to forest planning,* he'd said, *and let someone else put out the fires.*

And now they were headed for the pine forests of Western Michigan. Ready or not, Dee would need his help to put out her "fire". The churning in his gut told him he was not ready.

CHAPTER TWELVE

They wasted precious minutes on the car rental problem. Without a driver's license Dee could not sign for one of the cars and the clerk would not allow Jeff to sign for both. So they both got in the Chevy and drove it all of fifty feet across the street to another agency. While he rented their second car, she looked up electronic supply houses in a borrowed phone book, found one that advertised two-way radios, and jotted down the address.

"The electronics store isn't far from here," she told him as they left the rental office.

"Good. You take the Chevy, I'll follow in the Ford. Don't make any sudden--oh, damn!" He stopped abruptly, slapped his forehead. "I forgot maps. I'll need a good one of the White Cloud area--preferably a Metzger. Your radioed directions won't be any good to me if I don't know where back roads and landmarks are."

"You can get a map at the sportsman's shop in White Cloud. Lots of good detail."

He nodded. "I'll be right behind you."

She waited until he backed his car out, then drove slowly out of the lot, checking the rear-view mirror to make sure he was still behind her. There had been a lot of new construction in Grand Rapids since her last visit, but she found enough familiar landmarks as she headed for the electronics store near the mall.

Jeff seemed to know exactly what he was looking for. "We want a set of long-distance two-ways. Hands free, clearest possible channel," he told the clerk.

"I have just the thing for you, sir. This model here can be keyed with switch or toggle. You can tune in any of the regular C.B. channels, or select one of three dedicated channels of your own choosing. They have good range and excellent squelch--"

"How good?"

"Up to twenty-five miles. I tried one myself over to Saugatuck Dunes a while back with my girlfriend and she came in five by five from all the way across the park."

"And how far is that?"

"Not more than two miles," Dee put in before the clerk could answer.

The clerk turned a little red, but quickly nodded his head. "'Bout right. I've also heard from a lot of satisfied customers. One fella took his up hunting--"

"What's the battery like?"

"Fully rechargeable. Comes with adaptors for A.C. or cigarette lighter. See this light? Tells you you're transmitting. Goes dim on you, you know it's time for a recharge."

"We'll take them. And pair of extra battery packs."

"Gee, I'm not sure I have any spare--"

Jeff had taken the other radio from the case to inspect it and had been about to walk to the front of the store. He spun back around, jammed the radio back into its case, regarded the clerk with a glare.

The clerk turned red again. "Tell you what I can do. I got a few more of these in stock. I'll just scrounge the battery packs from one of them, then replace them..."

Jeff picked up the radio again, turned, and walked toward the cash register at the front of the store. "These are probably the best we can find here, absent an agency source," he told her while they waited for the clerk to join them. "I think I'll forget checking into that motel, though. No point in putting an extra four miles between us."

"Here we go, sir. Will that be cash or charge?"

Dee felt a touch of sympathy for the clerk. She had experienced Jeff's impatient glare, knew something of the very real threat one could feel when those eyes went cold and dark. At that moment, though, she was grateful they had been spared more of the salesman's time-wasting chatter.

Jeff displayed none of that chill outside the store when he handed her one of the radios and a spare battery pack. "I saw a gun shop up the street near where I parked. Why don't you wait in your car for me, familiarize yourself with the radio while I get what I need."

He emerged from the shop a short time later and beckoned to her, then stood beside his rental. She started the Chevy, waited for the traffic to clear, then executed a pair of u-turns to pull up beside him.

"Use channel A on your radio," he told her when she lowered the window. "We'll check them for distance when we get to the highway. Drive carefully."

She started to reach for his hand resting on

the door sill, but he'd already turned away.

He stayed close until they were on the freeway, circling the city to the north. She noticed him dropping farther behind her at the same time his voice burst forth from the radio.

"Do you read me?"

It took a few tries before she felt comfortable with the radio, learning to release the "talk" button so she could hear his responses. They drove north from Grand Rapids on M37, Jeff dropping farther behind her to check the radios' range as she led him through very familiar country.

The constant radio checks kept her from slipping into a nostalgic state. She'd clocked a lot of miles on this stretch of highway and it was surprising to discover how little it had changed over the years. The little roadside stands that dispensed fresh produce in the summer and fall and served as shelter for school children waiting for the big yellow bus in blustery winter weather looked much the same as they had when she was a child. The farmhouses which stood behind them still held the same fascination for her, but on this trip there was no time to muse about the lives they sheltered.

At one point he advised her of a minor change of plan. "It might be safer if you just leave your radio on 'send' once we get to town. I won't have anything important to say, and it will protect us against the possibility of your forgetting to throw your switch."

While she did not care for the implication, she had to admit to herself he was right. She *had* forgotten to do that once already. Still, she was not happy with the idea of one-way communication. She did her best to keep the disappointment out of her voice as she sent him a cheery "Roger!"

As they neared the crossroads south of town she keyed her radio. "Did you say you're not staying at the motel?"

"Right. But we'll check it out--Rico might be staying there. Are we near?"

"Yes."

His tan Thunderbird appeared in her rear-view mirror only seconds later and they pulled into the parking lot of the Pink Flamingo together.

"Is anyone here likely to recognize you?" he asked when she stepped from her car.

"Not likely. Why?"

He stopped in the act of moving off toward the motel office, turned back to her with a puzzled frown. Her question had been automatic, but his response made her immediately regret it. They had agreed on a partnership, but that didn't mean he had to explain every little action, give her a complete run-down of his thinking at every turn. She was about to tell him it didn't matter when she noticed his grin. He encircled her waist with his arm and set a slow pace across the graveled parking area toward the motel's office.

"Two reasons. First, I'll be able to use Carter's I. D. again. It should insure a straight answer. Second, if someone does exhibit signs of recognizing you and that someone fits your description of Rico, I'll save valuable seconds by being able to act immediately without checking with you first. I take it this is your local hot-pillow establishment?"

His words chilled her, but his arm around her and the cooperative tone of his voice rendered the chill negligible. She answered his question without thought. "Only for the very foolish. Locals who spend the night here might as well wear the Scarlet Letter the next day."

"Small towns." he muttered.

They were back in the parking lot less than two minutes later. The couple who owned the motel had happily described the people--all six of them--who had checked in within the past week without even seeing Jeff's stolen agency I. D., apparently assuming from his manner that he was some kind of official. None of them came close to Rico's description.

Dee held back tears of disappointment but was unable to stifle the moan that formed deep in her throat. She hadn't realized how much hope she had placed on Jeff's gamble that Rico would be at the motel. "There's a hotel in Fremont," she suggested.

"No. It was a bad guess to begin with. He wouldn't take the chance of being seen with a young girl--it would be too risky. More likely he'll be in his car near your mother's house, or maybe in some deserted barn or cabin."

"There must be a hundred empty cabins within fifteen miles of town. Most people will be back in the cities. He could be anywhere."

"Where's the sports shop you mentioned? The one with the good maps?"

"On your left as you cross the bridge going into town. First building. You can't miss it."

"Give me about five minutes head start. Make it ten. I want to be back in my car, near the radio, before you arrive at your mother's house. You can turn the switch on now, and leave it on. Check the light from time to time to make sure the battery is still good. You won't see me or hear from me again until..."

Disappointment welled up in her at the thought of being separated from him. Not since his reawakening had he given any indication of personal feeling for her. He had expressed admiration and respect for her abilities, and his being here at this moment certainly suggested a concern for her well-being, and that of her sister; but there had been a distinct absence of anything even remotely resembling tenderness or affection.

She went up on tiptoe and stopped his words with her lips. She filled her senses with the taste and smell of him, pressed herself to him and held onto his muscular shoulders. When his arms wrapped around her she pressed even closer.

The intensity of his response startled her. He held her tightly, pressed his mouth hard against hers, and groaned deep in his throat. A roaring noise in her ears drowned out the sounds of traffic on the highway, yet she could hear his labored breathing.

When he released her mouth and moved her away with his hands on her shoulders she didn't resist even though she wanted the moment to last. He held her at arm's length, his dark eyes studying her, then moved his hands down her arms, his thumbs pressing the sides of her breasts. He continued the caress until he captured her wrists, lifted her hands to his lips, kissed her fingertips.

"Ten minutes," he said in a voice gravelly with emotion.

Then he moved abruptly away, toward his car. She stood there, warm and happy with the realization he wanted her as much as she wanted him.

Perhaps, she thought, they'd have time to express their feelings more clearly. That is, if she lived through the coming encounter with Rico.

CHAPTER THIRTEEN

Dee turned the car into the familiar driveway, then bit down on her lip to forestall the tears. Everything looked exactly as it should, with no outward signs to indicate the terror that now gripped her family. The maple in the front yard was still green, a few weeks away from showing the first signs of autumn, the lawn neatly mowed, the porch swept clean.

The first sign of trouble within came as she stepped from the car. Light flashing across the three window panes in the top of the front door indicated the door had swung open but her mother did not come onto the porch to greet her. Even with the sun behind her Dee could not see her mother through the screen door. At that moment the difficulty of the role she must now play became clear to her.

She must pretend Jeff did not exist, appear to be less confident and more fearful than she actually felt, and at the same time try to offer comfort to her mother without tipping off the presumably eaves-dropping Rico. Nothing in the roles she had played in Hollywood had prepared her for this, but Inga's life was at stake, and that meant the rewards for a well-played role here were far more important than anything the glitz and glamour of Hollywood had offered.

Her mother stood a few paces back from the open front door, a handkerchief clutched in front of her, her eyes red and watery behind her glasses.

"Thank God you've come," she whispered through quivering lips.

"Mama." Dee wrapped her arms around her mother's shoulders and let the tears come, all thoughts of role-playing washed from her mind at the sight of her mother's pain and anguish. The two women held onto each other and cried.

"Hush now, Mama. Hush. It's going to be all right."

Dee was surprised at the force with which her mother wrenched herself away. "All right? You have no idea what I've been through these past three days. I've been afraid to go out of the house. Three days of waiting to hear they've killed Inga--or worse!" She slumped into an armchair.

Dee knelt in front of her and held her hands. "I thought you told me he took her yesterday."

"That man *called* yesterday. She hadn't come home the night before. What difference does it make? They have my baby!" She pulled her hands free, lifted her glasses and dabbed at her eyes with the handkerchief.

Dee was hurt by her mother's tone, but tried her best to not show it. "I'm just as frightened as you are, but it's going to be all right. He doesn't want to hurt Inga, he just wants me. As soon as I find out where he is, I'll go to him and we'll work things out. Then I'll bring Inga home and everything will be all right again."

"You talk like you know this man. What kind of people were you mixed up with out there in California?"

Dee ignored the implied criticism, tried her best to soothe. "If it's who I think it is, I do know him. I wasn't exactly mixed up with him, he's just someone I worked for.   We had a....misunder-standing."

"You call kidnapping an innocent girl a *misunderstanding*?   I guess I don't know you any more , Dee Johansen.   And I see you don't care about me or your sister all that much."

Dee felt suddenly tired.   She lurched to her feet, slumped into the cushions of the nearby couch. Years of living on her own in California, of talking to her mother only during rare phone calls, had dimmed her memory.   Mama's gratitude at those times, after receiving the occasional checks Dee had been able to send--"to help out with Inga's fall wardrobe" or other flimsy excuses to avoid the taint of charity--had made those phone calls pleasant experiences, had enabled her to forget the argumentativeness that had characterized far too much of their relationship.   This exchange brought it all back in a rush, reminding her of her mother's habit of taking words and phrases out of context, twisting their meaning, and then throwing them back in Dee's face.

If only Jeff could have come with her to the house.   Mama wouldn't badger her if someone else was present--she never argued in front of company. Dee glanced at her purse, wondered how her mother would feel if she knew her every word was being transmitted to a stranger's ears.   The thought did not cheer her.   From somewhere deep within her a sense of loyalty to her parent surfaced.   It became her duty to put an end to the bickering for her mother's sake. She took a deep breath, let it out slowly as she searched for words.   "Mama---"

Her apology was cut off by the ringing of the phone. They both jumped.   Her mother's hands went to her mouth, the handkerchief muffling a bleating cry. Dee propelled herself off the couch, the heavy purse banging her hip as she crossed the room in two strides.

She closed her eyes, took another deep breath and let it out while the phone rang a second time. "Hello?"

It was Mrs. Peterson, their nearest neighbor, in the house across the highway. The woman answered Dee's greeting, then gushed, "Dee, is that really you?"

"Yes. Hello Mrs. Peterson. It's nice to hear your voice." Dee listened impatiently as the woman went through her usual song-and-dance about having called *just to chat*, pretending she hadn't been watching from her front window as Dee drove in moments before, and ending with a flow of questions about The Coast.

Dee considered asking the woman about any suspicious characters in the neighborhood--if anyone had seen Rico it would have been her--but decided against it. Not only would it encourage a lengthy conversation and invite more curiosity and speculation from one of the town's more notorious gossips; such a conversation would alert Rico if he was, as Jeff suspected, listening. She cut the woman off, pleading travel fatigue and the need to talk with her mother, and promised to drop in for a brief visit soon. It was still another full minute before she returned the receiver to its cradle.

As she turned she met the disapproving, superior look on her mother's face. "Emily doesn't miss much."

"Have you talked to her since...?"

Her mother shook her head slightly,

smoothing the handkerchief in her lap. "I've been afraid to talk to anyone--especially Emily."

"Mama, do you have any coffee?   And maybe a cookie or two?" The diversion seemed to work. The feeling between them grew less tense, if not exactly relaxed. She'd have to be careful about reopening the subject of the kidnapping. Perhaps a little gossip about Emily Peterson would help to ease the tension further.   There'd be time to get whatever details Mama could relate about Inga's kidnapping later.

* * * * *

Rico lifted the headphones from his ears, turned to look at the girl propped up on the couch. "Well, Baby Sister, looks like Big Sister made it home. Bet you're happy about that, eh?"

The kid didn't answer, of course. The gag made it difficult for her to say anything. And she gave no other sign of reacting to the news.

She'd caved in right from the start, this one. The minute he'd shown her his .45 she'd shut down, checked out, turned to jelly. Not spunky like Big Sister, not even like the old geezer who'd at least had a little fight in him. The old guy had been too damn nosy for this own good, snooping around like that, asking questions about the people who owned the cabin.

"You'd better answer, Baby Sister, or you'll wind up in the lake with the old geezer!"

The kid bobbed her head and made that funny wheezing noise through her nose. Boring. No fun at all.

Deeana's Old Lady sounded like she had a

little fight in her, just like his own mother. The way she tore into Deeana the minute she walked through the door made him wish he'd snatched her instead of the kid. Of course, that wouldn't have done him any good. Baby Sister would probably have panicked, called the cops, and queered the whole setup if she'd been the one left behind with instructions to fetch the blonde.

He crossed to the couch, checked the ropes. Still nice and tight. The kid hadn't even bothered to try them. "Time for me to go have a look-see," he told her. "You stay right where you are and maybe I'll give you a little something to eat when I get back. Give me any grief and..."

He let her see the gun again. She just closed her eyes. No spirit.

Rico locked the door of the cabin with the old man's keys, slipped them into the pocket of his hunting jacket. He checked the nearby woods for signs of intruders, then walked to his rented Cadillac and got behind the wheel. He'd much rather have borrowed a limo in Chicago, the way he'd done in Oregon, but even if they'd let him he didn't want anyone--family or not--to be around as witnesses.

He missed having a limo, and the convenience of a mobile phone. Not that he had that much use for a phone any more--his last call to the office had been answered by a stranger and there was little doubt about what that meant. The raids on his operations had been increasingly serious, not the usual election-time political show. There was no question about it--the blonde's friends had been very thorough and surprisingly determined. Whoever they were--the sketchy reports he'd received hadn't been too clear on that score--they'd set their sights pretty high and their questions about the blonde made it clear she was the source of their information.

Even the family had cut him off, covering their own asses rather than coming to his support. This mess showed him just how little he could count on their loyalty. They probably wouldn't even go his bail if the pigs caught up with him. Not that that was a worry, of course. The pigs weren't going to get a chance to slap iron on Rico. He'd exact his revenge on the blonde, then disappear for a while until things cooled off.

Maybe he'd go down to Miami when he was through with the blonde, maybe all the way to South America. Yeah. He could lay low for a while, maybe even put a new organization together, come back bigger and stronger than before.

He drove slowly up the dirt driveway and onto the gravel road that circled the lake and took him toward town. On the way he entertained himself with thoughts of how he'd teach the blonde her lesson once he had her. It was going to be a nice, long, slow process.

CHAPTER FOURTEEN

Jeff could still taste her on his lips, smell her on his sleeves and lapel. Dee's embrace had shaken him more than he would have thought possible, leaving him with little doubt about his desires. But he had to stop daydreaming about her if he was going to operate at peak efficiency. He bought the map he needed, hurried across the street to grab a burger, then drove to a nearby city park to await Dee's arrival at her mother's house.

The greasy burger and salty fries erased some of the lingering aroma of Dee. As he finished the last of the fries and brushed crumbs from the map spread across his lap, he felt some return of sanity. The burger sat like a cold lump in the pit of his stomach, deadening the butterfly feeling. He hoped the black coffee would cut the grease a little, took healthy sips of the warm brew as he continued to study the map.

Newaygo County formed a tall rectangle of land about 25 miles wide and a little under 40 miles tall with the single highway bisecting it on a fairly straight north/south line with White Cloud placed near the center of the county. Other roads in the county were either laid out "on the square", following a zigzag course around farms: three miles east, then one mile north, then another mile east, and so forth; or were curved roads that followed rivers or circled lakes.

The upper two-thirds of the county lay

within the Manistee National Forest, and the map was designed for hunters and fishermen. Creeks and rivers and lakes were clearly marked with boat ramps, which was usual; but there were also many patches of "marsh" and other features which would probably be of interest to hunters in all seasons. His thirst for information was being nicely slaked.

He reached for the paper coffee cup on the dash and noticed the police car making another slow circuit of the park. "Damn," he muttered. The cops had made a drive-by shortly after he had parked the Thunderbird on the edge of the wide stretch of lawn between the road and the river, and he had given them a tight-lipped nod. A few kids were splashing in the river at the other side of the park, and he had reacted instinctively to the scrutiny of the police, hoping they would accept his acknowledgment of their presence as indication of his friendly intentions. This second pass, however, made it clear he must either move to a less public place or set their minds at ease.

He could, of course, simply flash his "borrowed" I. D. and settle the issue of his right to park there. They would leave him alone after that, even if he spent the night waiting for the phone call Dee was expecting. But it was also possible-- depending on variables he could only guess at-- they would check him out with either the Detroit or the Chicago office, and he couldn't allow that.

He flipped the button on his radio, cutting off the conversation from the Johansen kitchen, as the car drew closer, opened his door and waved them down. They pulled alongside and he climbed out, taking his map with him.

"Afternoon, officers."

The driver busied himself with the radio, the sergeant riding with him acknowledged his greeting with a curt nod. "Can we help you, sir?"

Jeff hunkered down beside the car and balanced the map on one knee. "Hope so. Been looking over my map, trying to find a good fishing spot. Figured I'd avoid the crowds at the state parks, but I don't want to be trespassing on anyone's private property."

"There are a couple of good places, but they'd take a bit of hiking to reach," the cop suggested, his eyes taking in Jeff's attire.

"That'd be okay. My gear's in the trunk. Drove up from Grand Rapids this afternoon. Needed to get the sound of the ticker-tape out of my ears for a while. I'd planned to go on up to Manistee, but I'm a little more tired that I thought I'd be. I've always meant to stop here before--never did."

The sergeant gave him a look that made it clear Jeff had been a fool to waste his time going to Manistee. He shifted in his seat, stuck a weathered hand out the window. "You see this road here, goin' west? That's about a mile north. You go out that road about three miles, there's a farm with a yellow house. Just past that is Larkins Lane. 'Bout here, see? That takes you up to Blue Lake. There's a couple of cabins on the south side, but the road continues past them, and then there's a wide spot, room for two or three cars. You park there and hike back to the lake. Guarantee you a nice catch to take back to Grand Rapids with you."

"Thank you, Sergeant. I sure appreciate it. Say, is there a restaurant in town that opens early in the morning? I'd like to get some breakfast before I head out there."

"You planning on spending the night?"

Jeff had counted on the sergeant being a good cop. He'd taken the bait nicely, gave Jeff just the right lead-in. "Yeah. I spotted a motel a few miles south, and that's what made me realize just how tired I am. I thought about heading back there, but figured these seats in my rental are probably just as comfortable as their beds. If I can grab an early breakfast and head out to that spot, it should be good fishing in the morning, right?"

The cop thought about it for a few seconds. Jeff was pretty sure he'd check out the car's license later, assure himself it had been rented in Grand Rapids. And he knew with a certainty that information would set the sergeant's mind at lease and give him the satisfaction of having earned his pay. Something Dee had said about people just waiting to be told what to do went through his mind as he waited.

"Well, if you're going to sleep in your car, best thing is for you to head over to the Country Kitchen. They open at six. The cook will probably shake you out when he's ready."

"Great. Where is the Country Kitchen?

They spent a few more minutes in idle chatter about the quality of food at the local restaurant and the size of the fish in local streams and lakes, then the two cops drove off. Jeff got back in his car, switched on the radio. Dee and her mother were still talking quietly about things just as inconsequential as restaurants and fishing. He breathed a sigh of relief. At least the expected call from Rico hadn't come while he talked with the police.

* * * * *

Dee rubbed sleep from her eyes as she swung her legs out of bed, then reached for the phone. She'd slept fitfully on the hide-a-bed in the parlor--she'd wanted to be as close to the phone as possible--and despite her careful preparations she fumbled around in the dark, knocking things over before she managed to find the phone. She'd expected Rico to call early--though not quite *this* early. The clock on the mantle read four-thirty.

Rico didn't waste time with preliminaries. She had barely pressed the receiver to her ear when she heard him say, "There's a store three miles north of town on the highway. Phone booth outside. Be there in five minutes or you'll miss my call."

"Wait! I'm not even...." but she was talking to a dial tone.

She scrambled into her clothes, cursing herself for not leaving them on all night, and made a dash for the door even before she'd put on her suit coat or sweater. She banged her knee when she tried to pull open the locked door, swore once as she fumbled for the dead-bolt lock in the semi-dark room. She heard her mother on the stairs behind her as the door finally came open, but didn't wait to explain. She was already in the car before the chill of the night air struck her, sending a shiver up her spine.

The Chevy wouldn't start on the first crank. She pumped the gas pedal a few times, then tried it again. The engine caught and roared to life. She let it race for a moment while she finished buttoning her blouse and slipped into her coat. She left the sweater on the seat beside her, pulled the gear shift lever down one notch and spun the tires on gravel as she backed down the drive.

"I hope you're listening, Jeff. He's sending me to the general store three miles north of town. He's going to call me at a phone booth there--with more instructions, I guess. God, I'm scared."

She forced herself to slow to a reasonable sixty miles per hour and tried to struggle into the bulky sweater. The unfamiliar dash arrangement of the Chevy defeated her attempts to find the heater. She kept watching for signs of Jeff's Thunderbird.

She scattered more gravel as she braked near the phone booth in front of the store. She flung open the door and started to run for the booth, remembered her purse, went back to the car. The phone wasn't ringing, so she forced herself to walk from the car to the unlit booth while she got her left arm into the sweater. The sky was black as pitch, the crisp night air smelling faintly of moss and swamp grass. She drank in the air, trying to calm jangled nerves.

* * * * *

Rico chuckled as he slipped the headset off his left ear and reached for the phone. "So, Big Sister brought her boyfriend along. Ain't that cute."

He turned to look at the teenager lying on the couch. She was pretending to be asleep, ignoring him, but he could tell by the way she was shaking she was awake.

The blonde hadn't said anything to her mother about Jeff being with her. They'd gossiped all night about their neighbors, talked about Baby

Sister now and then; but he could tell from the old lady's tone, and by the way she kept insisting that they bring the police into the picture, that she thought Deeana had come alone. Old Lady Johansen didn't trust her daughter any more than he did, and that attitude earned her his grudging respect. It hadn't made him any less cautious, though.

And his precautions had paid off. Making the short trip to town last night to plant a second bug on the blonde's Chevy had been a smart move. No mistake about that message she'd sent, even with the noise of the car's engine. Unless this Jeff character had slipped into her car during the short time between his planting the bug and getting back to his radio here, that meant she was wired, or they were using radios. The thought gave him pause. If they were smart enough to wire the blonde they might have spotted his own bugs, might be aware he was listening. It wouldn't do them any good, though. He'd thought out his plan to the last detail. Let Jeffie-boy follow her.

"I think I'll have a little fun with Big Sister before I bring her here," he told the kid. "Pay attention. You'll get a kick out of this."

* * * * *

Dee checked her watch every fifteen seconds, became convinced she had somehow missed Rico's call. She shivered uncontrollably in the open phone booth. She'd been standing here for nearly five minutes, and it couldn't have taken her more than four minutes to get here, even counting the hassle with the locked front door. She wanted to talk to Jeff, but he had been adamant about her using the radio only when she was inside the car with the windows closed. She hadn't needed an explanation of directional microphones to understand his caution. A movie studio is a veritable jungle of sound equipment and she'd witnessed for herself how well a good directional mike could pick up a conversation from a distance. But she was now beginning to wonder at the wisdom of their separating. If Rico was...

The phone made a soft burring sound just before it rang, but the strident tone of the bell startled her in spite of the warning. She grabbed it immediately. "Yes?"

"Phone booth at the Mobil station. Five minutes." The line went dead.

"Damn you, Rico!" she screamed at the dead phone. It was a short drive back to town and the engine was now warmed up. She'd make it with time to spare, but that didn't ease her anger--or her anxiety. Her tires spat gravel again and squealed when she reached the pavement. "I'm going back to town--to another damn phone booth. The Mobil station. I guess he's going to run me around for a while, make me sweat."

It took her a long moment to realize Jeff wasn't going to answer her. She considered releasing the button on her radio--there seemed little point in holding them to a one-way conversation at this stage of the game. But then, what could he say to her? Words of encouragement might calm her, but they wouldn't change the situation any. She left the radio as it was despite her growing fear that Rico would find a way to separate her from Jeff, leave her to fend for herself.

She left the car running at the gas station so the heater would warm it up. Her more leisurely drive back to town had given her time to find the controls. She didn't forget her purse this time, either, though it seemed silly to bother with it since she couldn't talk to Jeff outside the car. There were an increasing number of things wrong with this plan, she mused. When she closed the car door behind her she heard the phone ringing.

She took two quick steps to the booth, picked up the receiver, but found the line had gone dead.

Dee replaced the receiver, then stood staring at the phone, wondering what to do now. There was nothing she could do. Rico had all the cards and she was completely at his mercy. She made a bet with herself he had planned to toy with her in this way right from the start. The thought calmed her. She turned to go back to the car, but before she could get the door of the booth open, the phone rang again. "I'm here, Rico."

"Back to the other phone booth."

"Wait!" He said nothing, but the line hadn't gone dead. She hurried on. "Rico, what is the point of all this? Can't you just tell me where you are, let me come to you? All I want is for Inga to go free. I'll do whatever you say. Please."

"Back to the other booth," was all he said.

She hung up, repeated his instructions for Jeff's benefit as she got back into the car, wasted no time getting back to the general store. The phone rang just as she stepped up to the booth.

"I'm here," she informed him.

"Take highway 20 west. A roadside picnic area about five miles out. Wait there."

"Yes. I know the place. I'll..." the phone was dead again. It was pointless to go on. She got back in the car. "Jeff, I'm headed west on highway 20. There's a small wayside about six miles out, just this side of Aetna. I'm supposed to wait there."

The wayside held three picnic tables and an out-house. She pulled into the parking area off the road and looked around for some sign of Rico. Of course, it was silly to expect him to be here since she had just talked to him on the phone not five minutes before. She tried to picture the rotund man, dressed in silk suit and ruffled shirt, sitting at one of the picnic tables, taking the phone from his secretary or his house boy. In other circumstances she might have found the image amusing. At the moment it only added to the sinister--and formidable--qualities she begrudgingly attributed to him.

Rico had picked the spot well. The highway was straight and flat at this point, offering a clear view of any approaching cards and practically no place, other than the wayside, for mile in either direction at which a car could pull off the road. A very steep ditch ran down the south side of the road, and pines grew so close to the north side they had to be sheered like a hedge each spring to keep them from growing over the road and obstructing traffic. It seemed unlikely Jeff would know about the service road a mile behind her. More likely the closest he'd be able to be at this moment without being spotted was over five miles away, on the highway.

The minutes ticked away and she fought an impulse to close her eyes, to smother her nervousness in sleep. She considered getting out of the car to stretch her legs, but decided against it. She was better off where she was. When Rico drove up she'd at least have a few seconds to advise Jeff of the fact, maybe describe his vehicle. She rolled her window down halfway, bathing her face in the cool air. The usual night sounds made by frogs and cicadas and an occasional bird reached her through the open window.

Something hit the car, startling her. She looked up in time to see a pine cone skittering off the edge of the hood. The morning breeze must be kicking up, she told herself, craning her neck a little to see the tree tops through the windshield. Their swaying upper branches confirmed her suspicion.

When she returned her eyes to the road she saw Rico standing beside the car, just in front of her door. He pointed a very large, ugly-looking gun at her through the open window, and he had the index finger of his left hand pressed to his lips, warning her to remain silent. His sudden appearance froze her with fear, and she was able to do nothing other than dig her nails into the palms of her hands wrapped around the steering wheel as she stared at him, transfixed like a deer caught in a car's headlights.

CHAPTER FIFTEEN

Rico's bulk loomed large through the windows, his massive frame made even larger by the hunting jacket he wore. He looked strange without his usual ruffled shirt and silk suit, but there was no mistaking the glint in his eyes, even in the dim glow given off by the car's interior lights. She had no choice but to obey his silent signals to get out of the car if she ever hoped to see Inga.

She unlocked the car door, swung it open slowly, and put her left foot on the ground. A little voice in the back of her mind told her she should make some sound to alert Jeff, but her throat wouldn't cooperate. She reached behind her for her purse but Rico immediately wagged a finger and shook his head, a bemused, almost triumphant, look on his face. She left the purse behind and didn't utter a sound as she slid from behind the wheel.

Rico motioned her toward the back of the car with his gun hand, then jerked his other hand downward in a clear signal for her to kneel or get down on all fours. Trembling with fear, Dee felt the gravel bite into her knees through the thin fabric of her slacks. Her hands shook so badly she could hardly get a grip on the bumper to steady herself. She kept her gaze on his gun, praying she would find the strength to scream if his finger tightened on the trigger--hoping Jeff would hear that, and that would at least give Inga a chance.

Without a sound, Rico backed up a few

paces, reached into the car and lifted the radio out of her purse. He turned an evil grin her way as he carefully replaced the radio and then very quietly closed the car door on her purse, the radio, and her hopes of aid.

At his silent direction she regained her feet and moved toward the back of the wayside. She stopped at the edge of the park but he prodded her in the back with his gun, forced her into the trees. A branch smacked her in the face.

His beefy hand grabbed her left shoulder just as she raised her arms to ward off any other branches, pulled her to a stop. He swept her arms to her sides, and then she felt him tug at the collar of her sweater, pulling it downward. Dee was already chilled to the bone, but she clenched her teeth and tried to remain cooperative as he stripped the sweater from her. A moment later she heard it fall to the ground with a rustle of leaves.

He started to do the same with her jacket, and she reached for the single button, ready to do anything he commanded if it would help Inga; but suddenly his arm was around her throat. She felt the pressure of cold steel in the hollow place below her right ear, heard his quiet hiss--barely distinguishable from the breeze rustling the pines, but clearly warning her against either movement or sound.

When the blood stopped pounding in her ears she recognized the sound of a distant engine. The idling engine of the Chevy had become lost in the night sounds. This new sound was of an engine under strain--a fast-moving car, she guessed.

The vehicle noise grew closer, then suddenly changed in pitch as it receded from them. She could tell it wasn't Jeff's Thunderbird. It had been a truck, a big one.

She heard his controlled exhale as he relaxed his grip, then felt him tug at her jacket again. She released the button and allowed him to rip it from her, heard the tell-tale rustle as it joined her sweater on the forest floor. Then the gun barrel was back at her ear.

She needed no further direction. He expected her to make like a statue. Nonetheless, she was unable to suppress a shudder as his hand snaked over her shoulder, beefy fingers pressed against her flesh through the thin fabric of her blouse. He reached for her breast, but she soon realized he wasn't just copping a feel. His fingers went along each edge of her bra, twisting it every inch or so from center to strap on each cup. He was looking for more listening devices.

Dee's skin crawled at his touch, regardless of his intent. She wanted to tell him his search was pointless, admit he'd been clever enough to outsmart them, cut off the only hope of aid she'd had. She suspected, though, that any words she spoke, any sound she made would be interpreted by him as a warning to Jeff; and she was sure she'd never live to see Inga if he thought that was what she was doing. She bit her lip and squeezed her eyes shut as he continued his repulsive search.

Apparently satisfied she wasn't wired, he prodded her in the back again, gave her a one-word command. "Move."

Dee's eyes were now accustomed to the scant light available in this forest and she could see they were on a narrow path of sorts--probably a deer trail. She'd shivered with cold and fear when they started, but the effort of walking and shielding her face from branches soon warmed her in spite of her lack of clothing. She tripped on roots or vines a couple of times but managed to keep her feet under her and set a pace that kept the gun out of her back.

They must have walked a mile when it occurred to her Rico might be in even worse shape than she was. If she increased her pace a little at a time she might begin to pull away from him, might even get far enough to make a break for it.

As if reading her thoughts he gave another single-word command from close behind her. "Stop."

She came to a stop, breathing heavily, rested her hands on her hips and hung her head. The gun barrel found her side, dug in deep beneath her rib cage.

"Don't move. Don't make a sound."

Not moving was easy. Breathing quietly after such exertion was a little harder. She did her best and, when he urged her forward again after a long wait, was relieved that her best had been good enough for him. Almost immediately they broke out of the woods and she collided with a black car parked alongside the road.

"Get in," he ordered. He closed the door behind her by leaning against it, then walked around the front of the car, making sure she saw the gun pointed at her. He closed his door in the same quiet way, then threw a switch that locked all the doors. "So much for your boyfriend," he said with a wide grin.

Had he not seen the two-way radio she might have tried to bluff it out. But he had been too thorough. She huddled into herself and tried not to shiver.

He started the Cadillac and put it in gear without turning on the lights. Less than a quarter mile down the gravel road he turned left onto another gravel road. She thought the road looked like the one leading to Long Lake, though she couldn't be completely sure. The hike had disoriented her.

He drove slowly, without lights. "Now for some answers," he said conversationally. "Who is this Jeff Westman character?"

The question startled her. How had he known about Jeff? How had he known the person on the other end of the two-way was a "boyfriend" and not the police? She looked out her window, tried to think of what she should tell him. She didn't notice his hand move. Her head snapped back against the seat and a searing shot of pain lanced through her left cheek. She sat up, then felt the sting of his blow warming her face, tasted her own blood in her mouth. Her vision blurred and she heard him speak to her as though from a distance.

"I asked you a question, Big Sister! 'Smatter, you think I'm stupid or something? You want I should spell it out for you? I planted a bug on your car last night, same like I put on the old lady's house a coupla days ago. You ain't been able to fart without me knowing about it.

"You traded in your car in 'Frisco, I knew about it the next day. You dumped the Toyota at Westman's little hidey-hole in Oregon, I knew about it as soon as the cops did. Now you want to tell me the rest, or do you want me to beat it out of you? How long have you two been planning this?"

Rico was obviously in possession of more

facts than she and Jeff had even suspected, and was clearly way ahead of them. His last statement, though, carried implications she could not even guess at. He knew about Jeff, so there was no point in trying to deny their relationship--but she needed to convince him Jeff was not a threat and that he could let Inga go and deal with her directly.

"Jeff doesn't have anything to do with you and me, Rico. I met him completely by accident-- literally. My Toyota went off the road near his house. He rescued me and agreed to help me when a cop started nosing around, that's all. We're not even sure who he is. He was in some kind of accident...he can't remember anything about his past beyond January of this year."

Rico lifted his hand from the wheel as though to slap her again. "Don't give me that crap about January. I seen the records. I already know about his cover story. I said I want the truth. Now you tell me how he's operating, how he got into my organization, or you ain't gonna live to see Baby Sister, get it?"

Dee felt like she'd followed Alice down the rabbit hole. Rico seemed to know a few facts, but they were all twisted. In a manner of speaking the life Jeff had been leading in the mountains was a "cover story", but that part about Jeff getting into his organization was pure insanity. They'd both been too busy running to cause anyone trouble. "I don't know what you want me to say, Rico. I'm telling you the truth."

"In a pig's eye!" He stopped the car, turned his bulk slightly toward her and pointed the barrel of his gun at her face.

Then just as suddenly he relaxed, a grin

spread across his pudgy face. "Okay. Fine. You just stick to that story. Maybe Little Sister can convince you to tell me what's going on--why strangers are answering the phone in my office, why my houseboy isn't around." He let the car roll forward again, turned off the road onto a gravel lane.

Dee felt tremors of fear race through her body but tried to ignore them as she puzzled his strange remarks. Jeff had been with her every moment since their first meeting--except for that short time in Seattle while she interviewed Sondra Culver--and Dee was dead certain he had not initiated any action against Rico. To the contrary, Jeff had admitted his underestimation of Rico during their flight out of Dallas. Either Jeff was a more gifted actor than anyone Dee had ever known, or Rico had gone completely mad. She decided the latter was far more likely.

Rico slowed the big car, turned into a narrow driveway. He stopped the car and then backed it toward the cottage which stood by the shore of Long Lake. Using his gun as a pointer he directed her toward the cottage.

She stepped into the gloom of the cottage interior, Rico close behind. He flicked on the lights and a chandelier made from an old wagon wheel filled the room with brilliance. When she opened her eyes from the involuntary blink she saw Inga lying on the couch, her legs and arms tied together at the wrists and ankles and bound together behind her. Inga had a gag in her mouth and the eyes looking up at Dee appeared to be as big as saucers.

Dee fell to her knees and tried to wrap her arms around her sister's shoulders. She couldn't stop her own tears, and when Inga began a tearless whimper through the cloth gag, they flowed even more freely. "Oh, Baby. I'm so sorry. Please forgive me. I'm so sorry."

"Okay, that's enough! Sit down over there," Rico commanded.

She turned to look at him without releasing her grip on Inga, tears and rage blinding her. To hunt her down was one thing, but to treat her little sister like this was quite another. Her hands curled into claws, ready to dig his eyes out, and she started up from the floor.

He was fast for a big man. Before she could get off her knees he had covered the distance between them and aimed a blow at her face. She couldn't avoid it but she saw it coming and was able to roll with it.

"That's more like it. I like a little fight in my women. Now get into the chair."

She was more than willing to go up against his fists, but she wasn't foolish enough to argue with his gun. It was pointed at her middle again, so she did as she was told. She lifted herself into the wooden kitchen chair at one end of the couch. Lengths of cotton clothesline lay in a heap beside it.

"You have a choice, Big Sister. You can tie your ankles to the chair nice and tight, or I can put you to sleep with this and do it myself." He brandished the gun.

She picked up one of the ropes, wrapped it around her left ankle and one the leg of the chair twice, and tied it in a secure knot. She did the same to the other ankle before she looked up at him, then sat up straight, fixing him with a glare.

"Good. Now, let's see what's on the radio,

shall we?"

He backed toward a desk near the front door, picked up a set of headphones and placed one earpiece to his ear. He kept the gun pointed in her general direction.

Was he going to leave her hands free? It might give her an edge if he thought she was helpless enough with just her ankles tied to the chair. She looked at Inga lying on the couch, tried to smile, let her know things would work out somehow. It was difficult to do when she didn't believe it herself.

She let her gaze wander around the cottage. Hope emerged when she spied a large glass ashtray sitting on the end table nearest her. She tried to calculate the distance, wondered if she could reach it with her right hand before she tipped over in the rickety chair.

She continued her visual search of the room in as casual a manner as she could summon, thinking all the while about the ashtray. If she held her left arm out while she reached for the ashtray with her right it would help with her balance. Better yet, if Rico could be distracted long enough for her to scoot her chair a little to the right...

"Well, Baby Cakes, it's all quiet on highway twenty. My guess is Jeffie-baby is running around like a chicken with his head cut off, trying to find you. But we're not going to tell him where you are, are we?"

"Rico, why don't you let Inga go? You have me now. She's no use to you. Mama's worried sick about her."

"That's a mama's job, to worry sick. Bellyache, bitch, and gripe. Too bad mama doesn't have a man around to straighten her out once in a while. That's what you all want, isn't it? *My* mother did. Speaking of mama, let's see what's happening at her house, shall we? Hey, isn't this fun?"

He turned a knob on his radio console. "Nope. Nothing happening at Mama's house, either," he announced a few moments later. "No little Jeffie and no bad policemans, at either of our two choice locations. Now what do you make of that, folks?

Rico was either turning into a ham actor with his "captive" audience, or he had gone off the deep end. Maybe he'd gone power-mad with the success of his scheme. The thought gave her an idea.

"I'll tell you what I make of it, Rico. I'm impressed. No, really. I still think you're a rotten bastard, but I'm impressed." *Had he straightened just a little? Was he buying it?* She did her best to maintain the same tone, careful to avoid laying it on too thick.

"When you told me back in L.A. what a powerful man you were, I quite frankly didn't believe you. But this is very impressive. You've pulled off two kidnappings in unfamiliar territory, managed to shake a tail--though losing Jeff probably wasn't *that* hard--and you've gotten away with it. To tell you the truth, I think I'm going to have to revise my opinion of you."

"So you still think I'm a rotten bastard, eh?"

His response told her more than she'd bargained for. He saw it as a compliment. She was on the right track.

"Well, sure. After all, Inga is my baby sister. You figured out the one thing you could use against me, and it worked."

She glanced at Inga. The look of disbelief in her little sister's eyes almost threw her off the track. Inga couldn't be expected to understand what she was trying to do. Dee returned her attention to Rico, watch for a sign of weakening. "It's impressive," she repeated.

"So...you think we ought to let Baby Sister go, eh? Then maybe you and me could have a little party, right?"

She did her best to avoid appearing too eager or too hopeful. "Well...we'll see."

"Okay." He turned toward Inga, a broad smile on his face. "Baby Sister, you can go."

Dee held her breath. Inga's frightened gaze darted back and forth.

He straightened, threw his head back, and laughed. "See? She doesn't want to go. She likes Rico. Takes after her big sister. I think we'll keep her. Maybe the two of you can be the start of a new stable of ladies for Rico. The foundation of my new organization, eh?"

He laughed again, subsided into giggles and snickers. Dee closed her eyes, realized she'd never had a prayer. Rico had no intention of letting either of them go. Her mother's worst fears were about to become a reality.

CHAPTER SIXTEEN

A long shudder wracked Dee's body, but she forced herself to stop shaking, willed her body under control. She was not going to be able to talk Rico out of killing them, nor could she convince him to let Inga go. There was only one option left to her--find some way to render him unconscious long enough for her to get herself and Inga free.

She tried to bring the glass ashtray into her peripheral vision without signaling her intent to Rico. She knew she would have just one chance. She'd have to reach it, throw it before he could react, and hit him hard enough to make him drop the gun. But that wouldn't do her any good...even if he dropped it, he could still pick it up again and shoot her before she could reach him. She'd have to knock him senseless, if not unconscious.

The ropes would tear at her ankles when she made her lunge, and the chair would probably slam against her legs, maybe throw off her aim. She'd have to steel herself to ignore the pain in her ankles and account for the drag of the chair when she took aim. It would be better if she didn't have to reach so far for the ashtray.

"Let me see. Which of my admirers do I start with? What do you think, Baby Sister? Shall I start with Big Sister so you can see what you'll be getting, learn to respect Rico properly? You can see Big Sister already knows, can't you?"

Dee tried to ignore him as he leaned toward

Inga, considered the possibility of feigning a protective lunge for her sister. She could pull herself closer to the couch, dragging the chair with her, and be closer to the ashtray when the maneuver was completed. Rico would probably slap her back into the chair, which was something she could handle. But would he also realize she was too mobile with her hands untied? That was the risk--a better fighting chance against no chance at all. If he tied her hands after her attempt, it was certain death for both of them.

"Big Sister knows how many people Rico has hurt, how many people he's killed."

His statement startled her. "You never said anything to me about killing people."

He didn't appear to have heard her. He was on one knee at the far end of the couch, his face inches away from Inga's. Dee thought she detected a fleck of spittle on his chin.

"Big Sister knows all about Rico's operation. She ratted on him, tried to close him down."

The Alice-in-Wonderland feeling returned, then Dee flashed on her conversation with Jeff during their flight to Grand Rapids. Her hunch had been right--Lila must have told Rico a whopper of a lie to ingratiate herself with him.

"Rico, what are you talking about? You never told me any of this before. And I didn't *rat* on you. Is that what this is all about? Are you afraid--"

"You shut up!" he screamed, his voice rising to a near soprano pitch. "You just shut up! I'm not afraid of nothin', d'you hear? Nothing!" He stabbed the air between them with the gun.

Despite the distance between them Dee could smell his foul breath, see the stains on his teeth as his lips pulled back. She fought the impulse to wipe at her face, kept her hands wrapped around the edges of the chair. Inga had screwed her eyes shut and Dee wondered if Inga would ever open her eyes again.

Rico's look had a hungry quality to it, and it occurred to Dee she might have one other weapon at her disposal...sex. If she started stripping herself, took off her blouse, then her bra, maybe Rico would get a better idea. She tried to will her hand to move, to reach for the top button of her blouse, and found she could not.

It might work, but then again it might not. He might be too far over the edge to be distracted from his murderous intentions. He might also prefer Inga. But it was neither of those considerations that stopped her. She simply could not abase herself any further. She'd rather die than let him use her. Why didn't he just kill them, get it over with?

"Yeah, I think I'll start with Big Sister." An evil grin spread over his face as he got back to his feet and stepped toward her. The blow came faster than she had expected, caught her just above her ear and rocked her. She fell sideways and only narrowly escaped having her fingers crushed between the chair and the floor.

"Whatsa matter?" he taunted. "No fight left in you? C'mon, let's try that again." He dragged her back to an upright position.

Without any conscious intent on her part she spat in his face before he could pull away. She steeled herself for another blow, but it did not land.

"That's the spirit! See that, Baby Sister? Hey!" In two quick strides he was back in front of

Inga again. Her eyes were glued shut. He reached down, dug thumb and fingers into her cheeks and shook her head. "Hey! Open those pretty peepers, Baby Sister. You have to watch this so you'll know how to act when it's your turn."

Dee couldn't watch. She turned her head away, and her pulse began racing. The ashtray was now within reach! Rico must have moved her chair when he lifted her off the floor. And he wasn't watching her now. The time had come.

And time slowed to a crawl. As though someone had a finger on the world's remote control switch, all action went into slow motion. Dee became aware of a part of her mind telling her to move faster, screaming at her to pick up the pace. Another part of that same mind noticed seemingly unimportant details like the small nick in the clear glass surface of the ashtray. And yet another part of her mind registered the fact that Rico was already moving...but turning *away* from her rather than toward her.

From somewhere off in the distance, a low moan was turning into a blood-curdling scream, rising in pitch and volume with each passing millisecond. She was not surprised by the calm realization that the voice was her own, the scream merely another manifestation of the tremendous surge of adrenaline pumping into her veins.

The ashtray moved in a wide arc from behind her now, the weight of it feeling very good in her hand. The strain of her arm muscles as she pulled, then pushed it up, up, and over her head felt wonderful. *Action is good*, she thought in the lazy observer part of her mind. *Feels good.*

It looked like her aim was true. It looked

like the ashtray would connect with Rico's head. But then something else was happening. Rico moved in an unexpected way, straightening as he turned. The ashtray bounced harmlessly off his shoulder.

The world snapped back into real time just as she slammed forward onto the floor. *Hurry!* she urged herself, pushing upward. *Move now before he can--*

The thought was jarred out of her as the chair hit her legs and back, driving her back to the floor. She shook her head, looked up.

Rico remained on his feet, but his attention was not on her. He was panting heavily, his gun pointed at the ceiling.

A cold, menacing, dispassionate voice cut through Rico's wheezing sounds. "Drop it!" Jeff ordered.

Dee craned her head , tried to focus through pain-blurred eyes. Jeff stood in a crouch just inside the door, his gun pointed at Rico, his left hand wrapped around his right wrist. His stance perfectly matched the menacing tone of his voice.

Rico must have come to the same conclusion. His wheezing turned to whimpers, and Dee expected to see his gun clatter to the floor in front of her. Instead, a single ear-piercing scream rent the air. "No-o-o!"

Before the sound of his screech had died away Dee heard a muffled retort. A second later Rico's gun--and Rico himself--fell to the floor.

Dee's distorted senses, and her rather uncomfortable angle of view from the floor, added to the confusion of the moment. Jeff remained in his stance, but a dumbfounded look clouded his features, and she was almost certain he hadn't fired his gun. A wave of pain washed through her and she closed her eyes momentarily. Before she could open them again, Jeff knelt beside her.

"He shot himself. He put that forty-five under his chin and...here, let me help you," he said, his tone changing from disbelief to concern. He holstered his gun and helped her with the bindings at her ankles.

When she was able to sit up she avoided looking at Rico, turned the other way as she struggled to her feet. "Inga."

Jeff was already working at her sister's bonds, removing the gag from her mouth. Inga stared at him, fear still glazing her eyes.

Dee moved closer, took one reddened wrist in her hands and gently massaged it. Inga whimpered.

"It's okay, honey. It's over. This is my friend Jeff. He's...Jeff, how did you find us?"

"Followed his tracks...heavy car...saw the lights." His face still wore a puzzled frown as he mumbled his explanation. "Jeez! I can't believe he did that--just blew off the top of his head."

Another frightened whimper escaped Inga. Dee put an arm around her sister's shoulders, coaxed her into a sitting position, then held her while Jeff finished untying her.

"He'd gone quite mad, Jeff. He babbled stuff about *you* wrecking his organization, and how he planned to use me and Inga to build a new one, and then later he decided *I* was the one who'd brought him down and he was going to kill us both."

"Wrecking his...the guy definitely had *both*

oars out of the water. Maybe that's why he..." Jeff trailed off as he glanced at Inga, tossed aside the ropes he had removed from her ankles, turned to poke a toe into Rico's side. "How did you get your hands free?"

"He never tied them. I think he wanted me to fight. He likes...liked to slap women around."

"Sadist."

"And then some. Jeff, let's get Inga out of here before the police come.

"Right. Did you touch anything other than the chair and the ashtray?"

The question caught her off guard. "I don't think so."

He was already wiping the ashtray with a cloth, and as she got Inga to her feet he picked up the chair and wiped it down. "How about you, Inga?"

There was no reply. He repeated his question in a gentler tone and Inga shook her head without lifting it from Dee's shoulder. Jeff went through Rico's pockets, transferred odd bits of paper to his own pockets, put other papers and items back into the dead man's possession.

"What are you doing?"

He glanced over his shoulder at her. "Take Inga outside and wait for me."

In spite of everything she balked at his peremptory attitude. "I asked you what you're doing."

Rico's left arm thudded to the floor as Jeff released it. He stood and turned to face her, a scowl darkening his features. He seemed about to stay something, then his eyes moved downward, taking in the shivering Inga huddled against her. A long sigh escaped him and he stepped closer, wrapped his arms around the two of them, and pressed the side of his face against her hair. "Sorry," he whispered.

He stepped back, one hand still on her shoulder, the other resting tenderly against Inga's. The warm look in his eyes made her want to go back to his arms, press herself against him. She tried to smile but felt her own lingering fear turned it into a grimace.

"I'm going to remove all trace of the two of you from this cottage. When the police investigate, find out who he is, they'll be more likely to conclude it was a gangland slaying. If any connection is made between him and you, if your names show up anywhere--police reports, local papers, anywhere--there's a good chance his friends will seek vengeance."

"I hadn't thought that far ahead," she admitted. "Rico said he'd planted a bug on my car," she added with a glance at his radio.

He merely nodded in response, and the non-verbal exchange reminded her of the closeness they'd experienced, the kiss they'd shared the day before when they'd parted outside the motel. She wanted to be in his arms at this moment, feel him holding her close--but Inga came first.

The rising sun bounced blinding slivers of light off the surface of Long Lake. She led Inga across the porch and around the side of the cottage, then held her. A sudden noise told her Jeff had wrecked Rico's listening device. He joined them moments later, asked her about prints on the car.

"Just the door handles, inside and out."

He was very thorough. He checked the

glove compartment for evidence, then wiped his own prints and hers off the car before leading them to his car a few yards down the road from the end of the driveway. He drove them back to the wayside, waited with Inga while Dee retrieved her jacket and sweater from the path. Inga was still shivering as Dee helped her into the Chevy.

"Inga, I can't tell you how sorry I am about all this," Dee said as she pulled the car out of the rest area. "I know it's been awful for you, but you have to put it behind you now. You have to forget about it and not talk to anyone--even Mama." At the thought of her mother she began to wonder if Jeff's care in eliminating evidence would be wasted. Convincing her mother to remain silent would not be an easy task.

"It's like a nightmare," Inga said. "Like it couldn't really have happened."

"Go with that thought, honey. It was just a bad dream. I'll try to explain some of it to you later, but for now, just don't talk to anyone about it, okay?"

"Okay, Dee. Is Jeff a movie star, too?"

Dee laughed in spite of herself. "No, honey. He's just a man I met while I was...running away from the nightmare. He's very resourceful."

"He *looks* like a movie star. I like him."

"Me too, Inga."

Dee pulled her car all the way into the driveway, noted with satisfaction that Jeff followed her lead and parked his car directly behind hers. She hoped the neighbors would still be in bed, and that she'd have time to prepare her mother before the nosy phone calls started.

"So this is the place where you grew up."

Jeff's observation startled her. It was the most intimate thing he'd said to her. Even his comment about needing her had not carried the force of his single statement about her roots. When his arm went around her shoulders it seemed like the most natural thing in the world for her to snuggle against him, and she knew in that instant she had made up her mind about her feelings.

"Mama's waiting," Inga pointed out from the other side of the cars.

Dee glanced at the window-lined utility porch, saw her mother standing in the doorway to the kitchen, one fist pressed to her mouth. "Go in, honey, let her know you're all right. But remember what I said."

Jeff gave Dee's shoulder one brief hug. "This should be interesting."

They were halfway up the steps before Dee comprehended his cryptic remark. He'd been listening to their conversation last night, of course, and was probably wondering if Mama would turn her wrath on him; or had he guessed Mama would wear a different face for "company" than the one she'd shown then, unaware that her every word was being broadcast to a stranger.

They waited while Mama hugged Inga, crooned sounds which fell short of being real words, smoothed her daughter's dirty, tangled hair. Dee became aware of the smells of the house: the furniture polish, the coffee steaming in the gurgling pot, baked goods.

Jeff put his arm around her shoulder again, pulled her close. A pulse of pain lanced down her arm, caused her to draw an involuntary breath. Jeff released her, a look of concern across his face. "It's okay," she whispered, "just a little tender."

"Mama, this is my friend Jeff."

Her mother stared over Inga's head.

"Pleasure to meet you, Mrs. Johansen."

A few of the hard, questioning lines on her mother's face eased, but her eyes held onto the wary glint. Dee groped for words to explain without revealing more than was necessary. "Jeff was with me in Dallas when I called. He arranged every-thing. He's been...helping us. But we're not out of danger yet. We need to talk."

Her mother seemed to go automatically into hostess mode. She bustled around the kitchen, poured coffee and put out cinnamon twists. Dee took charge of the conversation while Inga devoured rolls and milk as though she'd been starved for a week.

It took a while to convince her mother of the necessity for keeping others: neighbors, police, anyone, in the dark about what had been going on. She renewed many of last nights arguments against going to the police, embellished them without going into any revealing details. It was clear that the scant information Dee was willing to share added to the difficulty, but eventually her mother began to relent. Jeff's quiet agreement with each of her suggestions helped, as did Inga's. Her mother's eyes told her she did not like the idea, but she seemed willing to go along--for now.

"Am I permitted to ask what you plan to do now?" Butter wouldn't have melted in Mama's mouth, but Dee was acutely aware of the anger and frustration her mother felt at having to take orders, even when disguised as suggestions, from her daughter.

"Jeff and I need to discuss that. Maybe after Inga has had a bath and a nice long rest in her own bed..."

"You're right. The poor child has been put through enough. Young Lady, you do look a fright. Come along. I'll pour you a nice hot tub."

Dee cleared the dishes from the table, rinsed them in the sink. When she turned Jeff was standing directly in front of her. "Let me look at that shoulder," he said. "It seems mighty tender after all this time."

"I think I smacked it again when Rico knocked my chair over. Let me get my jacket off."

Jeff followed her to the parlor, waited while she took off the suit jacket and tossed it on the rumpled bed where she had spent the short night. She tugged at the collar of her blouse until the bruise showed above the fabric. He murmured a sympathetic sound as his fingers gently explored the tender spot.

An aching need swept through her. She wrapped her fingers around his wrist and moved his hand lower until it covered her breast. "Jeff. Please."

His hand immediately closed around her breast. His mouth sought hers, his other hand pressed them together.

Dee answered his passion with an equal intensity, dug her nails into his shoulders, his neck, the back of his head. She thrust her hips toward him, her need turning to a wanton lust at his acceptance.

When Jeff released her to pull the sliding doors of the guest room closed, she wasted no time in coyness, quickly removed her blouse and slacks.

He carefully placed his gun and holster on one of the chairs, but his own clothing joined hers in a heap on the floor.

He moved her to the bed, his dark eyes wide and his nostrils flared. A throbbing vein in his neck caught her attention and she focused on it until his descending mouth found hers. She dug her nails into his shoulders again, wrapped her legs around him, gave herself to the life-affirming passion he inspired.

Her need proved greater than his, but she didn't mind. She caressed his shoulders while the spasms rocked him, kept her lips pressed to his so his cries of pain would not be heard. Somewhere between desire and satisfaction the need had turned to tenderness, and the only thing that mattered was that they were together.

Jeff didn't collapse onto her. He slid a hand beneath her buttocks, held them close as he turned them to their sides, her bruised shoulder uppermost. He trailed his fingertips over the moistened flesh of her hips, her side, her neck, planted tender kisses across her forehead.

Dee's ragged breathing returned to normal, her not-quite-fulfilled hunger subsiding in the warm glow of closeness. She kissed his chest, tickling her lips against the curly black hairs. She tried to think of words that would tell him how she felt, let him know how special he was to her.

Her warm thoughts evaporated when she realized he had stiffened beside her. His hand stopped moving on her body, his face turned upward as though he listened to something outside the dimly lit room. Dee imagined her mother outside the parlor doors, but she soon sorted out the sounds from upstairs and she knew that was not so. Perhaps Jeff, not as familiar with the house or its other occupants as she, was concerned about the propriety of their lovemaking.

"It's okay--"

"Shh! Someone's outside," he warned.

With a speed more attuned to his new concern than to the tenderness of their lovemaking, he separated them, left the bed, and crouched down in front of the window. Dee fought back tears as she joined him and followed his gaze.

A man in his late 30s or early 40s, dressed in a business suit, stood at the bottom of the porch steps. His sandy red hair was touched with gray at the temples and a dusting of freckles covered most of his face. Dee had an awful feeling she knew who the man was.

Jeff confirmed her suspicion with a single word that sounded more like a growl than human speech. "Brian."

CHAPTER SEVENTEEN

She joined Jeff in dressing quickly, opened the parlor doors as he clipped his holster to his waistband, stepped aside as he strode purposefully toward the front door.

She was about to follow him outside but was stopped by his command that she remain in the house. Then she noticed Mama standing at the bottom of the stairs leading to the second floor. The look her mother gave her carried enough venom to stop a horse. As surely as though Mama had spoken the words aloud, Dee sensed the condemnation. *I know what you two have been up to,* the look read, *and I see you're still a brazen hussy.*

Dee was torn between her need to support Jeff and her desire to explain to her mother that this was different--that she loved Jeff. Mama made the choice more difficult by turning abruptly and stomping back up the stairs. Dee turned to the front door, looked through the thick pane of the window with her hand poised above the knob.

The well-insulated house prevented her hearing anything the two men said, and she watched their interaction unfold as though viewing a silent movie. The early morning sun had not yet reached the front lawn and the grass was covered with a layer of dew, a row of staggered dots in green marking the passage of Brian's steps to the porch.

They talked, and she tried to interpret the conversation using their body language. Jeff paused at the top of the stairs, then descended as Brian backed away. Both men had their hands at their sides, but tension vibrated in their shoulders.

Brian's hands lifted away from his sides, palms upward. Jeff's left hand shot out, chopping the air to his side as though rejecting the suggestion of the other, then both of his hands folded into fists.

Would the two start slugging each other, rather than use guns? Would Jeff try beating the truth out of Brian, instead of killing him as he had promised to do?

They moved in a slow arc, facing each other more like wrestlers looking for a hold than like boxers getting ready to punch. Brian's hands repeated the palms-up gesture a number of times, and each time it was answered by a chopping, or jabbing, motion from Jeff. Were the jabs becoming less severe, less emphatic? It seemed so. She tried timing them, became distracted by the play of muscles in Jeff's neck as he shouted responses to accompany his gestures.

A wide wheel of dark green lawn was now showing through the dew, the inner circle punctuated here and there with the suggestion of spokes as one or the other of them had shortened the distance, momentarily, between them. Jeff had his back to her once again, Brian was visible to his left.

She jumped involuntarily as Jeff gestured back over his shoulder, his thump pointing directly at her. Whatever he had said seemed to take the wind out of the other man--Brian's shoulders slumped, hands hung limp at his sides.

Dee opened the door and stepped onto the porch.

"...couldn't have known that," Brian was

saying. "If you'd contacted me--"

"Before or after Hobart's goons lobbed a grenade into the motel?"

"I've told you I don't know how he found out. Maybe there's a plant on my team, maybe he was watching Sondra. I only know *I* didn't tell him. Hell, would I have gone to all that trouble if I'd just wanted you out of the way? My *only* concern was to find you, stop you from doing something foolish."

"So you've said," Jeff intoned.

Her footstep on the creaking boards of the porch alerted them to her presence. Jeff glanced over his shoulder, then turned his back on Brian and mounted the steps.

Dee almost knocked him back off the porch with the force of her embrace. He corrected their balance, then pressed her head against his chest. She had promised herself she would remain calm and cool through this ordeal but she had suffered far too much trauma to let mere promises take precedence over her emotions. She did not relax her grip on him until he kissed her.

Both she and Jeff were breathing hard when they separated. Brian had joined them on the porch and was the first to speak.

"So we meet at last. You've led me on a merry chase, Miss Johansen."

She took his extended hand, decided she liked his blue eyes, but was puzzled by his comment.

"Brian thought you were an enemy agent. He traced you through Rico's organization," Jeff explained. "He's half-convinced me he had my own best interests in mind when he let his witch-doctor wipe out my memory and then stuffed me into that hole where you found me."

Jeff's words and tone made it clear his truce with Brian was an uneasy, and possibly temporary, one. She put aside the questions his comment about Rico's organization brought to mind, groped for a subject they might be able to agree on. "So it *was* Hobart in Seattle?"

"Maybe," Jeff shrugged.

Brian flashed her a wary look. "How did you know about Hobart--ah, you two have become very close, I take it?"

"Dee gave me back my life, Brian. The life you took."

Her mother's shrill voice broke into the charged air between them. "Dee Johansen, what is the matter with you? Don't you know better than to leave the door wide open like this? Were you born in a---oh!" Her mother cut herself off as she caught sight of Brian.

"Sorry, Mama." Dee felt a pang of sympathy. Just when Mama had decided Jeff was no longer a stranger, another visitor had arrived. Dee could imagine the internal struggle the poor woman was going through.

"Good morning, Mrs. Johansen. Sorry for the intrusion. I'm Special Agent Williams. Perhaps Special Agent Carter has mentioned me?" he added with a nod toward Jeff. "I wonder if we could come inside?"

Brian took Mama by the arm, charm oozing from every pore, and led her back into the house. Dee was impressed and said so in a stage whisper to Jeff.

"Yeah. He's very good with people. Just

like you."

"I'm glad it wasn't him. I know how much he means to you. Did he explain how it happened?"

"Said it was Ash. Claims Hobart ordered him to cancel my ticket and he decided to tuck me away for a while until he could sort things out, clear my name. The doctor at that hospital used some combination of chemicals and hypnosis to block my memory. Apparently I'd still be in that state if we hadn't stumbled on Sondra."

"That sounds reasonable."

Jeff did not look convinced. "Yeah, I guess so."

"You two coming?" Brian called cheerily. "Mama Johansen's going to fix breakfast." He stepped back into the doorway and lowered his voice. "What's the scoop on this Rico character?"

"Dead," Jeff told him. "He kidnapped Dee's sister two days ago. We tracked him down and he wound up taking himself out--just a little over an hour ago. We told Dee's mother she'll have to keep quiet about it to prevent retaliation."

Brian nodded his assent. "Probably a good precaution. We thought at first he was just a small-time hood, but it turns out he was into everything dirty you can imagine--O. C. connections, the whole bit. Too bad he's dead. I'd liked to have picked his brains, see if we missed anything in the process of shutting down his operation."

The revelation shook Dee. She clutched at Jeff's arm for support. "Sh-shutting down," she stammered. "Did you say you shut down Rico's operation?"

Jeff shot her a concerned and puzzled look as he reached out a hand to steady her. Brian appeared to be simply puzzled.

"Yes, we might have missed a few of his ancillary businesses, but he wouldn't have had much to go back to...if he'd lived. A couple of his minor functionaries, and one red-headed bimbo are singing like canaries even as we speak."

"So he wasn't insane. He kept insisting Jeff was behind it all, and in a way he was right." She looked up at Jeff. "If you hadn't saved me from that wreck..." She drifted off, the tangled web of circumstances becoming too complex to put into words.

Jeff put his arm around her as another shudder rumbled through her. "Given what we've learned about him, I don't think Rico would have stopped chasing you in any case. He might not have gone to the extreme of kidnapping Inga, but he was pretty tenacious."

When the tremor subsided she turned an angry glare on Brian. Jeff was right--Brian's ham-handed way of ripping through Rico's gang had tipped the scales, thrown him into a rage. "You damn near got my sister killed," she accused him through clenched teeth.

Jeff leaned toward Brian, his dark eyes glinting. Dee felt he would have lunged at his former partner had he not been helping her to stay on her feet at the moment. Brian's hands went to his sides, palms up--the same gesture she had witnessed earlier from behind the door.

"I'm sorry. I didn't know. Believe me--"

"You didn't know!" Jeff cut in. "I'm getting sick of hearing that from you. First you rip off eighteen months of my life, then you damn near get Dee and Inga killed. You never used to be so sloppy."

"I've never been ordered to kill my best friend before," Brian shot back, just as angrily. "And please keep in mind that I've been operating without the brains of the outfit--you! I can't keep saying I'm sorry, and we can't undo what's been done. You're upset by what I did to you, I'm upset that Dee wrecked my plans, Dee's upset that I put her sister in danger. The point is we're all alive, safe, and relatively sound now. Can't we just call it even and start from square one?"

Dee wasn't sure what game board Brian played with, but she was inclined to agree with him, probably more because she was tired and hungry than she was convinced of his sincerity. They could argue about it later.

"Jeff, he has a point. We handled it, and it's water under the bridge now. Besides, there's unfinished business with your Mr. Hobart to be considered. Let's give it a rest for now."

Jeff nodded his assent.

"We can't talk here," Brian pointed out. "How about that pink motel south of town? I'll take care of the local police, tidy things up after breakfast, just to show you I'm on your side. Then I'll meet you at the motel."

Jeff sighed noisily, then nodded again.

"Promise?" Brian flashed his charming grin.

Jeff took his arm from around her, turned his back on Brian. He stepped to the front window on the driveway side of the door and surveyed the glass, then went onto the porch and scraped at something with his fingernail. Rico's listening device, she concluded.

"We'll be there," she assured Brian.

Brian did a minor double-take. His reaction told her his remarks about meeting and talking had been meant for Jeff alone; but he quickly adjusted. He nodded, seemingly satisfied that everyone was in agreement.

Dee wasn't sure she agreed with much of anything beyond finding a chair to sit in. Brian Whipple was far too slick for her tastes, and there were new questions about her relationship with Jeff to be answered.

Brian's comment about Jeff being "the brains of the outfit" told her a great many things about their former partnership she had only guessed at until now, but it also raised the issue of where she stood with Jeff in that regard. Would it be correct to infer that Jeff no longer needed her ability to handle people the way Brian did now that the two men were together again? And what about the personal side of their relationship? Brian had interrupted what could have been a solidifying conversation in the aftermath of their love-making. Of course, it could also have be a coda rather than a prelude.

She needed answers, but at the moment the aroma of bacon, eggs, potatoes, and toast demanded their immediate presence in the kitchen.

She'd have to put her questions on hold for now while she studied Brian and tried to ignore the piercing looks her mother was sure to direct her way. Rico's demise hadn't uncomplicated her life one little bit.

CHAPTER EIGHTEEN

Brian charmed her mother so thoroughly she did not even object to the three of them leaving immediately after breakfast. Not only was Mama convinced by that time that Brian, Jeff, and Dee had been working together on the "operation" from the start and that it had been Brian's mistake alone which had led to the momentary danger to Inga; he seemed to have convinced Mama she had played a crucial role in the successful completion of the operation to rid the country of one of its most vicious criminals.

Her attitude as she saw them to the door made it clear she would maintain a tight-lipped silence about the whole affair while priding herself on her imagined participation. Dee could picture Mama's friends and neighbors being puzzled by her new aura of confident self-importance.

Dee and Jeff drove to the motel in the rented Thunderbird while Brian headed for the police station. Dee passed the time during the short drive creating a mental list of the questions she wanted to ask Jeff. As they entered the sparsely furnished, damp-smelling room, she surprised herself by asking a question not even on her list.

"Did you ask Brian about your...about Sondra?"

Jeff's reaction did little to assuage the anxiety the question had raised within her. He turned to look at her and his unfocused gaze and slack expression told her she had opened the wrong can of worms. "No. That subject...wasn't raised."

She sat on the sagging edge of the bed, toyed with the knots of the chenille bedspread, tried to sort out the conflicting emotions warring within her. She felt she had a right to know where he stood, but also felt she had no grounds for pushing him into making a declaration.

Jeff pulled the curtain away from the window and gazed out at the nearby trees. With a sigh he let the curtain fall back into place, then turned and looked around the room. "Cold in here," he muttered.

"There's a wall heater," she pointed out, "but I don't see a switch anywhere."

While he conducted an over-acted search for the heater's thermostat, she felt the emotions shutting down inside her as palpably as though doors were being closed on noisy rooms. It was clear the subject of Sondra Culver nagged at him as well, and it was also clear he did not want to discuss her. She chewed at her lower lip while she waited for the inevitable change of subject.

The heater came to life with a series of pinging sounds. Jeff stood in front of it, alternately holding his hands in front of the grating and rubbing them together. He kept his back to her.

When she could stand the silence no longer, she asked one of the questions from her mental list. "What about your status with the agency?"

"That's still unresolved, too."

His non-answer was, at least, better than the maddening silence. She decided to try to keep him talking, for no other reason that to avoid thinking about her own desires.

"Are you convinced it was Ash and not Brian who ordered your--uh, being taken out of the picture?"

He turned to face her, but just as quickly turned away and strode back to the window. She was reminded of the way he had acted when he first "awoke" in that Seattle motel room.

"I guess I believe him. I'd forgotten about that charm of his, though. He never tried to use it on me before, but..."

"But?"

He uttered a low growl, slapped at the window curtain.

"*Goddamnit*! I don't know! I thought when I found Brian I'd get the answers to my questions. Now I have more questions than I had before. If it *was* Hobart...I just don't know."

"You asked me a question a few days back, about Rico, that maybe we should turn back on you. Why is Ashton Hobart afraid of you?"

He sputtered, then stared open-mouthed at her for a brief moment. Then he began pacing the short distance between window and door.

"Yes! You're exactly right. And the situation might even be perfectly parallel. If Ash is so afraid of me he ordered me terminated, it could be that I posed some real danger to him, or it was just imagined, the way Rico got that crazy idea about you.

"One possible scenario is that Hobart is connected to Walburg in some way. If he is, though, I should have seen it. Maybe I was getting rusty. Maybe I missed something."

His anger and frustration helped her to overcome the sense of loss she felt, gave her a new focus.

"You said you and Brian were working on different aspects of the Walburg investigation. Were either of you actually looking for a connection between him and Hobart?"

"Good question." He waggled a finger at her as he stopped his pacing, then stood gazing at the ceiling.

Dee had a moment to reflect on the way things had turned around. Whereas they had once avoided conversation about the past, she now apparently had to be almost as careful to avoid discussion of the future. Now that her past had been laid to rest and his had been resurrected, everything had gone topsy-turvy. She wondered if there would ever come a time when they would be comfortable dealing with both past and future while they negotiated the present. The prospect was downright heavenly and gave her a new goal.

"I was working on Walburg's business connections," Jeff said. "He was involved in a lot of different companies--most of them incorporated in Delaware--so I was using the Philly office as my base. I'd uncovered a few money-laundering operations and some other minor items with a strong suggestion of drugs and/or arms dealings, but I hadn't managed to get any proof."

"How close were you?"

"You have any idea how hard it is to prove wrong-doing on the part of a politician? They've exempted themselves from so many laws you have to practically catch them in the act of raping a nun in the Supreme Court chambers before they can be charged...and even then the worst that happens in most cases is they get a slap on the wrist and run out of office."

"You must have been close to finding that nun."

"Brian worked out of the Chicago office, making like a bull in a china shop with his investigation into campaign contributions in the big industrial states. We hoped the noise he was making would distract Walburg and his people from noticing what I was doing on my end."

Jeff's fists worked at his sides. "To answer your question--no. I don't think either of us suspected he had connections inside the agency. I know *I* didn't. He's on the appropriations com-mittee, but he isn't...or wasn't at that time...the chair, and..."

"And?"

"And we were stupid. Damn! How could I have missed that? Dollars to donuts, Hobart already had the goods on Walburg. Walburg was probably paying off Hobart with guaranteed funding, maybe a little personal bonus on the side.

"Ash set us up. He probably thought he'd use us to give Walburg a little heat, just enough to get him to increase the funding--public and private. But he hadn't counted on us finding as much as we did."

"So when Walburg heard your footsteps, he told Hobart to call off his dogs, get rid of you--whatever."

"Exactly..."

"But wait," Dee cut him off. "Much as I'm loathe to suggest this, I can't help wondering why Hobart didn't try to get rid of you himself. Wouldn't it have been simpler and safer to do the job himself and cover it up in some way? Why turn the job over to your partner, your friend?"

Jeff flashed her such a look of...what? Admiration? Respect? Whatever it was, she found herself melting under the gaze.

"You are sharp," he said. "But you're not devious enough. Ash probably figured he could kill two birds with the same stone. Call it a double-bluff. He not only gets me out from between him and Walburg, but he runs a loyalty test on Brian at the same time he's throwing a smoke-screen in his eyes where Walburg is concerned."

"Oh...that is twisted."

Tires crunching on gravel outside the room alerted them to Brian's arrival. Jeff opened the door just far enough to wave Brian to the room, then moved to the room's single chair and slumped into it. Dee noted his relaxed manner and offered a silent prayer of thanks that he'd apparently decided to accept Brian's good intentions. It was one less thing they'd have to worry about, one less variable complicating things. If only they'd had time to discuss some personal issues...

"Everything's taken care of," Brian announced as he entered the room. "I tried bluffing my way with the locals but they're sharper than I expected. In the end I decided to tell your Chief Towne a modified version of the truth, Dee. Seems he's a great admirer of yours and asked me to let you know he'll take special care of your mother and sister. And he sent a message to you, Ger--Jeff. Says to tell you, you didn't fool his sergeant for a minute, whatever that means."

Dee was equally puzzled by the message but decided against asking Jeff for an explanation when she noticed the redness creeping upward from his collar. "We've been discussing the problem of Hobart and Walburg," she told Brian.

Brian stuffed his hands into his pockets as he leaned back against the door, a look of anticipation on his face.

"Just a minute," Jeff said. He cleared his throat, then turned a slightly belligerent look on Brian. "I'd like to get a few items cleared up first. What about Sondra?"

Jeff's question seemed to upset Brian almost as much as it upset her. She'd asked the same question of Jeff; but somehow hearing her question coming from him and directed toward Brian put it in a different light. She wasn't at all sure she wanted to hear the answer Brian might give.

Brian took his hands out of his pockets as he drew in a sharp breath, lowered them by degrees as he exhaled. Dee held her breath.

"I'm truly sorry about that. She...I...look, is your memory completely restored? I mean, every-thing?"

"I think so. There's something about smoking I don't understand, but the rest of it..."

Brian's brow furrowed. "You haven't smoked since Cambodia, or Kampuchea, if you like. What's the--"

"It's not important. My question was about Sondra, Brian, not about smoking."

"I hate to have to tell you this, in just this way, but you might as well know. Sondra was remarried within a month after Ash told her of your death. I know, I should have told her myself, but I couldn't run the risk. She had to be convinced it was real or Ash would have known something was fishy. But she didn't waste any time finding another husband."

Dee wondered if Jeff had picked up the unspoken *assuming she had to find him*, but the only sign Jeff gave was a continued glare.

Brian pressed on. "She always hated this life, and you know it. When she called to tell me about her wedding she confessed she was...I think the word she used was relieved, or maybe it was released. The guy she married is a nice, quiet, sedate kind of guy. Home every night at the same time, never out of town, no problems worse than a bad case of crabgrass in the front lawn."

Jeff got to his feet and Dee tensed herself, ready to throw herself between them to keep Jeff from using Brian for a punching bag. But Jeff didn't approach Brian. He stepped to the window and looked out at the forest.

"Sounds a lot like the life you carved out for me. And I didn't even have to worry about crabgrass."

Brian seemed about to say something, but closed his mouth and stuffed his hands back into his pockets.

Jeff turned from the window. "Let's say, for the moment at least, that I decide to believe you. What do you expect me to do now--go back to my little cabin in Oregon and wait around for you to finish your investigation?"

Dee welcomed the change of subject. "I don't think there would be much point in that," she put in.

Both men regarded her with surprise.

"Have you forgotten the other thing that happened in Seattle?"

"The motel room," Jeff acknowledged.

"What about that, Brian? Were you dis-appointed to learn we'd survived?"

She hurried to head off his anger. "Jeff! That's not what I meant and you know it. You told me yourself it looked like an Ashton Hobart job."

"She's right, Jeff. Sondra called me in Chicago right after Dee left her. She'd seen the van, described it, and I figured it was the same van we'd provided you with. I ordered a team to locate and keep an eye on the van, ordered another to check on the cabin in Oregon--which is where we stumbled onto Rico's organization--and I headed for Seattle. The motel bombing took place while I was en route."

Jeff snorted but said nothing.

"When I got to Seattle I learned an unmarked, unlicensed sedan drove by and launched a couple of grenades from a rifle without slowing. Like Dee said, it had all the earmarks of an Ash Hobart job. Frankly, I haven't had time to think about it. My men said they thought Dee had been outside when the explosion occurred."

Brian turned to her. "I tried to find you, to see what you knew about Jeff. I later learned there were no bodies in the motel room, but I still didn't know where you two had gone. And I was groping in the dark, without my usual team, because I realized if Ash knew Jeff was still alive he'd know I'd betrayed him, and my own life wouldn't be worth a plug nickel. All I had to go on was that one slim lead Sammy had uncovered."

Dee wanted to believe him, in part because she was aware of the depth of the relationship between the two men--a friendship neither of them seemed willing to admit to at the moment. But a red flag had gone up inside her mind and she now wondered if she should have been so ready to defend Jeff's former partner.

"An interesting story, Brian. Believable except for one small item. You said you traced me to White Cloud through Rico."

"That's right. That's the lead Sammy uncovered."

She marveled at his ready agreement. He'd do well on the stage with that innocent, freckle-faced countenance. He looked for all the world like a Scoutmaster verifying the fact all his little scouts were thrifty, brave, and reverent.

"If you didn't know where we'd gone, or what we had been up to, how is it you knew to refer to Jeff as Agent Carter--rather than Westman, or Eastman--when you introduced yourself to my mother?"

CHAPTER NINETEEN

It took less than the space of two heartbeats for Brian to react. His face screwed up into a look of grudging admiration and be began to nod his head. Dee was appalled at his smug attitude.

But it was Jeff who pulled the rug out from under her accusation. "I told him. Matter of habit. Remember me telling you it didn't matter what name you called me? We switch names so often we're used to letting each other know what name we're using any time we meet. As soon as I was sure I wasn't going to kill him on the spot, I told him about Carter."

Dee's embarrassment couldn't have been more acute. Then she noticed the two men grinning at each other. Even if the joke was at her expense, she decided, it had been worth it. The tension in the room dissipated quicker than a Hollywood snowstorm.

Brian suggested changing their location for a local restaurant where they'd be more comfortable, but both Dee and Jeff vetoed the idea on grounds of privacy. In the end they decided to drive back to Grand Rapids, divest themselves of at least one of their vehicles, and find more comfortable quarters where they could do some planning.

Dee wished she could talk with Jeff on the radios as they drove, but their conversation could be heard by anyone with a similar C.B. setup and all of the subjects she wanted to cover were either too personal or too confidential to be trusted to the airwaves, so she had to shelve that idea.

The atmosphere among them as they checked out of the motel left her with the feeling they were now a team of three; but she wanted a moment alone with Jeff to assure herself he had truly put aside his lingering doubts about Brian's intentions.

She had no such doubts herself--especially after watching Brian retrieve a gun from under the front seat of his car and clip the holster to his belt before sliding behind the wheel. Brian's evident willingness to face them in an unarmed state spoke louder than all his slick words and glib apologies. She was now certain he had acted as he had for exactly the reasons stated.

Jeff's intentions were another matter. He seemed willing to accept Brian's suggestion that the *divorce* from Sondra had been inevitable, but had he truly put that marriage behind him? Had their lovemaking in her mother's parlor been an indication of a new commitment between them, a personal commitment above and beyond their agreement to "help each other"; or had it been a purely physical response to their shared danger, a celebration of the fact they'd both survived the threat to their lives? The untimely appearance of Brian had interrupted the conversation which could have followed--the words and touches and looks which could have settled the matter in her mind.

Her own intentions were only slightly less obscure. When she'd fled L.A. her only motivation had been to get as far away from Rico as possible. Given that, the bizarre chain of events that led to her antagonist's demise should have ended it for her, yet stopping now had all the flavor of getting off a roller coaster halfway through the ride.

As they approached Grand Rapids it occurred to her it would be possible, perhaps even acceptable, for her to announce her intention to take a bus back to White Cloud while the two men went on to Chicago for their confrontation with Ashton Hobart. She couldn't envision either Jeff or Brian objecting.

She also knew she'd never propose such a plan. On the one hand there was the matter of her commitment to Jeff--a perfectly reasonable and logical consideration. Jeff had helped her--at times just by being there--and now it was her turn to offer the same assistance. The memory of how she had felt when she thought Rico had cut her off from Jeff's aid reminded her of the importance of even moral support in a situation like this.

On the other hand there was the completely unreasonable and totally illogical fact that she was falling in love with Jeff Westman, had been falling in love with him even before he announced his intention to help her escape Rico's grasp. It didn't make any sense. He was moody, unpredictable, undemonstrative, and probably had more hang-ups than a dress shop.

Riding roller-coasters didn't make any sense either, yet people waited in long lines for the chance to do it. She'd come along for the ride and she intended to see it through to the end. She wasn't getting off, nor did she plan to squeeze her eyes shut and grip the bar--she'd do it with her eyes wide open, no matter how terrifying it turned out to be.

They had to do a reverse-shuffle at the rental agency, with Jeff driving the Chevy the last half-block to turn it in while she waited in his car. When Jeff rejoined her in the Thunderbird after turning in her car she attempted to clear up a few of the unanswered questions that had occurred to her on the drive south.

"Did you notice Brian wasn't wearing his gun when he joined us at the motel?"

"Doesn't surprise me."

His comment told her nothing. "It seems to me that's a pretty clear indication he trusts us."

Jeff drove in silence for a few moment, then turned a steady gaze on her at a stop sign. "You're fishing, Dee."

She considered denying the charge, but decided it wasn't worth it, gave him a smile and shrugged her shoulders in mute acceptance of his accusation.

"I could tell you a few things about Brian and his gun that would change your mind, but I'll leave that to Brian. Instead I'll answer a question you *didn't* ask. I've decided to accept Brian's version of what happened to me, and why."

Dee marveled at the way he could rebuke her and support her all at the same time. She considered broaching more personal subjects, but they'd already arrived at the motel where Brian had promised to meet them. Brian was waiting at the curb outside the office. Dee lowered her window and he handed her a key. "Seventeen and Eighteen. Down at the end."

Dee looked at the key he'd given her. Eighteen. Jeff drove to a parking spot near the room while her mind raced ahead. Had Brian given the second key to Jeff, rather than to her, the arrangements would have been more clear: she and

Jeff in one room, Brian in the other. As it now stood, it was clearly up to Jeff to decide which room he'd share with whom. Maybe it wouldn't require any conversation at all for her to learn something about Jeff's intentions.

Room eighteen, large and airy, contained two queen-sized beds and the usual furnishings of a reasonably good motel. She was reminded of their room in Dallas.

Jeff followed her into the room, raising her hopes they'd have a chance to return to the intimacy Brian had interrupted that morning. Here, she thought, there'd be no worries about Mama's reaction. She turned back to Jeff, but he went into the bathroom with a mumbled comment about her mother's strong coffee.

She put her small bag on the suitcase rack and hung up her coat. Her fingers toyed with the top button of her blouse, but before she could act on the impulse the connecting door to room seventeen opened and Brian appeared.

"Anyone for a drink?"

Dee shook her head.

"I'll hold off, then. I never drink alone. Unless I'm by myself."

Jeff rejoined them.

Brian didn't offer Jeff a drink, but turned to her with a look that clearly indicated he'd had something on his mind and had only waited for Jeff to join them before speaking.

"I've misjudged you a couple of times, Dee. If my actions seemed odd to you, maybe you can take my misunderstanding into account. When I first heard about you, from Sondra, I thought you were an agent for the other side. When we sweated out Rico's men I changed my mind and thought you were one of Ger--Jeff's old contacts. He uses a lot of actresses as informants."

The inflection he put on the word "actress" did not escape her. He was talking about call-girls and not about women who worked in the theater. She bristled internally, but kept a cool exterior.

"When I finally realized you two had met by accident, no pun intended, it kind of threw me for a loop. I'm still amazed at how you managed to do all you've done in such a short time."

"Chalk it up to an *actresses* ability to quick-study a new role." She pointedly used the same inflection he had, but he didn't seem to notice her sarcasm.

"Let's get to business, shall we?" Jeff trailed a finger across her shoulders as he walked behind her to the small table and sat in one of the chairs. He stretched out his legs. "Where's Ash now?"

Brian eased himself onto the edge of the nearest bed, did an exaggerated stretch that ended with his hands clasped behind his head. "Chicago, last I heard."

"Could I interrupt? I have a question or two that may have a bearing on the plans we're about to make." She joined Jeff at the table. "How did Hobart *know* we were in the motel in Seattle?"

"Much as I hate to accept it, someone on my team has more loyalty to Ash than to me," Brian said. "Could be someone in Chicago who overheard me talking to Seattle, or it could be someone in the Seattle office. Either way, the word got back to Ash and he put out the termination order."

"It could also be he didn't trust you from the start," Jeff put in, "and had someone watching

Sondra--just in case I showed up. And what about your people in Portland?"

Dee saw the hole in Jeff's theory and pointed it out before Brian could. "Couldn't be from Portland, Jeff. If Hobart had known about the cabin he would have tried to kill you there. And having someone watch Mrs. Culver doesn't fit, either. If he'd been that suspicious of Brian carrying out his orders in the first place, it seems likely he would have known something sooner than he did. I'm afraid I'm the fly in the ointment, here. Clearly I bungled my approach to Sondra and that's what must have set it all off. But in the end we're only guessing and I'd say we'd be well advised to trust no one other than ourselves."

"Point taken," Brian agreed. "Probably both of us are now targeted. I would have put my trust in a few people before the Seattle business, but now..."

Dee wanted to clear up one other point. "If no one knew where we went when we left Seattle, how is it those two agents were waiting for us in Denver?"

"Probably coincidence. I don't know what Carter and his partner were working on, but I have a hunch it wasn't you. I figured you to head for San Diego, or to drive back to Oregon."

"Carter *was* awfully lax for someone who'd been warned about a turncoat. I'll go along with you on that point." Jeff got to his feet, took off his suit coat and hung it in the closet. "Any more questions, Dee?"

She shook her head, distracted by his action, which she took to be a sign he had accepted this room as one he shared with her.

Jeff nodded, then addressed Brian. "Where

are you keeping that dossier you have on my contacts you've been interviewing?"

"In my apartment. It's nicely disguised among a pile of boring paperwork I never seem to get around to completing. I don't think anyone could find it even if they were looking for it. Why?"

"I'd like to check it in case there's something you've overlooked--something we could use to help us flush out Ash. But I'm not comfortable with the thought of visiting your place. That third-floor walkup is a ready-made trap."

"That's one of the reasons I like it. I never can allow myself to get too comfortable, drop my guard. And there are ways out of there I've haven't even shown you."

Dee began to get a more complete picture of Brian. For all his appearance of affability he was constantly testing himself, always alert. The freckle-faced, boyish exterior covered up a forever insecure man. The discovery did not make him more appealing.

Jeff rubbed his eyes with his hands and returned to his chair.

He must be so tired! As much as she wanted to share one of those beds with him, to take up where they'd left off that morning, she might have to put her own desires on hold. No matter where their present conversation led, she would insist on an early dinner and a good night's rest for all of them.

"You mentioned flushing Ash out, and earlier you talked about getting to the truth. Those phrases are a little too vague for me, Jeff. Would you spell it out? I'm not exactly clear on our ultimate goal. Since your Mr. Hobart has put this business on a kill-or-be-killed basis, what's all this talk about papers and evidence?"

"I'd rather not kill him though I feel I have enough justification for doing so. I'd rather gather enough evidence to insure he spends the rest of his life in a small, dark, cold cell. But regardless of how we ultimately handle him--with bracelets or bullets--we'll need enough evidence to clear ourselves with the agency before that happens, or we'll just be hunted down by others."

An involuntary shudder shook Dee as she considered all the in-fighting within their agency. She was moved to wonder how much tax money was wasted on such internecine warfare, on spies spying on spies, while they were ostensibly engaged in protecting the country from *enemies, foreign and domestic*. The old saw about who will guard the guardians never seemed more appropriate.

"And you can clearly include yourself in that scenario. If your theory about Sondra's phone call being the event that tipped Ash to our whereabouts has any merit, I'd say having me help you handle Rico has only put you in even greater danger. Out of the frying pan and all that."

Brian chimed in with more bad news. "When I ordered the watch put on the van, I used Sondra's description of you, Dee. I had no idea what the situation was, of course, but clearly Ash and his people are alerted to the fact an attractive blonde is part of the mix."

"I'm in this to the end, anyway. This isn't the first time today I've been told my life is in danger. How do you plan to get your evidence? And what *is* the evidence you need?"

"The business about Ash ordering Jeff's termination is established fact, so it doesn't mean much. He could always claim it was an honest mistake, unless we could show he got his orders from someone else--Senator Walburg, for example--or that he knew Jeff was clean."

"Tough assignment."

Jeff's sour look had eighteen months of lost time behind it. She reached across the table to give his hand a squeeze. He flashed her a weak smile in return.

Brian protested. "It's not impossible, buddy. If you can remember which aspect of the case you were working on at the time it might give us a clue to what brought the heat your way."

"You know how I work. It could have been any one of five or six different angles. We're going to have to establish the connection between him and Walburg some other way. What about the angles you were working, Brian? All that noisy stuff about the campaign contributions."

"I dropped it over a year ago--concentrated on your materials. The way I figure it , if I'd uncovered anything important, Ash would have ordered *you* to terminate *me*, rather than the other way around."

Listening to the two men eliminate one possibility after another gave Dee a headache--and an idea. "All this talk about your files, and Brian's files--what about Hobart's files? Could you figure out a way to get the evidence you need from them?"

Jeff regarded her with a puzzled frown. Brian rubbed his chin for a moment, then cast a negative vote. "Any stuff we need would be stashed at his house rather than in the office. His house in Evanston is more carefully guarded that our Chicago offices. I'd rather risk trying t get into the office unseen--and you know how impossible *that* would be."

"Yeah," Jeff agreed.

They shot down that plan, but the idea behind it remained intact. She pressed her point. "How about getting to Hobart to force the truth out of him?"

Jeff vetoed her idea. "Sorry, hon. Even if we could get to him, put the cuffs on him, take him to some quiet place where we could shoot him up with babble-juice, and force his confession, it wouldn't hold up. And he's probably built in safeguards against such action--instructions to destroy his records if he turns up missing or the like."

"We need either solid physical evidence, or an admission of collusion with Walburg given without duress," Brian added.

She exulted--twice. Once because they'd given her the perfect opening for her proposal, and a second time because she hadn't missed Jeff calling her *hon.* Using a pet name wasn't exactly hearts and flowers, but it would do for now.

"Too bad we can't think of some way to trick him into talking to someone he thinks he can trust."

Brian linked his hands behind his head again and leaned back on the bed. "That's not a bad idea. Someone he thinks is in his pocket, but who is, in fact, on our team."

"Do you have someone like that?" she asked Brian, trying to ignore the hard stare Jeff was giving her.

"I believe you were the one who just pointed out that we can't trust anyone but ourselves. There's no one we could trust to play such a role now."

"I disagree," she said mildly, trying to hide the butterfly-churning in her belly. When she'd told them she was in for the long haul she'd not envisioned playing so active a role, but now she'd thought of it she was determined to sell the two men on the idea.

Jeff seemed to be a half-step ahead of her. "I smell a rat. If you're thinking what I think you're thinking--"

Brian sat upright, hands on his knees, glanced back and forth between them. "Did I miss something?"

"You both agree it would be the perfect solution. Make him believe there's someone he can trust, someone who can give him something he wants very much. Someone who, in exchange, asks only for...oh, a little insurance policy."

Jeff was now sure about the rat. "Forget it!"

"Will someone please tell me what's going on?" Brian pleaded.

Dee turned on her gum-chewing hooker's voice for Brian's benefit. "Lissen, Sugar. I know where this Gerry-fella and his freckle-faced friend are hidin' out, an' all you hafta give me in exchange for the information is some kinda 'surance I'll live long enough to spend my ree-ward."

Brian stared at her, open-mouthed. Jeff seemed unimpressed with her performance. "No!"

She ignored Jeff, worked on Brian. "You said yourself Jeff is known to use hookers as informants. I could pull off a perfectly believable act for Ash's benefit, as one of Jeff's girls. I'll give him a story to explain my treachery. I'll gain his confidence. We'll talk, you'll get it on tape, and he'll go off on a wild goose chase. Then you'll..."

Brian surprised her by raising an objection of his own. "He wouldn't go anywhere. Ash gives orders, he doesn't execute them. Once you went into his office you'd never come out."

"He's right," Jeff chimed in. "You wind up in that room we were talking about, your veins full of pentothal. Once you'd told him everything, there'd be an accidental overdose. Forget it."

Dee wasn't willing to give up so easily. "How about my meeting him in a public place? Surely he'd leave the office if the bait was fresh enough."

Jeff fumed, and though Brian's objections were stated in a more reasonable voice suggestive of less personal grounds, he seemed as reluctant to go along with her plan as Jeff was.

"He might. But I still don't see what good it'd do."

"You could wire me--with something less conspicuous than those radios Jeff and I used--and record everything he says. I could draw him out a little by letting him know I had heard about the Walburg business from you two, and tell him I want confirmation from him before I let him know where you are."

"Absolutely not!"

Jeff's unrelenting opposition to her plan irritated her, but she did her best to keep her temper.

"I can't force either of you to accept my help, but unless you come up with something more rational than *forget it* I don't see why we shouldn't try it."

It took a concerted effort on her part to withhold comments about the male ego, but confronting them with their own chauvinism was not the way to win arguments.

"Why don't we just think about it for a while? Maybe we could relax over dinner, let it jell. If you two can think of a better plan, or show me why this wouldn't work..."

She trailed off on that note, waited while the silence hung heavily in the room.

Brian was the first to speak. "I could use a drink. What do you say, shall we try the restaurant here?"

"I'll get my coat," Jeff said, his scowling features clearly indicating his agreement was limited to the drink.

Dee discovered her knees were trembling as she stood to retrieve her purse from the dresser. She hadn't realized just how tense she'd become in the last few moments. Maybe she'd be the one to change her mind after giving the idea more thought.

Jeff was busy rearranging his suit coat as she opened the door. She started to smile at the young man lounging against the car outside the door, but her smile was quickly erased by his swift movements. Before she could voice a warning he closed the distance between them, brought a very large gun from under his jacket, and jabbed it into her belly.

"Back inside, Blondie."

CHAPTER TWENTY

Dee stood riveted in the doorway, the taste of fresh air gone sour in her mouth. The transition from hopeful expectation to dead-end threat had come too quickly for her thoughts to adjust. The burnished silver gun jabbing into her midsection, however, left little room for alternate explanation.

"I said, move it."

She took one tentative step backward, heard a curse from behind her, wondered what, if anything, she could do.

For the second time that day she seemed caught in a crazy time-warp. Without any clear awareness of the time it took or enough com- prehension to do anything about it, she found herself being moved inside, spun around so she was facing Jeff and Brian, and had her throat clutched in a grip that threatened to cut off her air.

A voice much too close to her left ear said, "Two birds with one stone. Carter and Whipple, right? Or is it Eastman and Williams? No matter. I'm sure to get a bonus out of this one. Lose 'em, boys."

She smelled peppermint. Was that his breath or was it from the cold steel pressed to her right temple? She couldn't tell. His fingers dug into her flesh and she wondered, idly and insanely, if her neck was bleeding or if he kept his nails neatly trimmed. The grip on her throat relaxed a little as Brian dropped his gun to the floor and put his hands behind his head.

"So it was *you* in Seattle," Brian said, raising his elbows even further.

"Yeah," the voice in her ear agreed. "Sorry I *missed* everybody. No miss this time, though."

Jeff was holding his coat open and reaching for his gun, very slowly. In a matter of seconds his gun would join Brian's on the floor and the three of them would be defenseless. She had to do *something* but it seemed her position was impossible. The man held her head in a vice-like grip, didn't telegraph his position behind her in any way. She couldn't see his feet, couldn't take aim with her heel to hit him where it would hurt, and if she happened to miss, his fingers would only dig deeper into her throat, cutting off her air completely.

She did the only reasonable thing she could do in the circumstances.

Her body became one hundred twenty-something pounds of dead weight in the man's hands. He did the only reasonable thing he could do--he let her fall to the floor in a heap. She stayed there, ignored her brain's commands to gulp in a lungful of air, remained as still as possible.

She heard a soft thumping sound above her, a gurgling noise which might have come from her own bruised throat, and then a very noisy thump like the sound of a body falling.

Jeff's voice: "Got him?"

Brian: "Yeah."

She opened one eye and saw a knee against the floor near the dresser, a pair of feet off to the left. She lifted her head from the floor and opened both eyes. Jeff crouched behind the dresser, his gun pointed at a spot over her head. Brian was in a strange sideways crouch, his empty hands outflung as though he was trying to balance himself.

"Check him. I'll cover. Dee, lie still." Jeff's air of command was clear.

She froze while Brian bent down to scoop up his gun, stepped forward and disappeared above and behind her. Jeff remained where he was, his gun never wavering from a spot just over her head.

"Yep, he's dead," she heard Brian declare a moment later.

"Okay. Dee, you can get up now."

She rubbed her elbow as she sat up, saw Brian's back lurch as though he was choking the man he had just pronounced dead. Then he straightened and she saw the stiletto in his left hand. The dead man wore a surprised expression on his face. A small ooze of blood stained his throat.

Brian's boyish expression as he turned to look at her was marred by a look of grim satisfaction. "So the faint was a feint, hey? You are some piece of work, lady."

"Yu...you're full of surprises yourself," she whispered through a raw throat. "What happened?"

Jeff examined her neck with gentle fingers while Brian wiped his knife on a clean towel. Brian appeared to ignore her question and addressed Jeff. "You recognize him?"

"He was in the mid-east section last time I saw him. Ash's man, wasn't he?"

"I thought he was mine. I recommended him to Ash to head up the Seattle office. Cute, huh?" Brian carefully fitted his stiletto into its sheath strapped to his back between his shoulder blades while he spoke. "The son of a bitch was in Hobart's pocket all along. Mystery solved. I'll get another towel for the egg on my face."

Distracted as she was by Jeff's gentle touch, she was still aware of an unspoken communication between the two men during their brief exchange.

Brian confirmed her observation. "Well, Dee, I guess you're officially part of the team now. No one other than my partners and dead men have ever seen this little trick, and since you're not dead I guess that makes you a partner."

Dee took Jeff's hand and got to her feet. Shaken, she tried to regain her composure, but wasn't entirely successful.

"This is going too fast for me. I'm used to people getting up after they've been killed, and heading for wardrobe before the next take. How can you take death so calmly?"

Jeff put a hand on her shoulder, gave her a comradely squeeze. "I'm developing a distaste for this kind of thing myself. Maybe I got spoiled by my extended vacation."

"You're just rusty." Brian slapped at his shoulder, then turned to Dee. "That fake faint of yours was perfectly timed. Another two seconds and I'd have been forced to go for his wrist. Risky."

"Do you do this often?"

Neither man acknowledged her question. They turned without a word to the dead man, seemed about to move him. Dee walked the length of the room and gazed out the window to the empty field which separated the motel from the airport. It wasn't just the killing, she told herself, it was the way they went about it. The two were a team with a clever, deadly, and probably well-rehearsed routine: Brian played the role of the frightened little boy, dropping his gun quickly and probably biting his lip while he raised his hands. Jeff played the tough guy, probably glaring at their assailant while he made a show of trying to decide if he should go for his gun or drop it as his partner had. The killer, having dismissed Brian as spineless, would concentrate on Jeff, which would give Brian the time he needed to draw and throw his weapon of choice.

The two men were as much actors, in their own deadly way, as she. And of the two she was, of course, far more interested in Jeff's role. His comment about his growing distaste was backed by experience. The way he had hesitated about shooting Rico, the look on his face when that action became unnecessary, the utter surprise in his voice over Rico's suicide...it all added up now. He didn't talk about *action* nearly as much as he talked about planning, organizing. She found herself wondering if Jeff had ever taken another man's life by his own hand, or if he always left that final act to Brian.

The men talked strategy in low voices. She caught bits of their conversation as she carefully swallowed and moved throat muscles to test the degree of injury she had suffered. Her own part in the blond man's death could not be ignored. If she hadn't pretended to faint Brian might have...

Fortunately, Jeff broke into her train of thought at that moment.

"Dee, let's go. We have to get out of here." He wasn't exactly issuing an order, but his voice still held that unmistakable tone of command. "We're going out through Brian's room. There may be back-up waiting, so I want you to wait until I honk the horn for you. When you hear it, come running. Okay?"

Did she have a choice?

He had already stepped away from her, but stopped, turned, and came back. He took her by the shoulders and looked into her face. "Are you going to be okay?"

"I'm fine. Really. Let's go." Her voice cracked a little but she gave him her best *brave little woman* look and he seemed satisfied. This was not the time for complete honesty.

Their exit from the motel went smoothly. Either no one else waited for them, or the way in which they left gave others no opportunity to stop them. Jeff drove the Thunderbird through the parking lot then raced up the street after Brian's car. They were already well over freeway speed as they climbed the on-ramp. Jeff tore down the right hand lane to the next exit, then slowed to a near-crawl as he drove into the parking lot of a shopping mall.

"We'll have to ditch both of these," Brian said as they joined him at the opened trunk of his car. "He had nothing on him to indicate which of us he was tracking, so we'll have to assume Ash knows everything about our present circumstances. Here's some I. D. for you, Miss Simmons. Use the Visa at the rental agency. And these are for you, Mr. Owens. I'll go with Fredericks. One car or two?"

"Better take two. If we pick up some company, we can use one as a battering ram."

Jeff's comment about using one car as a battering-ram registered in her mind only as a caution to rent the largest car she could get. Dee took the tidy, rubber-banded packet from Brian and inspected it. It included a worn driver's license with the faded photo of a blonde woman, two credit cards, and a thin sheaf of crisp bills. The outer bill was a hundred.

Brian transferred two briefcases to the front seat of his car, then returned. "I'll wait here. If I'm not here when you get back, just go."

She and Jeff got into the Thunderbird and drove away without a word. She wondered why Brian hadn't come with them, but was too dazed to formulate the question. She took the rubber band off the packet and slipped it into her purse. As they neared the airport complex again, Jeff's eyes grew more alert. He constantly checked mirrors as well as front and side views.

"No sign of anyone," he said. "We'll use Hertz this time. Get--"

"I know. The biggest car they have."

"Right." He glanced at her with approval as he pulled to the curb a few doors from the Hertz office. "Go ahead. I'll be along after I've parked this in their lot. Don't recognize me."

"I understand. I'll wait for you and follow you back to the mall."

He put a hand on her arm as she reached for the door handle. "You don't *have to* come with us, you know. If you'd rather go back to White Cloud, we could meet later."

"I've already considered the idea. I'm part of the team now. Let's get going."

She took her bag, which Jeff had thoughtfully carried out of the motel room for her, from the back seat and did a quick march to Hertz. She had to keep moving now, bury thought under action. If she stopped to think about what she was doing, she could easily lose her nerve.

* * * * *

Jeff slept from Grand Rapids to the Indiana-Illinois border. As they left Gary behind, he put his seat erect with a soft whine of electric motors and looked around before speaking.

"Where's Brian?"

"And good morning to you. He's behind us." She and Brian had played tag on the drive south and west from Grand Rapids, with Brian making all the moves: pulling ahead of her and matching her steady, cruise-controlled pace for a while, then dropping behind and doing the same thing from eight or ten car lengths. Watching him go through these maneuvers every ten or fifteen minutes helped keep her alert on the otherwise boring drive. "Sleep well?"

"Yes." He rubbed at his eyes with the heels of his hands. "How are you doing?"

"Fine. Where exactly are we going?"

"We'll be on the tollway in a few minutes. Signal Brian to turn into the first service area. I'll take the wheel from there."

"Don't trust my driving, eh?"

"You don't want me to bring up that Toyota again, do you?"

His wide grin was more welcome than anything she could imagine at the moment.

"We'll take a round-about route to our next stop. It will be easier for me to drive rather than give you directions every few blocks."

"I'm glad to see you've regained your sense of humor. The rest did you good."

Brian followed them into the rest area, but parked well ahead of them. After she and Jeff swapped positions, Brian pulled out again, leaving them behind. Jeff caught up to him without exceeding the speed limit. He went past the other Lincoln without a sign of recognition. When they left the toll booth near Markham she noted Brian had dropped still farther behind them. "What's going to happen now?"

"There's a motel in Elmhurst where we'll meet. If we're lucky, we'll be able to get to Ash tomorrow and have this wrapped up by tomorrow night."

She fervently hoped he wasn't being overly optimistic.

"I still don't like dragging you into this. I warned you once your life would be in danger, but..."

"I remember. I came of my own free will I just wish I had known enough to ask the right questions, that's all."

"You can still back out."

"And let you have all the fun? Forget it!" She liked the way the corners of his eyes crinkled up when he smiled. "I always honor my commitments."

He touched her shoulder with the back of his hand. "I just wish you were somewhere safe."

The console between their seats prevented her from snuggling against him. She touched his hair, stroked the back of his neck instead. He kept his eyes on the road.

The moment lasted longer than she expected, not as long as she'd hoped for. He reached for her hand, put it back in her lap, but gave it a gentle squeeze before letting go.

Reluctantly she turned her thoughts away from personal considerations. "If that man back at the motel in Grand Rapids was the same one who tried to kill us in Seattle, why didn't he use the same technique? Why a gun instead of a grenade?"

Jeff snorted and favored her with an appreciative glance. "Maybe I should have studied drama instead of forestry. You don't miss a thing. Fact is, he *was* carrying a grenade. It was in his coat pocket. You'll remember the only windows in that room faced the field out back. To launch a grenade from there he would have made himself too vulnerable--especially since he would have had to hit two rooms at the same time to be sure of getting all three of us. I think he intended to kill us all, then drop the apple in the room and run like hell."

"Then why didn't he?"

"Just drop the grenade once you'd opened the door? He probably got cocky when he took you hostage. Probably decided to crow a little. Killing us would likely have earned him a cushy promotion in addition to whatever cash reward Ash was offering. You could say it was his own ego that killed him."

She closed her eyes against the image of the man slumped in the corner of that room, the trickle of blood staining his throat. "Have you and Brian killed many men that way?"

Jeff kept his eyes on the road when he answered. "Contrary to what you seem to think, most of our work is boring--long, tedious hours of searching for information. It's not in our best interest to kill people. Dead men can't talk. It's far better to capture, interrogate, get all their secrets, then lock them away until they're brought to trial or used for an exchange."

"You make your job sound like a game of

chess."

"That's a fairly accurate metaphor. In this case one of the players--Bishop Ash if you will--got greedy."

Dee wondered if he saw himself as a Knight or a Pawn, decided against voicing the question. He hadn't really answered her earlier question, and she decided to let that one lie as well. The past was, after all, something they were both trying to be rid of, not dredge up. "What about Ash?" she asked, instead. "Will he know his assassin is dead, know you're still alive?"

"In all likelihood, yes. It won't take long for the local police to find the body and file a report. And our stripping him of I. D. will only slow things slightly. The minute the locals put his prints on the wire Ash will be flagged."

Her question had not been idle curiosity. She pursued her thought. "And he'll be worried, right? You've escaped him twice--three times if you count the cabin. That should shake him up a little."

"Yeah, he'll be worried."

"Wouldn't that make him ripe for the kind of shake-down I proposed?"

"Maybe. It will also make him a lot more dangerous."

"Speaking of that, how can you be sure he won't find us, the way he did in Grand Rapids?"

"Grand Rapids was my mistake. Using Carter's I.D. to rent the cars, buy the gun--I might as well have sent up a signal flare. All they had to do was ask the locals to watch out for either of our cars. Remember the deputy Sheriff back in Oregon? Same kind of system, except we don't have to pay off the police with cash the way Rico must have."

"Are you saying Rico paid off the Oregon--"

"He probably had an in with some department in the L.A. area. They'd do all the footwork for him. The LEDS system is pretty sophisticated these days, with terminals in practically every police station and jail in the country. It's designed to provide instantaneous information on everything from known felons to stolen boats and it works well, most of the time. Unfortunately it's also subject to abuse."

"By someone like Rico, paying off a cop?"

"Not necessarily a cop. A lot of people who aren't sworn officers have access to LEDS: parole officers, corrections personnel, clerks. Some operators make a nice second income by running checks for private investigators--which is illegal-- and it wouldn't take much for a guy like Rico to pay off someone to enter your car as a *vehicle of interest* and be informed any time it was spotted."

Dee remembered Jeff's earlier characterization of Rico as a fearful man. Fear and greed made a dangerous combination. "And who shall guard the guardians?"

"Not all of the abuse is criminal, or even significant. Take your friend back in L.A. who checked up on potential boyfriends as an example."

"Touché."

"Ash could legitimately enter the three of us, any cars we drove, credit cards we used, guns registered to us--darn near anything--into the system and be informed of a *hit* any time one of those items was spotted by an alert agency. If your local police chief in White Cloud meant what he told Brian about protecting your mother and sister, he'll see to it that the advisory on us is ignored, and further, he'll also bend the law a little and not report Rico's death in such a way that it could be connected with you or your family."

"We can trust Chief Towne. I used to baby-sit his kids when I was in high school."

"We can't trust the Grand Rapids police to keep things quiet, though. As soon as they discover the body or Brian's abandoned car, Ash will be informed. To get back to your question, we won't make the same mistake in Chicago. The I. D. we used to rent the cars is fresh, and it isn't connected to the agency. Once we get there we use cash only. And finally, we won't park the cars at the motel. They'll be close enough for us to use in a pinch, but not close enough for anyone to be able to pin-point our location easily."

"You mean we'll be able to get a good night's sleep?" She pictured the two of them in bed--no excuses, no apologies between them.

"You and Brian will, but I've had my rest. I'll be watching from my own room. Three rooms, no contact."

"I'll miss you." She tried to keep the hurt out of her voice, but felt she wasn't entirely successful.

"Me too."

Dee looked out her window as she fought for control of her emotions. The brightly lit living rooms and dining rooms of the suburban neighborhood they were passing through seemed like a different world to her. Families were eating dinner there, sharing small talk about their day, making plans for the weekend. She wondered if she'd ever taste that kind of life. So far it had eluded her, and her chances for capturing it did not look very bright at the moment.

Jeff broke into her reverie as they neared an average-looking motel. "That's it. I'll let you out at the next light. Take your bag, *Miss Simmons*. Get some sleep. I'll wake you early in the morning."

"Good night, Mr. Whoever-you-are."

"Owens. Good night, Dee."

Her legs felt like leaden weights on the short walk to the motel. She registered and took her key, ignored Brian who ostensibly examined a post card rack in the lobby. When she entered the room she glanced at the bathroom but decided against a shower, stripped out of her clothes and crawled into bed.

* * * * *

The sound of gunfire awakened her.

She sat bolt upright, surprised by the bright light pouring in around the edges of the ill-fitting curtain, then realized the "gunfire" was actually someone rapping on the door. "Miss Simmons?" called a muffled voice she could not immediately identify.

"Just a minute!"

She slipped into her slacks and blouse, bunching the material in front of her instead of taking the time to button it. She left the chain on the door when she opened it.

Jeff stuck his face into the opening. "Hi! Coffee shop across the street. Bring your bag."

"Good morning. I think. Do I have time to shower?

"Make it a quick one."

She tied up her hair and stepped into the

255

small cubicle. She would have loved to have had time to fantasize sharing a shower with Jeff, but she fought against the impulse. A brisk toweling brought her to a more appropriate frame of mind.

She took a change of underwear from her bag and concentrated on appreciation for the available clothing. "You're getting downright civilized," she informed her image in the bathroom mirror.

A quick brush through her hair, a dab of lipstick, and she was out the door. The morning air reeked of automobile exhaust and other stale odors, but it felt good. So what if it wasn't the smell of Michigan Jack Pine or Oregon Douglas Fir? She was alive and rested and about to participate in another adventure. The horror of death and danger seemed remote.

"That coffee for me?" she asked, slipping into the booth next to Jeff.

"Finest coffee for blocks," Brian quipped.

A bored waitress approached their booth. "You folks ready to order now?"

Jeff and Brian ordered scrambled eggs and bacon. Dee asked for a large glass of grapefruit juice and a poached egg on English muffin. The waitress never took her eyes off her pad and quickly turned away as though they no longer existed.

Jeff scowled at his coffee cup, an idle finger moving it through slow arcs on the Formica surface. She turned toward him in the seat and, in her best imitation of the waitress' bored tone, asked, "You folks ready to talk now?"

Brian grinned broadly, saluted her with his coffee cup. Jeff stopped toying with his own cup, his attempt at a smile a mere shadow of Brian's grin.

"We've decided to go with your plan."

She managed to get her coffee cup back to the table and her hands into her lap before they started trembling. Her world had just turned cold, gray, and dangerous again.

CHAPTER TWENTY-ONE

"Well, Sugar--" Dee cut herself off. Maybe she could fool them into thinking she was ready, willing, and able; but she couldn't fool herself. She dropped the gum-chewing accent and continued in her own voice. "You might as well know I'm scared as hell about this."

"We're not exactly happy about it ourselves," Brian said, "but after a year and half of getting nowhere we're agreed we have to try something different. And we've discussed a few additional safeguards."

Brian glanced at Jeff and she saw that unspoken communication pass between them again. A twinge of envy went through her. The years of close partnership had given them something she had yet to discover for herself with any other person.

Jeff took a deep breath, then turned to meet her expectant look as he slowly exhaled. "We'll wire you, as you suggested, but Brian thinks we can go one better than simply listening in--and make your job easier in the bargain."

"We already suspect everything you're likely to learn from Ash," Brian explained. "If you can just get him to admit some connection with Walburg, and we can get that information to others, the seeds of doubt we'll plant should do the rest of the job for us."

"Brian is going to set us up to pipe your conversation right back into our Chicago offices.

This is going to take careful timing and additional help on the inside." Jeff paused while their waitress deposited her load and left them again, then finished, "But you don't really need to know those details."

"Why don't you fill me in anyway? Maybe it will help to relax me."

Again that look between them. Jeff's tight-lipped countenance bothered her. She slipped a hand beneath the table and caressed his leg just above the knee. With her free hand she picked up her juice and sipped.

"There are two parts to my plan," Brian offered. "The easy part is to find someone in the office who will be ready to get the radio room to tune into the right frequency--the one you'll be broadcasting on--as soon as Ash leaves the office. Then she'll get as many people as she can round up to listen in."

"She?" Dee had assumed a male society within the agency--for no good reason, she now realized.

"Yes, the agent I'm thinking of happens to be a woman. I'm pretty sure she won't believe whatever rumors Ash may have started about me in the last day or two, and she's persuasive enough to get others to at least listen--whether or not *they* believe those rumors.

"The second part of the plan involves the meeting place and it's a lot trickier. Ash will make sure he's covered when he meets you. He'll have his men in place before he arrives or he won't show up.

"I'm going to have to break our rule and find a few more people I hope we can trust...in addition to the woman I mentioned. We'll need them to make sure that everyone Hobart contacts after your call to him is tailed and covered to keep them from putting you in greater danger. Jeff and I will be nearby, but we'll be concentrating on protecting you from Ash and we won't be able to watch for his backups."

Jeff seemed to relax a bit under her casual massage. Brian appeared not to notice. She ignored her poached egg, addressed a question to Jeff. "Do you expect Hobart to be wired, too? So he can communicate with his men?"

Jeff cleared his throat. "No. He probably won't want them to hear his conversation with you. He'd rely on a hand signal, probably."

"Have you picked a place for this meeting?"

Brian gave her his best little-boy grin before answering. "On that point we have a small disagreement. I'm in favor of an open place, like a park, where we can see more of what's going on. Jeff prefers something more crowded, with places for you to duck into out of danger if any shooting starts."

"I don't know much about Chicago, but I like Jeff's option. We talked about Hobart's hit-and-run techniques on the drive last night. It seems to me an open place would work to his advantage."

"Majority rules. In this case, you're a majority of one. But you're right. If we went with some place like Daley Plaza he'd be forced to use stationary backups and they'd be easier to neutralize."

As though by mutual consent all three of them turned their attention to the food in front of them. Dee took two bites of her poached egg, then returned her fork to the plate. Brian's use of the word neutralize had sent her mind off on a jumble of unrelated thoughts about beauty shop perms and chemical transformations. She recognized the process for what it was--a way to sidetrack her from the looming danger. "How will you neutralize them?" she asked as she picked up her fork again.

"Now that we've uncovered the major fly in the ointment I'm fairly confident I can put together a team we can trust. At the first sign of trouble, my men will move in, pose a more immediate threat to Ash's backups. If things start to look bad, you can give our guys an edge by saying something to alert them."

"You mean something like, *'Why Mr. Hobart, honey, why are you pointing that great big gun at me?'* ?.

Jeff's coffee cup banged against the table, sending a small slosh of coffee over his whitened knuckles. "Yeah, something like that."

"How close will your team be to Hobart's men?"

Both men looked puzzled.

She amplified. "It occurs to me there maybe a way to neutralize them without using guns or grenades. Your people will have radios so they can hear me, right? Well, if Hobart's men could hear what he'll be saying to me right from the start, like the people back in the office, maybe we won't have to neutralize them..."

Jeff stopped chewing his mouthful of bacon, gave her an admiring look that warmed her from head to toe. Brian beamed. "Well, I'll be damned. That's brilliant! Remind me to put you in for a pay raise."

"I'll need it. I plan to blow most of this

261

money you gave me at a beauty salon this morning. I'm going to turn myself into a flaming redhead again, but if I have time I'm doing it the right way, instead of with that awful strawberry mousse I used in Denver."

"You'll have time," Jeff assured her. "Brian needs a few hours to put together his team and the equipment. Plus, you've just handed him an additional assignment."

"One I gladly accept."

"What will *you* be doing?"

"I'm sticking with you, even if it means reading women's magazines all morning. I'm not going to leave you unprotected."

Brian pointed a fork in her direction. "Jeff tells me you're unarmed. Would you like me to pick up a nice little lady's gun for your purse while I'm shopping?"

"A *lady's* gun? What's that--something for shooting ladies with?" She didn't bother to hide her disgust over the chauvinistic comment, however unconscious it might have been.

Brian turned a shade of red she'd not seen since leaving the beaches of Southern California. "Christ! That was insensitive of me. Will you forgive me?"

"Eventually."

Jeff applied jam to a piece of toast with all the care of an artist working oil onto a canvas.

She let Brian stew for a long moment while she watched Jeff work. "I'll pass on the gun. As Jeff pointed out to me recently, I'm more likely to make the right defensive move if I don't have the false security of a gun. Besides, my best weapon is my wits."

"You can carve that in stone," Jeff remarked around a mouthful of toast.

"I thought it wouldn't hurt to offer. Just wish I'd put it another way," Brian apologized again.

"Don't worry about it," she told him. "Just put together a team to help us clear Jeff's name without getting us killed and all will be forgiven." She flashed him a brief smile to further ease his discomfort, then returned her attention to her own breakfast.

* * * * *

Finding a salon wasn't difficult. Finding one which would agree to a complete makeover in under two hours was another matter. After four unsuccessful calls, Dee talked to a woman who agreed to do only a color change without a set. When Dee assured her money was no object she consented to call in her part-time assistant who could handle the makeup at the same time and get Dee out of the shop on schedule.

She and Jeff took a cab to the shop and found it void of customers. Two operators lounged in the chairs, one of them the owner she'd spoken to on the phone, and a teenager joined them as Dee and Jeff entered. The "assistant" turned out to be the owner's daughter who was still studying cosmetology, but Dee figured the girl could handle creating the brassy look she wanted, given it didn't require a great deal of subtlety.

As she settled herself into a chair, an inspiration came to her. "Say Honey," she called to Jeff, raising her voice to insure all three women heard her. "Since we're going to be here for a while why don't you turn yourself into a blonde? I'm sure these people could handle it, couldn't you, girls?"

The women immediately agreed. Jeff wasn't as positive. He raised a hand as though warding off a blow and shook his head.

"No one at the *party* would expect you to show up as a blonde. You'd have them all guessing. And it would only take a few minutes, wouldn't it, girls?"

Between her badgering and the encouraging words of the three women, Jeff finally relented. The color they settled on for him was actually a sandy brown, a significant departure from his near-black color yet still plausible given his skin tone.

* * * * *

When they met Brian outside the Brookfield Zoo three hours later he summed up his reaction in a single word. "Wow!" His eyes took in the bright yellow mini-dress Dee had bought for herself, and continued on down her legs. She didn't mind the scrutiny, even turned an ankle at the appropriate moment. Her legs had landed her more than one role, and she had decided to use them to advantage.

When Brian completed his appreciative inspection he took a long, hard look at Jeff's lighter hair. If he had any witty quips about beauty salons in mind--and Dee was sure he had--he chose not to use them. She gave him points for discretion.

The bug he had prepared looked exactly like a round-headed straight pin. On closer examination she saw the shaft was a little thicker than the kind she'd used to tack up a hem before stitching, but the difference was hard to detect. She got into the back seat of Brian's Lincoln to insert the bug along the seam of her bra, then rejoined them.

"...and I was surprised at how many of them expressed interest in learning the whole story," Brian was saying as she returned. "I was just telling Jeff we have our team assembled, and it's larger than I had expected. Ash may have his own team in the field but I think we'll easily outnumber them."

"That's a comfort. Jeff filled me in on the things I'll want to get Ash to talk about, so we might as well get started."

"One last thing. You remember my little secret?" Brian patted the back of his neck for emphasis.

"All too well."

"Ash's favorite toy is a little over-and-under derringer fitted to a drop-holster up his left sleeve. If you're close and he decides to use it, he'll try to distract you with gestures of his right hand. He's tall and very distinguished-looking--"

"Yes, Jeff told me about that."

"Jeff's never seen him in action, though. He'll turn on the charm, start waving his right hand in the air like a senator while he drops his left arm sharply. Those little twenty-twos don't kill very often, but if he's close enough to aim for your head..."

"I get the picture." Dee fought back a wave of cold terror. "Anything else?"

Jeff put a hand on her arm, turned her to face him. "He's a black belt or better. You won't be able to throw him off balance with a faint, like you did with that guy in Grand Rapids. If it comes to a fight-or-flight situation, run like hell."

She nodded and gulped, then drew herself

erect. "Let's go." She felt considerably less brave than she tried to appear.

Jeff handed her into the front seat of the Lincoln, then closed the door. Brian had started around the back of the car, but she saw Jeff grab his arm. She thumbed the window control, dropped it a few inches.

"Are you sure you have *everything* covered?"

She couldn't see Brian's expression, but his tone carried an unmistakable air of hurt pride. "Of course. I already have people in place around the plaza, and others standing by to tail whoever Ash contacts after he gets Dee's call. Gervais will have the intercoms on and the tapes rolling the minute he leaves the office. I've left *nothing* to chance."

"Except for what surprises he'll have up his sleeve...and I'm not talking about that derringer. If anything happens to Dee..." Jeff left his implied threat unfinished.

Brian said nothing. A moment later Jeff released his arm. Dee thumbed her window closed. When Jeff got into the back seat behind her, she turned to him. "It's going to work."

They passed the ride through Berwyn and Cicero and into central Chicago in silence. As they neared The Loop Brian offered last-minute instructions. "I'll be dropping you and Jeff off at some phone booths near the plaza. You make your call to Hobart, then go straight to your spot. Jeff will follow at a discreet distance. I'll join him as soon as I get rid of the car. Remember to let Ash know you won't wait more than fifteen minutes."

"Now honey, don't you worry none about me. Y'all just take care of your end of things...but keep your eye on *my* end, y'hear?"

Brian chuckled. She heard nothing from Jeff. She hoped he'd be able to relax once they swung into action. *One* of them ought to be relaxed.

CHAPTER TWENTY-TWO

Dee fished a quarter from the bottom of her cheap plastic clutch while Jeff attached a small listening device to the phone with a suction cup. Jeff had selected the contents of her purse himself and she had diplomatically said nothing about his knowledge of what a street-smart woman's purse should hold. Inside was only a lipstick, a few wadded tissues, a small amount of cash, and the keys to the Lincoln they had left in Elmhurst.

She turned and rubbed the quarter in her hand like a worry-stone.

Jeff stepped to the side of the open booth. "Ready."

The woman who answered her call first attempted to learn "the nature of her business", then put her on hold when Dee refused to discuss it. A man came on the line and asked the same series of questions without identifying himself. Jeff gave her a negative signal from outside the booth.

"Sugar, you listen and you listen good. I have some information for Mr. Ashton Hobart and if he wants to hear it, you better get him on the phone pronto. Y'hear?"

The all-too-familiar click of a hold button was his only response. In less time that it took her to switch her wad of gum from one side of her mouth to the other, a new voice spoke in her ear. He didn't identify himself, either.

"Yes?"

"Is this Ashton Hobart?"

"What can I do for you, Miss?"

Jeff nodded, his lip curling upward in a silent snarl.

"Well, if this is you, Mr. Hobart Honey, I got some information for you, 'bout somebody you're lookin' for. You want to hear what I know you meet me in Daley Plaza in fifteen minutes. I'll be standing under that Pee-caso. I'm wearin' yellow and I got red hair wavin' like a flag. You can't miss me. Fifteen minutes, y'hear?"

He could have been a friendly loan officer discussing collateral. "I'm not sure I understand you, Miss. Just what is it you have?"

"You're tryin' my patience, Sugar. I've got just two things to say to you. One is Eastman. The other is, you're down to *fourteen* minutes."

She hung up the phone and cocked an eyebrow at Jeff. "How'd I do, Sugar?"

He grinned at her as he reached into the booth to remove his device. "Just fine, Miss. Now get moving. And be careful."

The afternoon sun felt warm on her back, but Chicago was living up to its reputation as the Windy City. A cool breeze from the lake chilled her as she crossed with the pedestrian traffic toward the plaza. She knew Jeff was behind her in the crowd, but wished he could be by her side. She felt more vulnerable in this crowd of people than she had felt in that cottage with Rico.

She vaguely remembered having learned in an acting class that people feel more lonely in a crowd. Lonely wasn't exactly what she felt, but the idea would do.

She walked around the Picasso sculpture,

looking for a likely place to make her stand. This was one of the few places in Chicago she recognized. Once, in defiance of her mother's opposition to her taking long car rides with boys, she and a guy and another couple had driven here, spent half their money on a meal near this very spot. Afterwards they sat in the plaza commenting on passersby as though they were world travelers inspecting the natives in their habitat. The trip had resulted in her being grounded for a month, but it had been worth it. She wondered what this second visit to Daley Plaza would cost her.

As she completed her circuit she spotted Jeff's newly blond hair. She started to flash him a quick smile, thought better of it, then realized it wasn't him after all. She chided herself, remembering she was supposed to be looking for no one other than the tall, distinguished-looking Ash Hobart. She shifted her small clutch to her other hand, dried a damp palm against the short skirt of her dress.

Dee considered taking her lipstick from her purse and applying another coat of bright orange to her lips to give her hands something to do. If she didn't find some way to calm her nerves the skirt of her dress would soon be soaked. She lifted the purse, but immediately dropped it back to her side. Coming directly toward her across the plaza was a tall, gray-haired man. She knew it was Hobart. His stride was long and unhurried, and he held himself erect. He could have been a bank president or an attorney on his way back to the office after lunch. He didn't look in the least bit sinister.

He stopped an arm's length away and regarded her with cool detachment. "Are you the young lady who called?"

"That depends, Sugar. Who might I have called?"

"I'm Ashton Hobart."

"So you say. Would you mind proving it?"

He reached inside his well-pressed suit coat.

She waved a negligent hand in his face. "Don't bother showing me your driver's license, Honey. I've seen enough phony I. D. in my time to know that don't mean nothin'."

"Then how do you expect me to identify myself, Miss...?"

"You can call me Sherry. And you can identify yourself by telling me a little about you."

Dee felt her nervousness leave her as though wafted away on the Chicago breeze. The trembling in her limbs stopped, her hands were dry, and there was moisture in her throat. The next few seconds would determine the success or failure of their plan so there was no longer anything to be nervous about. Either it would work or it wouldn't.

His hands remained at his sides. No reaching for a pocket or clamping them behind his back. He didn't even flex his fingers. "What exactly can I tell you? And why should I bother?"

"Tell me about Paris."

"What exactly--"

"Stop pussy-footin'! You tell me about four years ago in Paris, or I take a walk. And I don't want to hear the nightly news version, either. What'll it be, Sugar?"

He took a half-step toward her and she found herself frozen to the spot by his glare. She could see little flecks of gold in his blue-gray eyes, but discovered she could read no emotions there.

Her gum had become a hard little ball against her tongue. She flicked it between her teeth and worked it again, tried to bring moisture back to her mouth. When he leaned back, she thought he was about to take a walk himself, but then he seemed to relax. He reached a hand upward, stroked the side of his face with the knuckle of his index finger.

Dee held her breath, prayed the stroking finger was not the signal she had been fearing. It took all of her will to keep her eyes open, to stand her ground against the fear.

The moment passed. There was no sound of gunfire, no tearing of her flesh.

"Paris, eh?"

She nodded, unable to speak.

He told her about the phony student riots, about his team's participation in events which hadn't made the newspapers. When she asked for more details, he gave them without hesitation.

"Satisfied?"

"You bet, Ash-honey. Now we got that settled, we can get down to bizness."

"Not so fast. You know you can trust me, but how do I know I can trust you?"

"Okay, Sugar. Fair enough. In the first place I've been on the payroll for years. Well, I mean I was up until about a year ago, when the party we're talkin' about disappeared. Then last night he shows up again and acts like nothin' ever happened, like I'm supposed to just jump right in and help him like I used to.

"Thing is, I got me a new boyfriend in the meantime, and when I tell this Eastman fella I ain't so sure I want to play any more unless he's willing to pay me a lot more, he gets downright mean. Tells me he's short of cash. When I don't buy his story, he starts roughing me up. See?" She reached up to grab the ruffled bodice of her dress at the left shoulder.

He seemed about to stop her, but when she tugged the dress off her shoulder, revealing the top edge of the bruise she had received in the cabin, his hand dropped to his side again. She let him look at the bruise, and the ample portion of flesh she had, uh, coincidentally, exposed for a moment, then covered up again.

"So I let him think I'm going to do his dirty work for him again, and I stick around while him and his freckle-faced partner are grumblin' about how you did 'em dirty and so forth. That's how I got the idea to come to you. See, them two just figure me for some kind of Chatty Cathy doll, y'know? I get a date with whoever they tell me to, then tell them everything I hear. They don't figure I got enough brains to figure a way out."

A bemused half-smile played across Hobart's features. "And what exactly have you figured out?"

His smile told her he had bought her persona. His cool tone told her he remained unconvinced about cooperating with her.

"Glad you asked, Sugar. This is what I figger. You give me a little present, y'know? Something with three or four zeros behind it, if you catch my meanin'? I tell you were to find them. Then, when you've taken care of them, you put me on *your* payroll. I can be a real help, like I used to be for him. Whadaya say?"

Dee had considered offering him additional

273

favors in return but could not bring herself to do so. It was not just her rationalization to avoid laying it on too thick that stopped her, either. Despite his distinguished appearance he was a killer and even more of a gangster than Rico. While such an offer would have been in character for Sherry, Dee did not trust herself to pull it off convincingly.

Her observations of his mannerisms, added to the cautions Jeff and Brian had given her, were beginning to give her clues to his emotional state. The slight shifting of his feet, the almost imperceptible shrugging of his shoulder told her he was on the edge--still uncertain about trusting her, but eager to obtain the promised information.

"You say you can tell me where they are. How do I know this is true? You might have known where they were last night, or this morning perhaps; but how do I know you can pinpoint their location right now, or an hour from now?"

"Sugar, you can rest you mind on that score. I was with them not more than an hour ago, and they're expecting me back. I know where to find them sure as God made little green apples."

"If they need you so desperately, why did they allow you to leave?"

She showed scorn for the gullible redhead and Jeff. "I convinced them it would be smarter for me to get things settled up with my new boyfriend so's he won't be comin' in at the wrong time and bustin' things up. They know I"ll be back 'cause they're sittin' on all my pretties right now."

"They're at your place?" His eagerness stuck out like a traffic signal.

"Uh-huh."

"And where is that?"

She had him. She allowed the smile of triumph to show on her face, confident her next words would cause him to interpret it as she intended.

"Nice try, Sugar, but no dice. I told you I'm not dumb. I'll tell you where they are *after* we get a few things settled, and not before."

She needed to hurry, set the hook while he was still eager, avoid giving him time to think.

"First of all, you got to cross my palm with some of them presidential portraits, y'know? And prob'ly it would be a good idea if you sort of let me know how we're gonna work together--so's I can get some idea of what kind of profit we're talking about?"

Greed seemed to be something he understood. He relaxed a little. She took her gaze off him, glanced at the skyline as though lost in thought.

"Say...how about the business you got goin' with that Senator fella?"

"Wha--I don't know what you're talking about."

Hobart reacted more forcefully than she had anticipated. His feet shifted and he moved toward her with a menacing look in his eyes. The sudden move caught her off-guard and she backed too quickly, caught her heel on something and lost her balance.

His hand shot out and captured her left arm in a painful grip.

She'd overplayed her part, hammed it up like a rank amateur. She'd done nothing to help Jeff, and had only succeeded in putting her own life in jeopardy once again.

CHAPTER TWENTY-THREE

The seconds ticked away in what seemed like a perfectly normal time-frame to Dee. Hobart's painful grip on her arm as she righted herself seemed absent of either malice or concern, but he gave no further sign of becoming more aggressive. She decided she'd better say something to keep Jeff from barging in too soon.

"Thanks, Sugar. Guess I caught my heel in somethin'. What were we sayin'?"

"You were about to tell me where you live."

The grip on her arm relaxed slightly but he showed no sign of letting her go. His voice betrayed little emotion, but the glint in his eyes made the depth of his desire to find and eliminate Jeff abundantly clear.

"No, I think you were about to tell me about this Senator What's-his-name business."

She'd already given herself up for dead, so she might as well push ahead. In the back of her mind she paraphrased an observation Jeff had once made, *What have I got to lose, seven seconds?*

"That's none of your business." He released her arm but did not step back.

She held her ground, put her hand on her hip, then shifted that hip to the side. "Now, is that any way to talk to your new partner? Like I told you, Sugar, if I'm going to give up my meal ticket for you, I need to know I'll still have steady work, y'hear? How much is he in for, this Senator?"

His cynical laugh--more like a bark--was devoid of humor, as was the look he gave her. Clearly he considered the idea of a partnership with *Sherry* a laughing matter, but she felt a new stirring of hope as he seemed to give her proposal serious consideration.

"Enough. He's in for enough, though I suppose it wouldn't hurt to increase the take. You do have brass, but I'm not sure you're his type."

"What type does he go for? Them cute little Senate Page Boys? I hear a lot of those guys like boys."

His lop-sided grin added to the impression their conversation had turned cooperative, if not quite friendly. She widened her focus momentarily to include a portion of the plaza behind Hobart, but saw no sign of Jeff or Brian. Brian, she realized, would probably keep his red head out of sight rather than risk being spotted by Hobart, but she expected Jeff to remain close, somewhere behind their adversary. She returned her focus to Hobart, acutely aware she was still on her own with the man.

"I can't say that I know anything about the good Senator's preferences, though the idea might be worth looking into. Perhaps that could be your first assignment. Right now there are other matters to attend to, don't you agree? Why don't we go to your bank and arrange a transfer of funds right now? Where do you do your banking, Sherry?"

The man was certainly smooth, she admitted to herself.

"B. of A." she said casually, revealing nothing. "Say, if it ain't sex, what is it you got on Walburg? He workin' for the other side or something?"

277

"I see your two friends have been feeding you their standard propaganda line. They've been a thorn in my side for far too long. As for you, I'm losing patience. Either you tell me what you know, or forget it. I'll find them sooner or later, so I recommend you use the information now while it's still worth something."

"Yeah, they told me you'd tried to kill 'em three times already. I can see where that'd make you impatient."

His shifting feet, flexing fingers, and a small twitch in one cheek muscle informed her he was beginning to get rattled. She decided to press him a little more, use his irritation to keep him talking.

"What'd they do to make you so mad? They try to muscle in on your deal with the senator?"

"Hah! You credit them with too much intelligence. Their sense of values remains stuck in childhood, I'm afraid, relying more on the Boy Scout Oath than on the wisdom of the marketplace. Had they tried to *muscle in* as you so quaintly put it, they might have escaped my wrath. And I would advise you to heed the same warning, you little tramp!"

Even without the insult, his menacing tone made it clear she wouldn't be able to stall any longer. Her seven seconds had run out.

Dee turned her right foot outward, put her weight on the ball of her foot and stood poised to run. Hobart raised his right hand to his cheek. Brian's warning of such distracting gestures came back to her, and she concentrated on his left shoulder, waiting for a sign he was about to draw his hidden derringer.

A stranger walked into sight behind him,

passed through her field of vision while the two of them stood staring at each other. Hobart's eyes widened by the smallest margin as he tugged at his right ear lobe.

In that instant the true significance of the action registered with her. It was his signal. He had just notified his waiting assassins to kill her--but no shots rang out in the plaza. He dropped his hand to his waist, repeated the motion. Still no shots.

The game was over. They'd beaten him, and the time had come to let him in on the secret. She dropped the Sherry persona.

"Looks like you blew it, Mr. Hobart."

Her own voice sounded strange to her ears, a jarring contrast to the drawl she'd been using.

He looked from side to side, still holding his ear. Confusion, and possibly fear, registered in his eyes.

Dee took a half-step backward. "I told you I know where they are. They're here. And they've put a stop to you. Your killers won't shoot me because they've been listening to everything you've said. You're finished. As the little tramp would say, *You been had, Sugar.*"

She expected to see a resigned look in his eyes, a sign of defeat. She had misjudged him. He slowly lowered his right hand, then abruptly changed the motion and reached for her. Before she could register the movement he had grabbed a handful of ruffled bodice in his fist. His left arm described a downward arc as he pulled her toward him.

"Jeff!"

She forced the single word through a bone-dry throat as she went into action.

She tested his grip by throwing her body down and away from him, was not really surprised when it proved unbreakable. He adjusted easily to the unexpected pull. There was only one direction she could go, and she took it. She bunched her tensed leg muscles and leapt.

His eyes registered surprise as she came at him, gave her the split-second she needed to pin his left hand, which now held the derringer, to his side. She locked her ankles together behind him, squeezed his arm tight against his hip with her thighs.

She threw her right hand behind his head, grabbed a handful of hair for purchase, then pulled. At the same time she pinned his right arm between them and dug her left thumb into the soft flesh beneath his chin, used the ridge of bone just below his eyes to anchor all four fingers.

As her nails dug into his flesh he let out a bellow of rage and tried to dislodge her with a twisting motion.

She compressed every muscle in her body, breathed heavily through her mouth, and continued to lever her fingers and thumb into his flesh. Her legs were beginning to quiver from the prolonged strain of holding his arm pinned. She knew if she gave him the slightest freedom of movement he'd turn his small gun upward and fire, risking a self-inflicted wound in his attempt to escape. The only thing he could possibly do to get free was to fall forward, try to knock the wind out of her as he slammed her back to the pavement, or attempt to do the same thing by smashing her into the massive metal sculpture behind her. She braced for either eventuality and prayed her legs would hold out.

The muzzle of a large gun appeared against Hobart's ear, followed by a head of sandy brown hair thrust in front of her face.

"Give it up, Ash. It's over."

Jeff's prediction proved to be premature. A sound like a little boy's cap gun, two little *snap! snap!* sounds, rent the air.

Jeff didn't even flinch as he made a second forecast.

"You're dead, you---"

"Hold it right there," another voice commanded. "Agent Reynolds, F. B. I. Ashton Hobart, you're under arrest. You can let go of him now, Ma'am."

Jeff pulled his blond head from between them, holstered his gun, then helped her disentangle herself from Hobart.

"You can't arrest me!" Hobart spat, trying to pull away from Reynolds and another man who had joined them. "Don't you know who I am?"

The FBI man ignored Hobart, finished clasping his wrists in handcuffs behind his back. "Read him his rights, Frank."

The action dissolved into a meaningless background buzz as Jeff wrapped his arms around her and held her almost as tightly as she had been holding Hobart. She couldn't tell which of them was shaking more violently as she buried her face against Jeff's chest.

When she regained control of her legs she pushed upward on tip-toe, lifted her face. His lips descended to meet hers. They shared a long, hungry kiss into which she poured every bit of tension, anxiety, and fear she had experienced in the encounter.

His kiss restored some of her equanimity, then threatened to destroy it again as he pressed her closer.

A third hand joined his two on her back. Brian spoke close to her ear. "I take it you two are okay?"

Jeff released her and they turned to face Brian. Jeff croaked something--not exactly a word--which carried a positive sound. She nodded her agreement with Jeff's sound as she slid an arm around Brian's waist, gave him a brief hug.

Over Brian's shoulder she could see Hobart being led away between the second agent and a uniformed policeman. Other men and women, some in uniform, ran toward them from every corner of the plaza.

"Okay, folks, you want to come with me?" Reynolds suggested.

Dee wasn't sure who the FBI man was addressing, or why. Brian's response clarified both issues.

"Bill, you're going to be busy with Hobart for a while. Why don't I take Owen and Sherry to the hospital and have them checked over. I'll bring them along to your office later and you can get their statements then."

"Fine. I'll need to check in with the team at Hobart's house, anyway. See you later, Brian. Nice work, Ma'am."

Agent Reynolds turned to follow the men leading Hobart away, waved off the others as he went.

The pleasant wave of relief washing through her was interrupted by an angry outburst from Jeff. "Since when are you so cozy with the FBI? And why'd you bring them into--?"

Brian waved a hand in Jeff's face. "Cool it, will you? I used all the men I had to cover Hobart's goons. I needed more support here in the plaza so I struck a deal with Reynolds. He gets Ash and any of the papers he'll need to put him away, permanently. In exchange, he's promised to ignore anything else he uncovers. It's a good policy. He owes me one now."

"And you owe me one! You expect me to just stand here and watch the man who ordered my death be led away? If your buddy Reynolds hadn't interfered I could have---"

"Maybe you could have, but when I set this up I wanted to make sure I wasn't taking any chances with your life--or Dee's. I'm sorry you were cheated out of your vengeance, but..."

The lingering tension, both physical and emotional, reduced Dee's tolerance level to zero. She stepped between the two men and cut them off.

"Excuse me. I know you boys are fond of your bitch-and-bicker sessions, but would you mind calling a truce long enough to get us to some place where I could at least sit down?"

Their flushed faces and gaping mouths made her think of fish out of water. Brian ended the stand-off by grabbing her arm and starting a quick-march across the plaza. Jeff scooped up her discarded purse, and caught up a few seconds later.

Dee's legs protested the headlong pace but her desire to get away from the scene of her brush with death overrode the objection. She continued the near-run between the two men in silence as Brian led them across a street and into a nearby parking garage. The Lincoln was just inside.

She slumped into the soft contours of the back seat, leaned back and closed her eyes. Jeff got in beside her as Brian got behind the wheel and asked, "Where to?"

"I thought you told your FBI pal you were taking us to a hospital."

"Jeff, please! Brian, just take us somewhere peaceful, okay? Maybe the lakefront."

She found one of Jeff's hands without opening her eyes, held it tightly.

The drive seemed all too short, but when Brian stopped the car and turned off the engine she opened her eyes and saw they were, indeed, at the Lake Michigan shore.

Brian turned to face them, his boyish face once again masking his emotions. "I'm going to take a walk on the shore. If you two want to join me, fine. If you'd rather stay here and...talk, that's fine too. Just give me a wave when you're ready."

Jeff's face was still lined with negative emotions. Dee gave his hand a squeeze. "Thanks, Brian. Maybe we'll join you in a little bit."

"Okay." Brian opened his door and got out, then leaned back in. "There is one thing you should know." He kept his eyes on her, but his words seemed addressed more to Jeff. "I've arranged things, despite what you may think, so you're free to do whatever you want. If you want to come back to work, there's a place for you. If you want out, no one will hassle you about it. There's only one other man who knows about the place in Oregon, and I trust him completely, so if you want to go back there, you won't be bothered."

"The way you trusted your man, or should I say Hobart's man, in Seattle?" Jeff challenged.

Dee was tempted to kick Jeff sharply in the shin, but Brian appeared to be unaffected.

"This is different. I believe you know Sammy. He's married to my sister. Whatever you decide to do, just let me know. I'll see to it you get everything you need."

He stepped back, closed the car door, and walked off toward the shoreline walkway.

Brian clearly understood Jeff's dilemma, she thought, perhaps even better than Jeff himself did. Jeff was finally free of his past; and had the right, and the responsibility, to choose whatever path he desired for his future.

The same was true for her. She became acutely aware that a significant portion of her own future might very will hinge on the next few moments.

CHAPTER TWENTY-FOUR

Overwhelmed with emotions, ambitions, cautions, and questions to be dealt with at the moment, Dee didn't know where to start. She half wished Jeff would take the initiative and say something first, give her a cue she could follow.

When Jeff stirred beside her she thought he was going to do just that. He rubbed his leg, just below the knee, and uttered a muffled groan.

She followed his action, saw the small tear in his pant leg, a darkening stain around it. "You've been hurt! Let me see."

"It's nothing."

She ignored his protest, carefully pulled up his pant leg and inspected the wound: a small, straight cut just above the top of his sock.

"See? No big deal," he insisted.

"Maybe not, but it should be cleaned to avoid infection. It must have been one of those shots from Hobart's little pistol. I didn't realize..."

"You're always taking care of me, aren't you?"

He put his hands on her shoulders, turned her slightly to look into her eyes with a gently penetrating stare. She wanted to protest his claim. He had taken care of her when she needed it, given her as much aid as she had given him.

He stopped her protest with his lips. Kissed her tenderly, then repeated the action.

"Don't deny it, Dee. Right from the start

you've given me just what I needed, just when I needed it. I mean that. When I found you in the wreck I felt something I didn't even know was inside me and I guess it took me a while to figure it out, but now I see it for what it was. You gave me a reason to step outside myself, do something for someone that had nothing to do with my job or my own limited goals.

"And then you just kept giving, sometimes at great peril to yourself, but always with that unquestioning resolve of yours. I don't know why you did it all, but now I need to ask you for your help again. I need to...to get this all figured out. Will you help me?"

"I've already told you I would. I don't take back my promises. And as for why I did it..."

Jeff tried to pull her close again, but she put a hand against his chest, held him off. As much as she wanted to be in his arms she had to say more-- before his kisses made her forget.

"There's something I have to explain." She took his hands from her shoulders, held them tightly as she moved them farther apart.

"This is difficult...bear with me please. When we were in that cottage with Rico something happened to me. Something about my time sense--I think time slowed down. At the motel in Grand Rapids, when that killer pushed me back into the room, there was a similar distortion. It wasn't the same as the first time, but things seemed to happen at a rate that should have been impossible."

He nodded. "That's your adrenal gland. It's the flight or--"

"Wait. There's more. Today in the plaza it didn't happen. Even when Hobart grabbed me and started to pop his little gun out, time stayed normal for me."

"You're getting used to danger."

"I believe that's exactly right. And that scares me even more than the danger itself, Jeff. I was scared when I thought Rico was going to kill me and Inga, but that was nothing compared with the terror I feel when I think about *getting used to danger*."

She closed her eyes so she wouldn't have to see the puzzled look on his face and clenched his hands more firmly. "Maybe this sounds crazy to you--I'm not sure I'd be able to justify it on a purely rational basis. But the very idea of my getting used to hurting other people, being involved in death or even injury to another human being, no matter how just the cause, makes me..."

Her throat constricted, cutting off her words. She tried to swallow, to force back the bitter taste her feelings had stirred up, risked looking into his eyes again.

"I understand," he said evenly.

She let go of one hand, wiped at a bead of perspiration on her upper lip with a finger tip. "The point is, you've asked me to help you sort things out. You need to know I couldn't possibly be objective about...that sort of thing. If one of the things you need to work out is your decision about rejoining the agency, anything I might say about it would be biased by my own feelings."

He held her look for a moment before answering. "I appreciate--no, that's not the right word. Right from the start I admired you for your honesty. It was one of the first things I noticed about you. I love you for your honesty."

Dee's heartbeat raced. She considered asking him if he'd mind repeating the last part without the modifiers, but he went on.

"I have a lot to sort out for myself. Who I am, what I am, where I want to be, who I want to be with. I *need* you to be there, to help me. When I get around to deciding what I want to do for a living, I'll remember what you said and take your feedback with a grain of salt.

"And at the same time I guess you'll be doing somewhat the same thing for yourself. You haven't said much about your own future, like whether you want to go back to acting. L. A. should be safe for you now that Rico and his organization are no more, so I guess that's a factor to be considered. But that's for you to say. So maybe we can help each other, you know, to sort things out. What do you say?"

She considered telling him she wouldn't return to L. A. on a bet. Not only had she lost her taste for pretending as a career, but the prospect of possibly running into treacherous Lila again was more than she could handle. But he didn't need to know all that. There was only one thing she could say. "It sounds like a plan I can live with."

He scooped her into his arms before she had time to appreciate the smile spreading across his face. He squeezed the breath out of her, then released her to arms' length again. "Then you'll fly back to Salem with me?

"Oregon?"

"Yeah, Oregon not Massachusetts," he affirmed with a broad grin. "That cabin in the Cascades is the only place I can think of where I'd feel secure. We'll have peace and quiet there, time

289

to think and talk without interruptions. Unless you have some other place in mind."

The cabin would certainly be a good place for thinking and talking. Its absence of distractions like television, radio, or even books or magazines made it ideal for those purposes. There was also a decided lack of creature comforts, she remembered, like furniture...but that could be easily remedied. "The cabin's fine."

"Great! I'll call Brian."

Brian drove them straight to Midway Airport and hired a private jet to fly them back to Oregon. The two men shook hands formally but affably. As Jeff transferred her bag from the Lincoln to the waiting plane, Brian offered his hand to her. She stepped inside it, put her arms around his neck and kissed him lightly on the cheek.

He returned the chaste kiss, then moved his lips closer to her ear. "Take care of him."

They were in the air somewhere west of the metropolitan area before Dee had a thought uncluttered enough to voice. "What time will we get to Salem?"

Jeff stirred from his reverie, glanced at his watch. "Somewhere around four or five, I'd guess."

"And then an hour up to the cabin? Guess we'll get there just in time for you to fix me beef stew for dinner."

He turned to her, a slow smile starting to light his face. "I can't remember what I have in my cupboards. You might have to make do with horse."

Her raucous laughter surprised her as much as him, proved to be contagious, and both of them seemed near tears before they could check themselves.

Long moments later Jeff shook his head and gave off a short snort. "Funny. The way I feel at this moment I could swear I never had a problem worth worrying about. Being with you seems to be all that matters."

"It's good to see you smile," she said. "Of course, once we get to Salem we will have some problems to take care of. A vehicle, maybe some furniture...stuff like that."

"Don't sweat the small stuff," he admonished, his grin still in place. "And you know what? That can be true about a lot of stuff...that business you brought up about the danger, for example. One of the first thoughts I had after we decided to go back to the cabin was that maybe I could get on with Manpower again, if Rosemarie will hire me.

"It wasn't a very serious thought, but I think that what prompted it is the fact that I found the work very satisfying. There's nothing like physical labor to give you a sense of accomplishment, and working as a temp has additional advantages, like being able to take off on a vacation any old time. And as for danger, well...

"Of course my work with Brian in the agency was never all that dangerous, at least for me, because I was largely a fact-finder, an investigator. I'm thinking maybe I could go into the private sector, make life even less dangerous, and a whole lot simpler."

"You mean like a private detective?"

"Well, I was thinking more along the lines of consultant, but I guess that's the same ballpark. What do you think?"

"I...well, I don't know. Consultant, or even detective certainly sounds a little less dangerous than government agent, and the big upside is that you'd be in control of deciding what jobs you take or turn down. In a way you'd have the same kind of freedom you enjoyed with Manpower. Do you think you'd be happy with that kind of work?"

"Ah...you missed my point. The question is, do you think *we'd* be happy with that kind of work?

"We?"

"I like being with you, Dee. I want to be with you day and night; and if the past week or so is any indication, we make a darn good team. So I'm thinking, why break up the team? Why not come up with a business that allows us to work together as well as play together?"

"Oh." There it was again, his way of seeming to be making a commitment, or asking her to make one, without actually putting it in so many words. She opened her mouth to give him an equally non-committal response but just then he turned his face just the smallest bit and the overhead light caught it just right. There was a sheen of perspiration on his upper lip and on his forehead. For all his pretended nonchalance he was actually sweating. He was nervous. She knew in that moment she meant a lot more to him than he would probably ever let on, and it changed everything.

She reached up a hand to stroke the side of his face, then let it fall to his chest and began undoing the buttons of his shirt.

"Sounds wonderful, Jeff. But let's forget both the past and the future for the moment, just focus on the present."

He let his own fingers answer for him.

292

Made in the USA
Columbia, SC
08 May 2017